DETOURS

Visit us at www.boldstrokesbooks.com

DETOURS

by

Jeffrey Ricker

A Division of Bold Strokes Books

2011

DETOURS

ISBN 13: 978-1-60282-577-2

THIS TRADE PAPERBACK ORIGINAL IS PUBLISHED BY
BOLD STROKES BOOKS, INC.
P.O. BOX 249
VALLEY FALLS, NY 12185

FIRST EDITION: NOVEMBER 2011

CREDITS
EDITOR: GREG HERREN
PRODUCTION DESIGN: STACIA SEAMAN
COVER DESIGN BY SHERI (GRAPHICARTIST2020@HOTMAIL.COM)

Acknowledgments

As much as they say writing is a solitary profession, I've had a lot of help along the way. It takes a village? In the case of my first novel, it took a small metropolitan area. This book would not have turned out the way it did without the support and input of many people. I hesitate to name them for fear of omitting someone, but I would be remiss in not thanking 'Nathan Smith, Rob Byrnes, Alexander Chee, Elizabeth McNulty, Pamela Merritt, Huntington Sharp, Timothy Lambert, Becky Cochrane, and Cindy Fehmel and everyone in my writing group, Writers under the Arch.

Thanks especially to my editor, Greg Herren, for his wonderful friendship, unflagging enthusiasm, and always-constructive advice.

Thanks also to my parents, for counseling practicality while reminding me also to dream.

Last, but certainly not least, thanks to Mike, who was a book widow on many nights when I didn't crawl into bed until hours after the lights were out. Sweet dreams.

For Brad,
who always believed, even when I didn't

CHAPTER ONE

We always think we know how the story ends. In the case of my mother's death, the end of her story coincided with—caused, really—the end of one story for me and the beginning of another. It was the sort of thing she would have claimed she did on purpose.

I might have believed her, but that says more about our relationship than I need to think about at the moment.

I wasn't thinking about my mother at all at the time. I had just gotten home from a vacation in London, and I was thinking about Philip.

We met at a secondhand bookstall under Waterloo Bridge. I had found an old Jane Austen and an out-of-print Paul Bowles. Philip was holding a beat-up Anne Rice paperback. I don't remember what he said, but he struck up a conversation when I tried to slide past him. The longer we talked, the easier it was to overlook his questionable taste in books. His lopsided smile, typically English, charmed me. He didn't bother to brush the fringe of brown hair off his forehead. The sudden flush of high color in his cheeks could have just been the wind off the Thames.

"How much longer are you in town?" he asked. His voice was deep, and I could have listened to his accent for days.

"Only until Sunday," I said.

He frowned, looked at the ground, and stroked his chin for a second. "Well then, I guess you'll just have to have dinner with me tonight, won't you?"

I smiled. Normally, I would have suggested a later date—but Sunday was only four days away. He didn't look like the sort of person who'd beat me up in a bed-sit or leave me face-down in an alley. As I debated, the wind caught the edge of his Nike jacket and exposed the crisp white T-shirt he was wearing.

I said yes.

We had a deadline, so we wasted as little time as possible getting each other's backstory. Philip was single, in his thirties, and a computer consultant. The job paid well enough for him to afford a flat in central London. It also required him to travel a lot. His parents were retired. His sister, a primary school teacher, lived with them outside the city. He went on dates about as often as I did—not very. He didn't have to tell me this, though; his goofy, crooked, unself-conscious yet earnest smile gave it away, making him even more endearing. So did the accent. So did the bottle of wine we finished.

After dinner, we lingered over coffee until we were the only diners left. We both got up from our seats reluctantly. Outside, Philip asked, "Tell me again, how long are you here?"

"Four days," I said.

I memorized as many details about that moment as possible. The chill in the air and the dampness threatening rain, turning our breath to fog. The curl in Philip's hair, also brought out by the humidity. How the shoulders of his coat bunched around his ears when he jammed his hands into his pockets. The spring dresses in the shop window across the street that made promises the weather felt unlikely to keep.

"What are you looking at?" Philip asked, glancing over his shoulder. Instinctively, I put a hand against his cheek and turned his face back to mine.

"Everything," I said. "You just look right here."

I expected a gentle kiss. Instead, we stumbled against the door hard enough to make the glass rattle. I looked behind me—

the waitress inside stared back, an upturned chair in her hands. Our glances intersected. She smiled and went back to stacking chairs. Philip guided my lips back to his. It felt like he was trying to outrun the end of the evening, as if he could somehow get us in front of it. I gasped when we finally parted, breathless from the race.

Philip laughed and pulled me close again.

"Let's go to my place," he said.

Four days equals ninety-six hours. We spent all of them together, and tried to spend as many of those hours awake as possible. On the last day, Philip was still in bed when I left his apartment to head for the airport. I told him I didn't want him to get up. I wanted our parting to be quiet and everyday, like I was slipping out to go back to my own place, with plans to meet up later.

"Coffee," he said, his voice still tangled in dreams.

"I'll make it," I whispered, and slid out of bed into the blue-gray morning. It was not quite seven yet.

Coffee and a shower woke me up. When I returned to the bedroom with Philip's mug, I stopped in the doorway. Like four nights before, I tried to memorize the contours of the moment: the softness of the gray world outside the windows, the clefts and valleys where the bed sheets flowed over the curve of Philip's back, the tangle of his hair against the pillow. I wanted to be able to take out this picture later and look at it when I couldn't recall a detail.

"Do you have to go?" Philip mumbled, reaching vaguely for his mug. I aimed it toward his hand.

"I've been gone two weeks," I said. "I hate to imagine what my in-box at work looks like." This did not answer his question exactly. *It's only been four days*, I tried to remind myself.

"Well," he said. He set his coffee on the nightstand and stretched his arms over his head, like a cat. "I have to say these have been the best four days of my year."

"That's not saying much. It's only March."

Philip rolled onto his side. His eyes had lost their half-asleep veil. "I figured that might be less unsettling than saying they've been the best four days of my life."

❖

I wasn't ready to be home yet, so I drove in the wrong direction.

Once I'd negotiated my way through baggage claim and picked up my car, I headed in the opposite direction of home, across the Missouri River through St. Charles.

Now that I was back, every direction felt like the wrong one. It made as much sense as anything else that I was heading farther into the suburbs. I rolled down the window for a blast of March air to wake me up. The exits passed by in a blur until I reached Wentzville about half an hour later. The temptation was to keep heading west toward Columbia and Kansas City. Beyond lay the flat emptiness of Kansas and eastern Colorado, both places I'd never visited. If I kept going long enough, I'd get to California and the ocean. If I went even farther, I'd be back in London again.

I could even keep going until I came up behind myself.

Instead, I veered east toward the city, back across the river and through the Chesterfield Valley, where the largest strip mall in the country—maybe the world—sprawled along the highway. In some ways, St. Louis was like that strip mall to me—trying to be bigger than it was, but lacking in originality and seeming distant and standoffish.

It was almost midnight when I finally got home. The apartment smelled of dust and neglect. On the kitchen table was a pile of mail, and a note from Carrie. She'd watered the plants and Dudley was eager to see me. On the answering machine was a message from Mom. She'd gotten my postcard, wanted to talk about the trip and a few other things. That could wait until tomorrow. Dudley, unpacking, sorting through the bills and junk mail—it could all wait until tomorrow. I filled the kettle, put a teabag in a cup, and sat at the table.

The phone rang. I felt for a moment as if I had dozed off, and glanced toward the kettle instead of the wall where the phone hung. I didn't recognize the number right away. It was a 207 area code, which my exhausted brain eventually realized meant Maine, and home. Home of a sort, at least. When I picked up, it was my father.

"Son," he said. His voice was small and distant. I had to strain to hear him. "I think you'd better sit down."

❖

The part I couldn't wrap my mind around was why she'd said nothing. She hadn't told my father about her cancer until he found her doubled over in the kitchen with the refrigerator open and one hand on the counter to keep her from falling to the floor.

The next day, she went to the hospital and never came out.

After promising I would book a flight right away, I hung up and sat for a moment at the table, unsure which way to move. The kettle whistled, so I made my tea and sat back down, waiting for it to cool. Again, I was sitting still when I should have been in a whirlwind of motion, frantic to get back out of town as soon as possible, the same way I felt when I'd been driving down the highway not wanting to come home.

Instead, I started to cook, which is a sort of forward momentum. The refrigerator contained little that was salvageable after two weeks away: a wilting head of lettuce, four bottles from a six-pack of beer, some eggs, butter, and a chunk of Swiss cheese that, amazingly, hadn't turned green and fuzzy while I was gone.

I shredded the cheese and melted the butter with some flour.

By one o'clock, I was back at the kitchen table. My tea had long gone cold, so I opened a beer and waited for the soufflé to rise. It seemed right to make something fragile.

I called Carrie and told her what had happened. "I'll be right over," she said.

"Bring Dudley," I added before she hung up. I needed my dog.

While I waited, I emptied my suitcases—two weeks of dirty clothes now separated into piles on my bedroom floor—and began filling the largest one with clean clothes for my trip home.

It was odd to think of Portland as home. It had been more than fifteen years since I'd lived there. After college, I'd moved directly to St. Louis for a job. It was supposed to be a temporary relocation. I pictured myself someplace bigger, like Boston or Chicago, maybe even New York one day. Even though I always meant to, I just never got around to leaving.

I didn't have enough clean clothes to fill a suitcase. I remembered I should pack a suit. I picked one at random and placed it carefully across the other clothes. The doorbell rang as I shut the case.

Carrie had brought Dudley and a twelve-pack of Rolling Rock.

She had also brought Matt.

"I hope you don't mind," she said after we hugged. "I figured there's strength in numbers."

"Numbers of friends or numbers of beers?" I asked, trying to prove I hadn't lost my sense of humor.

"Both," Matt said, hugging me as well. He always smelled freshly washed. Even though he spent his days at the nursery up to his wrists in dirt and fertilizer, he seemed fresher now than he ever had as a lawyer in tailored suits and silk ties. We'd dated then, and he'd always seemed exhausted. Now, the lucky bastard glowed.

While Matt and Carrie offered their condolences, Dudley

grew tired of waiting. He shuffled over to his empty food bowl, then arranged himself on the corner of the sofa.

We each cracked open a beer and waited for the soufflé. I gave Dudley his belated welcome home. He agreeably rolled over onto his back, consenting to a belly rub, which was about as demonstrative as he ever got. After, he hopped off the sofa and returned to his bowl, looking back at me.

"Okay, I get the hint," I said.

I dumped a scoop of kibble in his bowl and he dove in. It dawned on me then that it was long past his suppertime, and breakfast wouldn't be due for another four hours. Already duped, I wasn't about to take his food away. The oven dinged and the soufflé was ready.

The first bite of soufflé is always the best. It never seems as light after that, and that first bite is like a cloud melting over the tongue. This one I'd pretty much knocked out of the park. It was company-perfect.

"Joel," Carrie said, "are you awake?"

I had closed my eyes for a moment to savor the cloud. "I'm awake," I said, but kept my eyes shut.

"Are you okay?" Matt asked.

"Not really." I tried to conjure up the image of Philip lying in bed yesterday morning. I felt a hand settle over mine.

"Thinking about your mom?" Carrie asked.

"Yeah," I lied. Telling them I was thinking about this great guy I had met on vacation would have deflated all the sympathy in the room. I ate another spoonful of soufflé, finished my beer and opened another. I said, "I should get online and book a flight."

When I opened my laptop, an e-mail from Philip was waiting in my in-box.

The world seemed suddenly much smaller than it had when I'd said good-bye to the man lying in the blue light. That was five thousand miles ago. The postcards I mailed on vacation hadn't even arrived yet, but here was this message arriving as if I had just left him across town—the way I had wanted it to seem.

I hesitated to open Philip's e-mail, and in that moment, a flood of other messages pushed it farther down the queue and out of sight. I shut my e-mail and bought my ticket. By the time I finished the next beer, I was booked on a flight later that morning, requiring an absurd connection through Raleigh/Durham, and an even more absurd amount of money.

Maybe it was Philip's e-mail—which could have said anything and existed only as potential so long as it remained unopened—but I was itching to start moving again. At the same time, though, I was so tired that I could barely keep my eyes open. Whenever I closed them, there was the tantalizing, unreachable guy across the ocean.

I sat back down at the kitchen table. This was another scene worth saving: my friends, my faithful dog. Carrie scooped some more soufflé onto her plate and asked us if we wanted any more. I held up my plate. Matt replaced my empty beer with a fresh one. Finished with his food, Dudley flopped on the linoleum under the table.

I wasn't ready to peer into the dark well of my mother's death. Instead, I said, "Let me tell you about my trip."

CHAPTER TWO

Carrie left at three thirty. She said she had to get home before her husband woke up and realized she was gone. Only a few beers remained by then, and I was a little buzzed. My flight out left at eleven thirty, so sleep seemed futile.

"So," she said, pushing her chair from the table, "what do you want to do about Dudley?"

"I'll take care of him," Matt said. I looked toward the living room. Once the soufflé was gone and the hope of any stray crumbs hitting the floor, Dudley had once again withdrawn from the kitchen and curled up on the sofa, feigning sleep; his ears still twitched when he heard his name.

"You're sure you're going to be all right?" Carrie asked, pausing at the front door. I wasn't sure of anything, but I said I would be. She gave me a hug, one lasting longer than the hug she'd given me when she arrived. There was a hesitation in it, as if she were on the verge of asking me something but changed her mind.

Matt stayed until the rest of the beer was gone, then pushed his chair back from the table as well. "I'm opening the nursery tomorrow," he said. He looked at his watch. "I mean today."

I started gathering Dudley's things—his bed, chew toys, bags of food, and biscuits. We loaded everything in Matt's truck and then took Dudley around the block to pee.

"How old is Dudley now?" Matt asked while Dudley sniffed the six-foot radius his leash permitted. "His nose is grayer."

"He's nine," I said. "Gray happens." It was happening to me too, creeping over my ears and getting harder to ignore. Matt was two years younger and hadn't succumbed yet.

"Nine? Already?" Matt asked.

I'd adopted Dudley when he was less than a year old. Dudley had been three when Matt and I started dating. The more years I spent with Dudley, the more I marked time based on how old my dog was when things happened. Met Matt: three. Broke up with Matt: four. Got my latest job: also four. Mother died: nine.

Once Dudley finished doing his business, we walked down Lindell Boulevard to Matt's truck. It was a relatively new Ford, but the battering it took on the job made it look older. The name "Randall's Nursery and Landscaping" was painted across the door. I opened the passenger door, and Dudley hopped in. He was always ready for a ride. I gave him a hug. I'd spent two weeks away from him and only a few hours with him, and was handing him off to the care of someone else. Again. *I am a responsible pet owner*, I told myself. Meanwhile, he sniffed my ear before licking it.

"He'll be fine," Matt said. He gave me a good-bye hug. Dudley glanced at me through the window before turning to face forward, eager to be going.

I tried not to take it personally.

"I'm not so sure about me."

Matt leaned back so he could look at my face. "You'll be fine too."

And, much to my surprise, he kissed me. It was a good kiss, but I was so surprised I nearly forgot to enjoy it. When I started to enjoy it, though, I realized I had been kissing someone else barely twenty-four hours before. Matt was my ex—past tense—and maybe this wasn't wrong, but it was so, so strange. Given all that had happened in the time I'd been home, it didn't seem surprising. I placed a hand on his chest and gently pushed until we separated.

Matt's ears were red, his eyes wide and white. "I didn't mean—"

"No, it's okay."

"Joel—"

"I've got to go," I said. "My flight."

"Okay."

"I'll call you."

I was breathless when I got back to the apartment, like I'd run up the stairs instead of taking the elevator. I sat on the sofa and tried to calm down. Once I realized that was futile, I printed out my boarding passes for my flight and opened Philip's e-mail. He was off to Spain for a week, then Brussels. In April, he'd be in New York.

I hit the Reply button and stared at the cursor. Beyond "Dear Philip," I couldn't figure out what to say. There were too many things, and none of them were right—certainly not in an e-mail. I closed the screen and hoped that later, Philip would seem foreign once more.

❖

I'd planned to nap during the flight, but sleep stubbornly stayed away. After a three-hour layover in Raleigh/Durham, I got on the connecting flight. I kept my eyes closed long after it seemed futile. Finally, I nodded off just before the flight attendant tapped me on the shoulder and told me to put up the seat back for landing.

Dad was waiting outside baggage claim. It took a moment to realize the old man scanning the arrivals board was my father. It was clear he wasn't well. He leaned on a cane and wore a coat that looked too heavy for March—even in Maine. His skin was the color of mayonnaise left out too long. His hair, gray going white, looked absentminded.

He saw me eventually. I realized I'd been staring at him. I shifted my backpack on my shoulder and headed over.

"I wasn't sure you were going to be here," I said, giving him a one-armed hug.

"Where the hell else would I be?" he asked, his voice a wet rattle. "I figured you shouldn't have to get into town all by yourself."

We walked toward the exit as fast as Dad's slow shuffle would carry him. "Did you drive?" I asked.

"Son, I haven't driven in years. I took a cab."

Taxis were few, but even fewer people were lining up for them. We waited quietly. As casually as possible, I scanned my father's face for a sign of how he was coping. Whatever I hoped to see remained concealed.

I slid into the back of the taxi while the cabbie loaded my bags in the trunk. The meter up front flashed zeroes and the radio crackled on an AM station. I was still wondering what the hell had possessed my mother to not tell me she was dying. It seemed so incredibly insensitive and selfish. I felt robbed of something she had no right to keep from me. As angry as I was, I couldn't even put into words how much it hurt that she didn't want to say good-bye to me.

Of course, I'd also been deprived of the chance to tell her exactly what I thought of her dumb-ass choices. It was easier to be angry now than risk a different emotion.

The driver finished loading my bags and slid behind the wheel. I gave him directions. My father remained outside, staring at the terminal as if it were a mirage. He looked lost, like he'd forgotten what series of events had led him here.

I rolled down the window. "Hey, Dad, it's time to go."

"Oh, right," he said. When Dad moved, his feet never seemed to leave the ground; he just slid them across the concrete until he could reach the handle and open the door. He was sixty-seven, but anyone would have guessed he was at least a decade beyond that. In dog years, he was about as old as Dudley. Ever since his heart attack and quadruple bypass five years earlier (also when Dudley was four), Mom said we would have to be prepared for "the inevitable."

I was not prepared. Neither, it turned out, was she.

❖

Actually, I was wrong. She was totally prepared. The funeral would be on Thursday, and she had already made arrangements with the funeral home, planned the service, and selected a minister. All my father and I had to do was call people and let them know when and where to show up.

I had hoped for a flood of details to distract me from anything else. I should have known she'd be thorough. She was a planner. Nor should I have been surprised I knew nothing about the plans. She and I had only talked occasionally about making arrangements for her. A few years ago, when she'd given me details for the power of attorney, she'd said not to worry about the funeral.

"Oh darling, why waste the money? It's not like I'm going to be around to raise a fuss and silently judge you." She was the same about burial: "It's not like I'm going to know or care how often you come to visit."

There was one detail she hadn't attended to, though. When we got home, a large recreational vehicle was parked in the driveway.

"What the hell is that?" I asked.

Dad was paying the driver. He looked at the RV. "What does it look like?"

I forced my shoulders not to rise up to my ears and kept my jaw from clenching. I was sure it was only the first time during my stay that I'd have to do it.

"When did you get an RV?" The more obvious question was *why did you get an RV?* But I left it unasked.

"When we were stupid and had too much disposable

income," Dad replied, answering the unasked question more than the one I had voiced. "Your mother was supposed to call you about that."

"I guess she never got around to it," I said.

Hearing her mentioned was unsettling. It was like she'd stepped out to run an errand and would be back any minute. I expected things like that would come up all week, bringing her painfully into the present until we both got used to the fact that she was now part of an irretrievable past.

Portland was supposed to be part of my past too. I think she'd been glad when I left for college and didn't come back to look for work after graduation. Not that there was a lot to be found at the time. Nevertheless, here I was walking back into my past, and my father and I were falling back into our old roles. It felt like putting on an old jacket that had shrunk—uncomfortable, but familiar.

"Why was she supposed to call me?" I asked.

Dad didn't answer. The cab had pulled away. He leaned heavily against his cane and bent down to pick up one of my bags.

"I've got it, Dad."

"I'm not an invalid," he snapped. "I can at least carry one of them."

I relented, ceding him the lighter bag. I kept my pace slow while we climbed the front steps.

He and Mom bought the RV just over a year ago, he said. It had been Mom's idea, and when she got one, she wasn't likely to be talked out of it. She thought it would be convenient, and maybe they would get out and enjoy their retirement more.

"*I* was enjoying my retirement just fine," Dad said. He dropped my bag inside the front hall and made his way to the living room, easing into his recliner and setting the cane within reach. He picked up the newspaper, which trembled a little in his grip. I didn't know how he could focus on the shaking words long enough to read them. Every time I came to visit since his bypass, I'd found Dad installed in his recliner. The chair had become an extension of him, whether he was reading the paper, or watching a game, or eating lunch. Whenever I came or went, he would always be in that chair. I couldn't imagine why Mom thought he would take to the road with her in an RV.

"You never did tell me why Mom was supposed to call me," I said.

Dad looked at me over the edge of his newspaper. "Go on and put your bags in your room. We can talk about that later."

❖

After I left for college, Mom had tried her best to turn my old bedroom into a guest room. On my first trip home, I came in to find my posters had been taken down, neatly rolled up, and placed in the closet. Where Duran Duran and the Pet Shop Boys had been, she'd hung a couple of Wyeth prints from the Portland Art Museum. She'd removed my child-sized bed and desk, replacing them with a daybed, wing chair, and side table. She'd kept my old dresser, which barely came up past my waist now. Arranged on top of it were my track and cross-country trophies from high school, little ivory towers topped by golden figures eternally in mid-stride, their feet never touching the ground.

I was still a fast runner.

She could never figure out why the room stubbornly refused to capitulate, despite all her efforts at change. I never did tell her that if she wanted to make it something other than her only son's old bedroom, she needed to steam clean the carpet or rip it out. I tossed my bags on the daybed, closed my eyes, and inhaled the stale memory of my childhood. It was a scent probably only I would ever find appealing.

Dad had set aside the newspaper and was watching the six o'clock news when I came back downstairs. I drifted into the kitchen with thoughts of cobbling together dinner. Culinary skills had never been my mother's strong suit, so there wasn't much to work with. Her idea of cooking usually involved the microwave or a takeout menu. TV dinners were a weekly occurrence, and Banquet lasagna was a fancy meal. She could make salads and arrange a mean cheese tray, but anything requiring the application of heat led to dangerous, and often inedible, territory. Home cooking meant Dad was either firing up the grill or making crepes, his one flawless kitchen creation.

When I asked her why she never learned to cook, she managed to turn the shortcoming into a sort of virtue. "Cooking is just this endless parade of ingredients and dishes and chewing and swallowing. It just gets you from one day to the next when you have to chop more ingredients and dirty more dishes and chew, chew, chew. I think that's why fast food is so popular, because cooking and eating waste so much time when you could be doing other things."

"But most people spend their time doing things like watching TV instead of cooking. It's not like that's such a better use of their hours."

"Yes, darling, but most people are sheep, just grazing and watching until they get sheared or turned into lamb chops."

As far as I could tell, the only difference between her and the other sheep was—well, I couldn't actually tell if there was one. Her grazing activities involved reading books and going shopping, though rarely for food. When I told her this, she smacked me in the back of the head. It would be a few years before I learned to keep my mouth shut.

For now, I took comfort in the consistency of Mom's kitchen. The spice collection was still in the same cupboard, still arranged alphabetically, and still mostly unused. The carton of eggs was still on the top shelf of the fridge along with the milk—skim for Mom, two percent for Dad. The deli meat drawer contained no trace of salami, ham, or sliced turkey, but was filled with a global tour of her favorite cheeses—Stilton, double Gloucester, Wensleydale, brie, camembert, a milky container of buffalo mozzarella, and a massive block of sharp cheddar still in its black rind.

I set a pot of water to boil for spaghetti and heated up pasta sauce from a jar. There was a box of garlic toast in the freezer. I put a few slices in the toaster oven and looked for anything resembling a vegetable. The only ones I found were in the pantry and canned. I also found a bottle of red wine, which was like discovering magic. I didn't realize how much I wanted a glass until I pulled the cork.

I sat at the kitchen table and stared out the sliding glass door. This was where I'd seen my mother smoke for the first time. I'd been doing my homework at the kitchen table; I must have been about fifteen. She had just put on the kettle for tea. She opened a drawer, removed a lighter and a pack of Marlboro Lights, and walked to the sliding glass door. She opened the door a sliver and lit up, careful to exhale through the opening.

I'd never known her to smoke before then. She looked my way and, rolling her cigarette between her fingers, winked at me and exhaled again. I was pretty sure Dad had no idea she smoked. At the time, I felt like I was being let in on a secret—like the time we went grocery shopping, and passing through the hair care aisle, she picked up a box of Nice'n Easy (number 104, Natural Medium Golden Blonde) and dropped it in the cart. She winked at me, put a finger to her lips and said, "Shh. Don't tell Dad." As if he cared whether her hair was not what it appeared to be.

Nevertheless, I kept both secrets.

By the time dinner was ready, I'd finished two big glasses of wine and there was only enough left for one more.

"Do you want wine or beer with dinner?" I asked Dad.

"You know, your mother never let me drink beer," he said.

"Then why is it in the fridge?"

"Because sometimes I go to the store myself. Gimme a beer."

After he finished the first beer, I opened another for him. I could imagine what my mother would have said about it: "I never forbade him to have beer in the house, I just forbade him to kiss me after drinking one. And in any case, is it my fault he was too lazy to get up and get one himself?"

Dad told me what Mom had been planning to call me about. They'd put the RV up for sale—they still owed money on it, the gas to run it cost an obscene amount, and Dad damn well didn't want to go camping. They'd found a buyer for it—in San Francisco.

"Who the hell buys an RV that needs to be driven all the way across the country?" I asked. "Don't they have RVs in California?"

"People with more money than sense," he snapped. "Kind of like us when we bought it. Remember the Millers who lived next door?"

"No."

"Nice couple, the husband was about your age. They moved to San Francisco, and when I mentioned we were selling it, he said he'd love to buy it if we could figure out how to get it there. Your mother was going to ask you if you'd be willing to drive it out for us."

"He can't come and get it, but he's going to have time to use it?" I asked.

"For all I care, he can park it in his driveway and live in it. He's paying for it and I'm not going to lose too much on the deal, so I'm not asking any questions."

I was surprised my frugal, practical father was selling something at a loss. He stubbornly held on to anything on the premise that its value would somehow bounce back. This explained why we had a Betamax for years after everyone had switched to VHS. He only got rid of it when they stopped making blank tapes.

"I don't know if I could take the time off," I said. "I just got back from two weeks' vacation and didn't even get into the office before…" I let the thought trail off. It sounded like I was complaining about how inconvenient Mom's death was. I slugged down the last of my wine and rested my forehead in my palm. I hadn't slept for almost twenty-four hours.

"You don't have to decide right now," Dad said. "We've got plenty to get through in the rest of the week. Just think about it."

❖

I wanted to focus on keeping Dad busy, but there wasn't much either of us had to do. Mom had made all the arrangements for her funeral, the lawyer in charge of the estate had already been in contact with Dad (I have no idea how he found out about my mother's death—Dad had never called him; maybe lawyers have an innate sense that I would have to ask Matt about sometime), and Dad had already called Mom's out-of-town friends to break the news. After breakfast, he suggested we start packing up Mom's clothes to give to charity.

"You sure you want to do that so soon?" I asked, not sure I wanted to handle Mom's things.

Dad waved his hand vaguely. "We're going to need a lot of time," he said.

He wasn't kidding. Mom was a clotheshorse *and* a pack rat. She'd turned one of the guest bedrooms into her own walk-in closet. The bed and nightstand had been replaced with a dressing table, armoire, and a second chest of drawers. A rolling clothes rack, shrouded in plastic, stood in the corner. The closet was filled with dresses, blouses, and skirts, many of which looked like they'd never been worn, their creases department store precise. The top shelf was stacked to the ceiling with shoe boxes.

Even Dad looked somewhat stunned. "I knew there was a reason she wouldn't let me come in here," he said. He brushed his hand along the dresses in the closet, pausing to inspect a sleeve. The price tag was still attached.

"She didn't have time to learn to cook, but she obviously had time to shop like a pro," I said.

"You sure you want to help?" Dad asked.

"As long as I don't have to pack up her lingerie."

"If you come across anything you want, go ahead and take it."

I looked again at the dresses. "Dad, I'm gay, not a drag queen."

His lips thinned into a dark, narrow line. "I meant as a keepsake." I had a feeling he wanted to append "you idiot" to the end of that statement but refrained. He dropped a stack of boxes on the floor and left me to work.

We kept at it most of the day, stopping only for lunch. As I moved blouses and skirts from hangers to boxes, I kept looking for things I might have remembered her wearing, with no luck. So much of her wardrobe still had price tags on it, I wondered whether her purchases were less of an extravagance and more of a compulsion.

Perhaps it was just as well I didn't find anything. Since I was putting away never worn clothes that never had a chance to pick up the scent of Mom's perfume or her hair spray, I could pretend they weren't really hers. It helped me keep my distance.

Until I got to the shoe boxes.

The Salvatore Ferragamo box was heavier than a pair of shoes should be. When I opened it, I found letters, still in envelopes, all in her handwriting. That struck me as odd. Why would she keep letters she had written but apparently had never sent?

The years had dulled the glue on the envelopes. They came open easily as I handled them, pulling out the smooth, cool gray paper. I unfolded the first carefully, worried I would be heard.

Dear Derek,

I walked past your house today and thought of you—can you imagine I almost stopped and rang the bell? You're not there, of course—I heard you and Mark are in Greece now—but I wonder how your mother would have reacted to see me on the front porch. My guess would be not too well, but then she's always been good at maintaining appearances.

So have I, which is why I will probably never send you this letter. I'll add it to the stack of other letters I've written to you but never sent. It should embarrass me to think of how many there are. If Arthur ever found them, perhaps then I would feel some embarrassment. He would tell me I've held on to this grudge for too long—that's what he'd call it, a grudge, and he'd tell me to just let it go, forget about it, tear these up or burn them. He'd probably be right, he's so practical.

Speaking of practical, did you ever find the ring? Or did you have to wait for spring and the snow to melt? I suppose, apart from the value, it wouldn't have been a great loss. I don't think it would have looked very good on Mark's hand, and I'm sure it wouldn't have fit.

I saw you both once, downtown. I guess it must have been a week or so after the thing with the ring. I was down on Congress Street, getting a refill for my fountain pen, and you had just come out of Porteous with Mark, and you were both carrying armloads of boxes and shopping bags, so I guess it was right around the after-Christmas sales. This will sound so silly, but I actually stood behind a Salvation Army bell ringer so I could watch you load everything into your father's Lincoln. And when you closed the trunk, his hand fell on top of yours and you both smiled. I doubt anyone else would have noticed it. But I did.

You'd probably find it amusing that my son is gay. Of course, it's such a different time now than when you and I were his age. He seems happy, though I wish he didn't live someplace as backwater as St. Louis. Chicago might be nicer, or New York certainly. He's single now, and I do worry he'll have a lonely life, like I said you would—though of course, you didn't have one, so why should he?

I stopped reading there. I folded the letter and tucked it back in the envelope before anything else about me could leak out. I took the box across the hall and slid it underneath the daybed. I didn't tell Dad about them. Later, while we were eating dinner—we had barely made a dent in Mom's wardrobe by the time we called it a day—I wondered whether she'd given the correspondence any thought before she went into the hospital. After her diagnosis, had she considered whether someone other than the letters' intended recipient might read them? She had been so particular about every other arrangement, it seemed doubtful this detail would have escaped her notice.

Unless she had intended they be found and read. The point of writing was, after all, to be read.

Wasn't it?

Still, the existence of the letters themselves was a puzzle. My mother had never displayed nostalgic tendencies. She didn't collect souvenirs from trips, kept only enough photo albums to deflect accusations of indifference, and family heirlooms were few. If an unexamined life wasn't worth living, my mother would have argued the examined life left too little time for actual living. It was hard to reconcile that view with a shoe box full of introspection. I wasn't sure I even wanted to try.

And who was Derek?

CHAPTER THREE

The next morning, I started hearing my mother's voice.

"If I had known this is what it took to get you into a suit, I would have died a long time ago."

I looked behind me, glanced around the empty room, and turned back to the mirror. I had chosen a charcoal gray Hugo Boss suit. I didn't know why I'd picked it instead of a black suit. I smoothed my hands down the lapels. I loved this suit, until I wore it to my first work presentation after my promotion. That was a week before my vacation, and when I uttered the phrase "maximizing synergies" with no sense of irony at all, things started unraveling for me. I'd started to think of this as my "synergy suit."

As soon as I thought I should have brought a different suit, Mom said, "But you look so dapper in that one. You need to straighten your tie, though. The knot's all wonky."

To my surprise, I found myself replying. "You must be the only person left who uses the word 'dapper.'"

"In a few moments, darling, the irony of that statement will occur to you." I heard the flick of her lighter, followed by a long exhale moments later. "Are you going to fix that or do I have to do it for you?"

"You might as well," I said.

She held her cigarette in her lips and exhaled out the side of her mouth while using both hands to adjust the knot. I laughed. When she raised an eyebrow, I said, "You remind me of a trucker with your cig like that."

"A trucker? In this?"

She was wearing a peach nightgown with matching robe, the feathery trim on the cuffs coordinating with her high-heeled slippers. She had started wearing these confections in the mid-eighties, about the same time she started watching *Dynasty*. While she didn't exactly admire or aspire to be like Alexis Colby, she did like what slippers with heels did for her calves. She always complained hers were like tree trunks. At least she'd been smart enough to eschew the linebacker shoulder pads.

When she finished with my tie, she straightened my lapels and brushed her hands down the jacket, standing back to take a drag and admire her handiwork. "How's that?"

"Better than I could do."

"You never were very good with your tie. Honestly, what would you do without me?"

❖

A knot of people stood near the funeral home entrance, their white and silvery heads bobbing like a cotton field in the wind. They turned as we pulled up—and standing there amid the cotton, smoking a cigarette, was Carrie.

Before I could ask what she was doing here—and why she was smoking again—one of those wisps of cotton floated toward my father. For an instant, when her outlines were still fuzzy, she looked exactly like my mother—and almost at the same moment, she morphed into someone else.

She didn't throw her arms around my father so much as arrange them delicately behind his neck. "Arthur, I just can't believe it," she said. Her voice fluttered like a hummingbird's wings. "We're all so shocked. How are you holding up?"

I didn't catch my father's response. I looked toward Carrie, who held up her cigarette and said, "I'll be right over."

The fluttery woman had released my father and now extended a hand to me. She dabbed her eyes with a tissue and said her name was Sylvia, gestured to a put-upon-looking man behind her as Gerald, and the other as Walter. They were old friends of my mother's, she said.

"Rachel told us so much about you." Her voice caught, but luckily she didn't dissolve into a crying fit right there. I looked toward my father, who remained stoic. I hadn't heard of any of these people.

"You just haven't gotten to those letters yet," my mother said.

"Let's go inside," my father said.

Carrie finished her cigarette and came over. She hugged me, perfuming the air with the odor of Marlboro Lights.

"When the hell did you start smoking again?" I asked. It was better to risk pissing her off than try to untangle the black knot in my gut. "And what are you doing here?"

She smiled, not happily, and reached for her purse again. She paused and pulled out her pack again. "I think I'll answer the second question first," she said as she lit up, "which will also answer the first question. You're never going to believe this."

Doug, her husband, was having an affair. He wasn't at the house when she got home the morning after my last night in town—she chalked it up to either another late night or another early start. When she called his office to see if he needed a change of clothes, his assistant Jason answered and asked, "Aren't you supposed to be in Cancun?"

"You would think a lawyer would be a better liar," she said. "Or at least better organized." He'd left her a note saying he was going out of town on business. Unfortunately, he'd left it in the kitchen, a room Carrie entered only to get coffee, leftovers, or cocktails (not unlike my mother in that respect). He'd told his assistant he was taking Carrie to Cancun, which turned out to be only half-true.

"He went to Cancun, all right," she said, "just not with me."

While Carrie went through two more cigarettes, she told me Doug's late nights at the office had nothing to do with work and more to do with an associate named Elizabeth Dawkins. As far as she knew, the two of them were still in Cancun. Carrie had gone to his firm and charmed her way into Doug's office (this I could somewhat believe) where she unearthed the incriminating e-mails on his computer. (His password was their anniversary date; she said he'd never been good at security.) From there, she had gone home, contacted a divorce lawyer at a different firm, and packed her bags, only to realize she had no place to go.

So she came to the funeral.

"How presumptuous yet strangely appropriate," my mother said. I cringed and tried not to address her out loud.

"I may not be in the greatest state of mind to offer moral support and comfort," Carrie said, stubbing out her cigarette against a concrete pillar, "but I figured I'd give it a shot."

"I'm sure we'll manage somehow," I said.

"That makes one of us," my mother replied.

We went inside. The chapel was cool and overwhelmingly beige, from the blond wood benches to the eggshell walls and the neutral gray carpeting. The minister had not yet arrived. My father stood in the middle of the aisle, leaning heavily on his cane, his gaze fixed toward the front of the chapel.

I wasn't prepared for the urn. Cool, porcelain, and white, it perched on a pedestal above a profusion of white roses, Mom's favorites. It was like a magnet, or a black hole. The crushing singularity of its presence drew every gaze until we all stared at it.

I had no words. Even if I had tried, the void would have swallowed the sound. The same void had already consumed my mother, pulverized her into a fine powder, her presence compressed into the brutally elegant container we stared at now. How could all of her have fit into something so small?

I reached for my father's free hand. We shuffled together to the first pew. Sylvia, Gerald, and Walter moved over to join us. "It's so silly to sit all spread out, isn't it?" Sylvia asked no one in particular. She sat on Dad's right side and placed her hand over his. He looked up and smiled at her.

"So help me," my mother said, "if that bony old fossil is hitting on my husband at my own funeral, I swear I will slap her into the afterlife."

I tried so hard not to laugh, I was certain I was losing my mind. To conceal the insane grin I thought would spread like a rash across my face, I glanced over the pew toward the door. A few more people wandered in and stood just inside, looking a little lost. My mother said, "I think it's customary for members of the family to greet mourners as they arrive."

I was about to get up when the doors opened again and a woman in a black skirt suit entered. Like the room, her appearance seemed calculated to not stand out, but failed spectacularly. Granted, she wore little makeup and her long gray hair was collected in a neat bun at the back of her neck, but somehow she managed to look sympathetic and intimidating at the same time. The combination was altogether ghoulish. She reminded me of a librarian of the dead, categorizing and shelving the titles away.

She walked briskly but silently up the center aisle and turned to face my father. Her mouth smiled while her eyes frowned. She held out her hand and looked constipated.

"Mr. Patterson, I'm so sorry no one was here to meet you," she said.

Her name was Gwendolyn Baker, and she was one of the owners of the funeral home. I half listened to her. There was no music playing. That was probably another of my mother's choices. She hated the endless soundtrack to life that played in every store from Shaw's to Macy's. It was the soundtrack to someone else's life and she didn't particularly like their taste in music. "Why do I have to listen to Sting on Muzak when I do my grocery shopping?" she once asked me. "Why do they think I need to listen to anything? For once, I'd like to pick out my bananas in peace and quiet."

"Where's the minister?" I asked Ms. Baker (she'd clarified her honorific after Dad called her Mrs. Baker).

"He just called. He's having car trouble but will be here as soon as possible," she said. She mentioned there was coffee in the vestibule, fussed around the flower arrangements without actually touching them, and exited.

"I think her bun is pulled a little too tight," my mother said.

We sat in uncomfortable silence for a few moments. Carrie got up and said she was going outside to have another cigarette. Sylvia began chatting with my father. From listening to her, I gathered she and Gerald lived in Sedona, Arizona. I also gathered, though it wasn't stated explicitly, that Gerald was gay as a goose.

A gay, grumpy goose.

"Gerald, darling," Sylvia said, leaning over and touching his arm, "would you care for some coffee?"

Gerald's gray caterpillar eyebrows tilted in surprise. "Yes, I'd love some."

"Well, would you be a dear and get me a cup while you're at it?"

He sighed histrionically. "Oh please, are your legs broken?"

That got a laugh from my father. "Nice to see some things never change with George and Gracie."

Gerald hauled himself up. "Better than George and Martha, I suppose."

In some way or other, everyone found a reason to step out, leaving my father and me alone. I wondered if they had done this on purpose, collectively but unconsciously, so my father and I could have a moment together with what was left of my mother and his wife. Perhaps this was the point where he and I were supposed to talk to each other about what she meant to us and how we were going to cope with her loss.

"Do you want some coffee, Dad?" I asked.

He cleared his throat. "No, son, I'm fine. I'm just going to stay here. If you want some, go ahead."

"I'm fine."

That was it.

My mother, however, was not content to leave it at that. "That's it?" she asked. "You can't come up with anything better than that?"

I looked away from her, at the same time looking anywhere to avoid staring at the urn, and wondered again if I was losing my mind.

There should be more people here, I thought.

My family had never been in the habit of accumulating a large number of friends. My parents didn't socialize with people from the office. They didn't have other parents over for dinner or go on vacations with friends. Whenever I brought a classmate home from school, to do homework or have dinner, my parents behaved as if they'd misplaced the script for that particular scene. My father always played the only role he knew anyway and refused to hit his marks, staying resolutely in his recliner instead. It embarrassed me, but as I got older I realized I was no better a thespian. The stage for this scene, my mother's funeral, seemed underpopulated.

The door opened again. I glanced back, hoping it was the minister so we could get this over with. The man who walked in was around my father's age and wore a black suit, but he couldn't have looked more different. Everything about him was square, from his jaw to his shoulders to his dark gray hair styled into an almost plastic sheen. I'd never seen him before, but something about him made me twitch. As my father hoisted himself to his feet, the man extended his hand. The moment before he spoke, I knew he'd say his name was Derek.

He introduced himself as an old friend of my mother's. *"Right,"* she said. My father shook Derek's hand, giving no indication of having ever met him or knowing who he was. Their exchange was low and whispered—everything in this room was—and Derek placed his hand on my father's shoulder and glanced over at me. I felt like I was caught in a spotlight. Derek simply smiled at me, though, the sort of smile that has nothing to do with happiness, and stepped into the row behind us.

Sylvia dropped her coffee when she saw Derek. That made my mother laugh. "She can't hold her coffee, much less her liquor." An edge of resentment I'd never heard when she was alive made itself plain in her comments, like she was growing bored with being dead and impatient with the living. I wondered how much of that was her and how much was me.

While Gerald hurried, as much as a septuagenarian could, to get something to clean up the mess, Sylvia extended her hand to Derek and retracted it too quickly, before he'd had much time to grasp it.

"I hadn't expected to see you," Sylvia said. Her flat tone indicated she hadn't hoped to see him, either. Before he could reply, she pointedly looked away and sat down again next to my father. I tried to feel a little sorry for Derek for the way Sylvia treated him, but for all I knew, she might have been acting that way for my mother's sake. I had no idea who knew what about whom.

Carrie sat down next to me but couldn't take her eyes off Derek.

"Stop staring," I whispered.

"Why not? He's a silver fox. Too bad the hot ones are always gay."

"He's old enough to be your dad. Besides, how do you know he's gay?"

"My gaydar spans generations," she said. She was stroking her purse. I was sure she already wanted another cigarette. I wanted to go outside and tell her everything I knew from reading my mother's letter, but the door opened and the minister arrived at last.

More low whispers passed between my father and the minister. His forehead was big, pink, and too shiny. He'd rushed to get here and was sweating. I stared at that furrowed pink balloon of a head instead of looking back toward the urn. I never caught the minister's name. He looked at me but couldn't muster any words of comfort. He pursed his lips, wrinkled his balloon, and scurried to the podium up front, off to the left side of the vessel containing what was left of my mother.

He started speaking, but I couldn't grasp a word of it. It was like listening to one of the teachers in a Charlie Brown cartoon. A Bible passage was read. I was pretty sure my mother would have laughed in the minister's face or told him to read from something else—the phone book, maybe. But I remembered this whole service was her idea. We'd done everything she'd asked.

The minister asked if anyone wanted to say anything about "the departed"—he actually called her that, as if she had departed us on a transatlantic trip, or had just left for the store. I resisted the urge to laugh. As everyone stared at me in the ensuing silence, though, I wondered if I actually *had* laughed out loud. It dawned on me they were looking at my father, who shifted in his seat. Of course he would be expected to say something. I don't know why that surprised me.

I leaned over and whispered, "Dad, do you want to say something about Mom?"

"What?" Dad looked up. I thought I should repeat the question, but maybe he was asking me what he should possibly say. Resting one hand on my arm, he leaned onto his cane and got to his feet.

There was a painfully long silence once Dad stood at the front of the room. I leaned forward. Everyone else did the same, as though expectation might pitch all of us onto the floor at his feet. The silence drew itself out ever tighter. I watched his jaw work, as if the words were lodged between his teeth and he was using his tongue to free them.

I couldn't watch any longer and started to get up. Before I could rescue Dad from the spectacle of silence, Sylvia glided up beside him. She slipped her arm through his and patted it with her other hand. Dad stared at her incomprehensibly for a moment. I waited for him to call her Rachel, at which point I was sure I would have been forced to kill her. Instead, his jaw ceased its gyrations and he stood there mute.

"She really is beyond the pale," my mother grumbled. "Look at that dress. What is this, a cocktail party?"

I didn't answer. Sylvia said something about how my mother was always the prettiest girl in school and made a comment attracting a scattering of laughter. I didn't hear enough of it to get the joke. She mentioned Dad's name, then my name. Carrie grasped my hand at that point. I tuned out completely then and didn't come back to the room until Sylvia and my father were heading back to their seats.

Eventually, everyone who wanted to speak had his or her say. People I'd never met knew things about my mother I never realized. It all washed over me until my ears filled with a roaring, tumbling sound like ocean over sand, one force of nature scouring the other.

"Son, are you ready to go?" My father stood with his hand on my shoulder. Everyone else was heading toward the doors behind us. The pink balloon had already drifted out. I realized I'd been staring at my mother's urn the whole time, almost like an out-of-body experience.

"I'll be out in a minute," I said.

The room felt stuffed with cotton once the door shut behind the last person. It was just her and me now. I stood and picked up the urn. Its lightness surprised me. I lifted the lid, half-expecting it to be empty. The tan and gray ash was grainy like sand, not the fine, talcum-like stuff I had expected. Was this all that was left?

"You know," my mother said, "I'm not really in there."

"Where are you, then?" I asked. She didn't answer. She didn't know the answer any more than I did.

CHAPTER FOUR

Darling," my mother asked, "how can you be sure I'm not just a figment of your imagination?"

"Because that would mean I'm losing my mind," I said.

We were sitting in my dad's boat of a Buick, waiting for everyone to leave the parking lot. Dad rode home in Carrie's rental car. I was going to the store because Dad had invited everyone back to the house, in an unusual display of hospitality.

"I can make us some coffee, at least," he said. "And maybe Joel could get something together."

Get something together. The phrase ran through my head as I started the Buick. The big old engine gurgled, and I watched the cloud of exhaust rise up in the rearview mirror. If I stayed there forever, in the muffled shell of that car, nothing else could possibly go wrong, just as long as I didn't put the car in drive and go.

My mother had never believed in an afterlife. I had asked her about it once, over the phone.

"Do you believe in God?"

She paused for a moment, then said, "No, darling, not really." I felt relieved and disappointed at the same time. If she'd believed in something beyond life, maybe that would have given me at least enough room to doubt.

I heard the flick of Mom's lighter, and the smell of cigarette smoke wafted across the bench seat. "Darling, we can't just sit here all morning," she said. I looked over. She was still wearing her peach nightgown and the fuzzy-heeled slippers.

"You look ridiculous riding around dressed like that," I said.

"This is my favorite outfit, and I am old enough to wear whatever I please." She exhaled toward me. "Now go."

At the store I gathered finger food: vegetables, shrimp, crackers, and salami from the deli. Some little puff pastries filled with—something; I didn't look too closely at the package. In the produce section I found big, bright white mushroom caps that would be perfect for stuffing. That would give me something to do in the kitchen so I wouldn't have to stand in the living room and be pitied.

When in doubt, cook.

I picked up shallots and Italian bread crumbs for the mushrooms. When I got to the cheese case, Mom took over.

"Get that tub of fresh mozzarella too. That looks good," she said as I reached for a block of Parmagiano. "Ooh, there's some Stilton too."

I let my hands be guided by her voice. Soon she had selected enough cheeses to fill the top basket of the cart. I would need more crackers. She'd always said there was nothing worse than running out of crackers when there was still cheese to be eaten. Of course, lack of crackers had never stopped her from eating the cheese anyway.

The smell of weak coffee greeted me when I wrestled the grocery bags into the kitchen. I peered through the doorway to the living room. A sea of black outfits had washed up, making the room look smaller. Carrie, alone in the kitchen, took cookies from a package and arranged them on a plate. She took a bite of one and frowned.

"These might be from last Christmas," she said. "And your dad doesn't really know how to make coffee. What did you buy?"

"Enough cheese to keep the dairy farmers of Wisconsin in business for at least another week," I said. "Also, a lot of wine."

Carrie left the cookie platter unfinished and began fishing in one of the bags. "Where's your corkscrew? I need a drink."

"Nothing like getting drunk for dealing with grief."

"Don't judge," Carrie said, pulling wineglasses from the cabinet. I got out a large platter and arranged the blocks of cheese.

"How's my dad doing?" I asked. I really wanted to ask where Derek was, and whether Carrie had talked to him yet.

She was struggling with the corkscrew and a bottle of Cabernet. "I couldn't say. As far as I can tell, underneath your father's gruff exterior is a gruff interior." At last the cork gave up with a loud pop, and she started filling two glasses. "I need a smoke. Care to join me?"

I went outside with her, but didn't smoke. I gave in to my curiosity and asked, "Has Derek had anything interesting to say?"

Carrie shrugged. She turned her head to exhale somewhere other than directly into my face. "If he has, he didn't say it to me. He's been talking to your mom's old friends. I'm dying to know what his story is, though. He was trying to talk to the one who's been hanging all over your dad, Sylvia, but she won't give him the time of day. I wonder what that's about?"

It was chilly outside, and the wine wasn't helping me keep warm. I stared across the lawn at the RV, beached against the garage like a whale of a mistake. I took a sip of wine and said, trying to sound casual, "Derek and my mother were engaged before she married my dad."

"Get *out*. Does your father know?"

"I don't think he has a clue," I said. I couldn't imagine why my mother hadn't brought up something as important as that, but she hadn't told him about her cancer, either.

Mom kept secrets. Sometimes they were little, like a box of hair color or a cigarette snuck out on the porch. Sometimes it was huge, like being enough in love with someone to consider marrying him before she'd ever met Dad. He and I never had a clue, never thought she could have had some sort of inner life we weren't privy to.

I knew she had an inner life, but I thought she'd shared it with me. In fact, the conspiracy of secrets we'd kept just between us had been nothing, and she'd never told me the things that really mattered, like *you can have love more than once in your life* or *I'm dying.*

Maybe I hadn't known her at all.

"Well, whose fault is that?" my mother asked, in that way she had—maybe all mothers had it—that accused without sounding like it.

As if reading my mind, Carrie said, "Sounds like your mom was good at keeping secrets." She stubbed out her cigarette. "I think I would have liked her."

"Everyone liked her," I said. I'd finished my wine and felt the chill even more now. "You two could have bonded over your bad habit. I just want to know what Derek knows about her."

"So ask him," she said.

Back inside, I managed to find plenty to do in the kitchen. I warmed up the oven for the puff pastries and began chopping ingredients to fill the mushrooms. Carrie circulated with bottles of wine. She and I reconvened on the porch as the afternoon lengthened into dusk. Carrie had a cigarette, and I downed a glass of wine. By the time the sun dipped behind the town houses across the street, I had a solid buzz going, and Carrie promised to try chatting with Derek.

"He didn't say much," Carrie reported later, when we slipped back out again. "Mostly, we talked about you."

"Me?" I set my empty glass on the porch railing, aiming carefully to avoid sending it over the edge into the yard. "Why were you talking about me?"

"Because I knew it would annoy you?" Carrie shook her head; she was kidding. "He asked me how I knew Rachel, and as it happens, you are really the only topic of conversation we had in common. Anyway, he was interested in hearing about you."

"What did you tell him?"

"That you're a big nelly bottom and hung like a horse, so he wants to have a three-way with you and his partner. Come *on*, dummy. I told him how we met and what you do for a living. He told me what your mom was like in high school. Apparently, she was well known but not known very well, if that makes sense. She was one of the prettiest girls in school too, if not *the* prettiest. He was surprised as hell when she agreed to go out with him, even if his family was rich and he was on the track team. Apparently, he was the fastest runner in school. Oh, and his partner's name is Mark. They've been together since college."

Carrie leaned against a pillar and stared at the town houses. She downed the wine still in her glass and took a final drag off her cigarette.

Across the street, lights were now glowing through tall, narrow windows. I watched for people moving through gaps in curtains or behind unblocked, unadorned panes of glass. Those were the ones that interested me the most. They didn't bother putting up anything to shield the private sector of their home from the public space of the sidewalk outside or the porch across the street. I looked over at Carrie and noticed her looking in the windows too.

She caught me catching her looking. Her cigarette was out and her glass was empty. She was out of props. She smiled and shrugged back. "What is it about other people's windows? I don't think of myself as a voyeur, but looking into someone else's domestic sphere…"

"Makes us forget for a little bit about our own," I said. "Personally, I've always liked a good set of window shades."

Much like hiding behind curtains, I concealed myself behind the stove for the rest of the evening. While my dad mingled and mourned, I sent out platters of pastries and cheeses and baby carrots. I could have spent the rest of the wake doing nothing but chopping and would have been as happy as possible given the circumstances.

Once the mushrooms were under the broiler, I poured myself another glass of wine. My fourth glass, maybe. I'd lost track of how many. Too many, probably. I didn't care. I did care about burning the mushrooms, though, and bent down to make sure I hadn't placed the rack too close to the broiler.

"Those smell good," someone behind me said. I registered it was Derek about the same time I tried to stand up and smashed the back of my head on the oven door handle. The crack of bone against metal sounded as if I was hearing it from inside my own skull, followed by my wineglass shattering on the floor. Derek gave a short cry of alarm—even through the haze of my pain, he *did* sound a little nelly. He helped me up and steered me to a bar stool away from the scattered shards of glass.

"Don't let the mushrooms burn," I said. I touched the back of my head and winced. There was no blood on my hand, but it felt like there'd be a knot the size of a doorknob back there tomorrow.

"Don't worry about those," Derek said. "I'll keep an eye on them. Where's your broom and dustpan?"

"In the pantry," my father said. He stood at the kitchen door along with Sylvia and Carrie. "You okay, son?"

"Darling," Sylvia said, "let me see—"

"That bitch did *not* call you darling," my mother's voice rattled from somewhere inside my head.

"I'm fine, really," I said.

"That's it, I'm cutting you off," Carrie said.

"Get him an ice pack," someone else said. Gerald, maybe.

"It was an accident. I was surprised."

"You're not feeling dizzy, are you?" Sylvia asked.

"No more than usual."

Dad decided I'd done enough work for the day. They installed me on the sofa, gave me a full glass of wine despite

Carrie's prior declaration, and handed me a towel filled with ice cubes. Someone put a plate of cheese and crackers on the coffee table. In a few minutes Derek returned with a platter on which he'd arranged the mushrooms. He dropped a couple on my plate and set the platter on the coffee table.

The pain in the back of my head had dulled to a cold, hard throb. The ice in the towel started to melt and soaked my collar. Everything seemed dull and thud-like, as if my head were wrapped in pillows and someone was hitting it with a book. As Derek leaned forward to peer at some framed snapshots on a shelf, I began shoveling the mushrooms into my mouth one after the other, chewing slowly.

"Honey," my mother's voice said, "snap out of it. You look like a cow contemplating a fence post."

"Is that your mother?" Derek asked.

"What?" Had he heard her voice? Had she really called me a cow? Then I realized he was referring to one of the photos. At the same time, the taste of the mushrooms registered. And they were awful. Too much garlic, and the shallots were underdone. I was tempted to spit out what I was still chewing. I couldn't find a napkin, so I swallowed it down, swilled a bit of wine, and hauled myself up to look at the photo.

"That's us," I said. I felt kind of dizzy but managed to stay on my feet. I leaned against the bookshelf.

I was five years old when the picture was taken. We were standing on the beach at Cape Cod, and behind us stretched the Atlantic, which had faded to gray in the picture. The waves that day were huge. I was terrified to go near the water, with the sea roaring like a monster and the noise flooding my ears. Shortly after he took the picture, Dad set the camera down, picked me up, and marched toward the water. He waded in just above his waist and dumped me. I was a good swimmer at the pool, but I swallowed a mouthful of briny water and went under. I popped back above the surface like a cork and promptly threw up. I swam back toward shore until I could stand, ran up the beach, past my mother, and into the dunes. I didn't speak to my father for the rest of the trip.

"She looks so much like she did when we were in school," Derek said.

She *did* look good. She wore a blue bathing suit, the skirt fluttering in the wind. We both were smiling. I hadn't been thrown in the ocean yet. Big Jackie O sunglasses obscured her eyes, and her arm was draped over my narrow shoulders. I knew that she was so pretty; people looked at her like she might be someone famous. Her beauty was some sort of spell that could keep me, *us* safe. Nothing bad happened to pretty people, right?

"Tell that to Jayne Mansfield," my mother said.

I started feeling dizzy then, and a swarm of little sparkles danced in front of my field of vision. "I think I need to sit down again."

As Derek guided me back to the sofa, I asked, "Did she know? About you, I mean?"

Derek's eyes inadvertently flicked left then right before he answered. His voice dropped a little and he leaned in closer, as if he were about to divulge something secret.

"I honestly don't know. When we broke off the engagement, she came over, threw her engagement ring in the snow, and I never saw her after that. Did she ever say anything to you after you told her about—well, about you?"

"No," I said. "I didn't know about you until…until this morning. You never saw her after that, not for forty years?"

Derek shrugged. "I think we may have seen each other at one of the high school reunions. And I saw her wedding announcement in the *Press-Herald* back when she married Arthur." He practically gushed when he said next, "She was *radiant*."

"Oh good God, how did I *not* know he was a queen?" my mother asked.

He scanned the shelf of pictures again, perhaps looking for the same wedding photo that had been in the paper. After a moment, he returned to the beach photo and picked up the frame, holding it closer to his face. Derek probably needed glasses but was likely too vain to wear them. When he looked back, his eyes were damp.

"She was happy, though, wasn't she?"

"Yes." I wanted to add *as far as I know* to give my statement the roundness of truth, instead of that blunt, unambiguous declaration. Even with her constant presence in my head, I had no clue whether she had been happy or not. And if she wasn't— well, as she might have said, whose fault was that?

❖

A short time later, people started to leave. My head kept throbbing, so I went upstairs to lie down. Carrie promised she would call or stop by before she caught her flight back to St. Louis in the morning. My mother's friends arranged to have lunch with Derek and his partner while they were in town. They invited my father, who begged off, mentioning all the things he had to do to get Rachel's affairs in order. There wasn't all that much to do, but I didn't point that out before going upstairs.

I don't know if it was the wine or the run-in with the oven handle, but shortly after my head hit the pillow, I fell asleep. When I woke up a few hours later, the room was dark and the house quiet. I got out of bed—I was still wearing my clothes from the day—and went out into the hall. My headache hadn't disappeared, but now it was more like a memory of having a headache than a feeling of real pain.

"Someday that's how you will feel about me," my mother said. "And I mean that to be a comfort to you."

"It isn't," I murmured.

"It will be."

I went downstairs. The dirty plates and pans from the evening were still piled in the kitchen sink and on the counters. The stacks cast long shadows in the streetlight coming through the window. It was enough to see by, so I didn't bother turning on the overhead light. I moved the dishes over to one side of the sink and began running water in the other.

"You want a hand with that?"

Dad was in the living room, his silhouette hunched in the recliner. He was sitting with his forearms resting on his shins, back bent forward. I couldn't see his face, but his voice sounded normal, without a tremor or a shake to it.

For a moment, the water filling the sink was the only sound. I thought of telling Dad I could handle it on my own and he ought to go to bed. Instead, I flipped on the light and asked, "You want to wash or dry?"

Dad dried, swirling the towel over the dishes in slow, careful circles. For a long time we didn't speak. I relaxed into the rhythm of cleaning, passing, drying, and stacking. Once the plates and glasses were done, I started on the pots and baking sheets, which took longer to scrub and scrape.

"It was nice to see your mom's old friends," Dad said.

I handed him a baking sheet and a new towel. "Yeah."

"Sylvia and Gerald live in Sedona. I told them about the RV, and they said if you make the trip, you should stop in and visit them. It's supposed to be pretty out there."

I was about to snap at him that I hadn't made up my mind yet, but instead just started to work on the sauté pan and asked, "So, had you ever met Derek before?"

My mother started to laugh. "I see you were paying attention when I was teaching you how to change the subject."

I expected Dad to answer gruffly. Instead, he kept drying the baking sheet and said, "Before today, I never knew he existed."

I handed him the sauté pan. Part of me would have loved nothing more than to put down the sponge, and say in a gossipy rush, "Oh my God, you had *no* idea she'd been engaged before, did you?" Right.

And later maybe we could paint our nails and talk about boys.

I picked up the last pot in the sink.

"Did he tell you—?"

"That they'd been engaged? Yes, and that she'd broken it off."

"She really never told you about him before you got married?" I asked.

Dad was looking at the sauté pan as if bewildered by it. "Not once, son. Neither did her parents." He laughed a little. "She finally kept a secret from me. Let me tell you something, son. Your mom was lousy at keeping secrets. She thought I didn't know she was smoking all these years, but I'm not that oblivious."

"Oh, I do *not* want to be here for this conversation," my mother said. She flicked an ash in the sink and walked out.

He finished drying the pan and put down the towel. I wanted to ask him what he thought about his wife's ex-fiancé turning out to be gay, but kept my mouth shut. Our relationship consisted of a lot of things I wanted to say but never did. When I was younger I thought it was because I was afraid of this guy who came home tired and taciturn and just wanted to watch the news and the ball game in peace, and maybe have a beer. Although the fear abated around high school when it seemed like overnight I became taller than him, the silence between us lingered. The older I got, the more it felt as if time had run out. If there had been an opportunity to talk, *really* talk, with my father, I'd either missed the signs or been too hesitant to go down that path, and now couldn't find my way back to it.

But then he asked, "Do you think your mom knew she'd almost married a gay guy?" and I had to wonder. To my surprise, Dad was smirking, as if he finally possessed a secret Mom never knew about. If he had figured that one out on his own, I wondered if I ever really needed to say any of those unsaid things, or if he'd known all along what I was thinking.

"That would be pretty funny if she didn't have any idea, huh?" I asked.

"At least as funny as I bet Derek felt finally seeing he'd been replaced with someone who was his exact opposite," he said.

"Do you think it would have bothered him?" I asked. I felt we were wading into uncertain, possibly hazardous, territory with that question. This was the sort of thing my father and I had never talked about before.

"Only if he's an idiot," Dad said. "If he didn't like girls, why should he care? You never really dated any girls in high school, did you?"

"No," I replied a little too quickly, and not wanting to lie, I added, "Well, there was one girl, but that was pretty hopeless."

"So how would you feel if you ran into her and found out she'd married someone who was everything you weren't?"

"I think by definition he would have to be, wouldn't he?"

I pulled the stopper out of the sink, squeezed out the sponge, and set it on the counter. My father lingered close by as the water gurgled down the drain, like he was about to ask me something. If it was the question I thought it might be, I'd already made up my mind.

Upstairs, I pulled the Ferragamo box from under the bed. I put aside the letter I'd read the day before and searched randomly through the remaining contents, shuffling the envelopes somewhat like playing cards and leaving my selection to the luck of the draw. Eventually, my hand found the one that felt right, that felt old enough, the paper the right texture. I pulled it out and began to read.

Dear Derek,

This has been a week of revelations. When I told Sylvia about you—how you were—she said she already knew. She'd known for weeks! And she'd never even thought for one minute to tell me! She looked at me as if I should have already known. I was so livid I had to walk out before I said something that would damage our friendship beyond repair, but not before she said

Gerald was the same way. I just don't know what to think anymore, I really don't.

I went home but they came by later and took me out to Grant's so I could drown my sorrows in a chocolate malt. I'm embarrassed to say it did make me feel better for a bit, but then I was even more embarrassed when I got to the bottom of the malt and, I suppose I was preoccupied, but I made the biggest slurping sound with my straw. The soda jerk apparently found this amusing because he told me I was only allowed one slurp and that any more would be unladylike. Of course, I told him it wasn't very gentlemanly of him to point this out, but he said that was okay, because he wasn't a gentleman.

Well, maybe I'm no lady.

I folded the letter and slid it into the envelope. Mom and Dad had met at the soda fountain where he worked. Growing up, I remembered hearing that story in passing more than once. How charming it sounded, so old-fashioned. Who drinks chocolate malts anymore?

I opened my laptop and started up my e-mail. Philip's message still sat there, unanswered, in my in-box. Maybe I'd send him a real letter, with a stamp and everything.

Though I'd been in his flat for four days, it occurred to me I didn't know his address.

I set that problem aside for now and opened up a new message window.

Dear Miranda,

This letter is to tender my resignation, effective immediately...

CHAPTER FIVE

The next day was Friday, and that morning I went to the Portland Art Museum and found myself standing in front of the Mona Lisa.

Not *the* Mona Lisa, perhaps, but she was *a* Mona Lisa, possibly painted by Leonardo's hand, according to the pamphlet I'd picked up at the gallery entrance. It had a photo of the Mona Lisa in Paris, and I looked from it to the canvas in front of me again. She was the same and yet, not the same. Her enigmatic smile was absent, but there was some difference more fundamental than that. I couldn't put my finger on what made one painting a masterpiece studied for centuries and the other merely an honorable mention.

I thought about that for the rest of the afternoon. I decided I was tired of cooking, and my head was still sore from the day before. I made reservations at an Italian restaurant not far from the house.

"You ever been here before?" I asked Dad. Slouched in his side of the booth, he looked like a shrunken version of himself hidden behind the tall menu.

"Not that I remember," he said. "We haven't been out since—well, a long time."

I hadn't told him I'd quit my job yet. I was trying to figure out how to bring up the subject when the waiter came to our table.

"Hi, my name's Lincoln, I'll be taking care of you this— Joel?"

I lowered my menu and looked up. Our waiter was Lincoln Walters. His sister was the last girl I ever dated. I hadn't seen him since he'd punched me in the face seventeen years ago. His expression now was somewhere between a smile and a smirk, not unlike the face I'd stared up at from the ground in front of the high school after he'd slugged me.

Thankfully, he didn't look like he was about to repeat the event. We stumbled through pleasantries, I introduced my dad, and Lincoln went over the specials. He took our appetizer order, suggested the lasagna—a house specialty—and disappeared into the kitchen.

I hadn't thought about Lincoln since high school. Nor had I thought much of high school since I'd graduated. (I didn't think much of it at the time, either.) Linda hadn't crossed my mind either. I couldn't call my ham-fisted efforts at being sociable with her in high school "dating." We'd hung out together after school, gone to the movies a few times, went out for pizza, usually with several other people, and made out between classes in the high-walled canyons formed by the banks of lockers.

Linda was only five-two, but even so, I always felt short around her. She was a force of nature, and I was just carried along on her prevailing winds. When she propelled me between the lockers and attached herself, it felt as if she towered over me, the attack of the five-two woman. She was more popular than I could ever have hoped to be, without any apparent effort. She was a bad influence, but parents seemed to have a blind spot to this aspect of her character. Her diminutive stature had something to do with that, and at the same time her round, fair face and wheat-colored hair made her look too wholesome to get up to any kind of trouble. She could turn that innocence on and off like a faucet, and when I was with her I felt even more invisible.

Linda, who managed to be intense and blasé at the same time, also took the initiative one Friday night when her parents went out for the evening and she invited (more like summoned) me to her house, and we had sex. It was my first time as well as my last time with a girl. I was pretty sure I wasn't her first. When I told her I hadn't brought any protection with me (later, I couldn't believe I had actually used the euphemism "protection," as if I needed a suit of armor), she whipped a condom seemingly out of nowhere and slid it on me with hardly a break in the action. I don't know how I managed to perform, probably saved only by the endless push of her jet stream and the inevitability of post-adolescent hormones.

Not long after that, we stopped dating—to say we broke up would have been an overstatement, since the duration of the encounter had only been a matter of weeks. The experience had left me dazed more than disappointed, and perhaps a little relieved—but feeling a little shorter, just the same.

"See," Linda said to me shortly before she dumped me, "your problem is you don't know what it is you want. Or you know what you want but you're too afraid to ask for it."

"Spare me the analysis," I said. Later, I did nothing but analyze it, and ended up wondering what the hell I'd been thinking. High school dating should have been like riding a bike with training wheels. Unless you were gay, in which case it was like realizing you didn't much care for bicycles at all and besides, you kept falling off.

At least if you were me.

Not long after, Linda started dating Darren, and I felt a surge of jealousy. Darren was on the football team and would have been nothing more than a big oaf if he weren't also funny, popular, drop dead gorgeous, and already accepted to the Naval Academy. I felt even shorter.

If I'd been more self-aware, I'd have realized I was jealous of that lucky bitch Linda.

But that knowledge was still months and miles away, in college. I didn't date anyone else senior year. I skipped senior prom.

The only reason I knew Lincoln was because of Linda. He and I hadn't been friends before that. We weren't exactly friends afterward, either, especially not after he punched me in the face. Lincoln hadn't explained or prefaced the assault—it had happened on the front steps at school, and Lincoln was carted off to the principal's office before I'd even stopped bleeding. Later, Linda made him apologize. Lincoln said he thought it was just what he was supposed to do when someone screwed his sister and dumped her, but Linda pointed out she'd broken up with me and anyway, if Lincoln planned to punch everyone she'd slept with, he was going to be busy for a while.

I wondered if he felt as small around her as I did.

Apparently, Linda and Lincoln had something in common when it came to the opposite sex. Lincoln was popular with girls, especially ones who put out. Or maybe they were popular with him. Either way, it was pretty much a given that he was getting laid on a regular basis, and not always by the same girl. He was a gentleman, he said, and never identified them.

"Who was that again?" my father asked after Lincoln left the table.

"An old friend from high school. You remember Lincoln?"

He shook his head. "Can't say that I do."

"Maybe his sister, Linda?"

"Son, my memory isn't what it used to be. And it never was that great to begin with."

I let it go then, and instead fiddled with the pink flower—surprisingly, real—set in a tiny vase in the middle of the table. A few moments later our drinks came out, followed by the appetizers, and we were distracted for a while trying to figure out the ingredients in them. This involved me making guesses, and my father shrugging at each one.

I would have expected Lincoln to leave town eventually, so I was curious to know why he was still here. But the restaurant was busy, and whenever I looked up throughout the meal, Lincoln was either in the process of turning away and heading to another table or back into the kitchen.

When we were finished, Dad balled up his napkin and dropped it on the table. As he slid out of the booth, he said, "When the waiter comes back, tell him I'd like coffee and a cannoli. I have to go to the can."

I looked at the dessert menu while the busboy cleared the table. When I thought Dad had returned, I looked up to find Lincoln sitting across from me.

"Before I forget, my dad wants a coffee and a cannoli," I said. "Make that two."

"Okay," Lincoln said. Though his order pad was in front of him, he didn't write it down. He hadn't written down any of our order all night. It always impressed me when waiters did that.

"So, what has it been?" Lincoln asked. "Fifteen years?"

"More like seventeen," I said.

"What brings you back to town?"

"My mom died."

I'd said it out loud only a handful of times before that. This loss felt more than personal. It felt almost sacred, like saying it aloud too often would dilute what was important about it. I really didn't want to be the guy who said it like he was looking for sympathy—especially not from a guy I only sort of knew in high school who'd punched me in the face, and was now a waiter in a white button-down shirt with a black name tag and was, to my surprise, placing his hand over mine where it rested on the table and saying, "Jesus, Joel. I'm so sorry."

The gesture made me feel like I was chewing on my own heart. "Thanks," I said. I briefly placed my other hand on top of Lincoln's and let go. His hands were rough. I started twisting my napkin around my fingers. "My dad's doing okay, I think. It's only been a few days, so, you know…"

He started writing on his order pad. "How much longer are you in town?"

"I don't know. I haven't really decided yet. It depends on my dad."

Lincoln tore the slip off his order pad and handed it to me. "Give me a call while you're in town. If you've got time, I'll make you dinner. Which reminds me, I'd better put in your cannoli."

When Dad returned to the table, he looked at me and asked, "Were you running laps around the dining room while I was in the can?"

"No, I've just been sitting here. Why?"

"Because your face is all flushed." He leaned back and exhaled heavily. "Mind you, after that plate of linguini, I could probably stand to run a few laps myself." He adjusted his waistband, and for a moment I was afraid he might undo the top button of his pants. Instead he looked around and asked, "Where's my coffee?"

❖

I called Lincoln the next day. I told him I was hoping to leave town soon, so we made plans to meet after he got off work that evening. And that was how I found myself standing, at the age of thirty-five, in front of my father, asking to borrow the car.

"I might be late," I said.

He gestured toward the kitchen. "Keys are where they always are. Not like I'm going to be getting behind the wheel anytime soon."

This had been a well-worn conversation between us when I was in high school, but it hadn't grown any more comfortable through repeated wearing. I didn't have a curfew back then, but not being home before midnight usually resulted in an interrogation the next morning. Trying to sneak back in without making any noise was hopeless too. The house, already old when I was a teenager, managed to rat me out every time with its vocabulary of creaks and wheezes.

"If you have too much to drink, don't drive," my mother

said. She was sitting at the kitchen table, flipping through a *Vanity Fair* and smoking a cigarette. "Take a cab, or just come home in the morning. Trust me, your father won't notice. He only knew when you were late coming in because I told him and made him put you through the twenty questions routine."

"Now she tells me," I muttered, grabbing the keys and heading out. It didn't surprise me in the least to find her riding shotgun when I got in the car.

The address Lincoln gave me was down in the Old Port, which used to be full of places my mother told me to avoid in high school but was now an arts district. "I don't know if there are any gay bars down there," my mother said. "You know, I haven't the slightest idea where there are *any* gay bars in town."

"Why would you need to?" I asked. I had no idea where they were either. I didn't start going out to the bars until college. Whenever I came home on breaks, I didn't want to go out and risk running into someone I actually knew.

Like a teacher.

"Anyway," I added, "Lincoln's not gay."

My mother shrugged. "Either way, a DWI right before heading across country would probably put a crimp in your plans."

Lincoln wasn't home. His roommate, a mountain of muscle named Rich, let me into their loft. Lincoln was still at work but had called to say he'd be home soon. He'd mentioned something about making dinner.

"With what, I don't know," Rich added, with a dubious glance toward the kitchen. He passed this along on his way out the door himself, telling me to make myself at home.

"Well," my mother said, once the door closed behind the roommate, "this is awkward."

I looked toward the kitchen. My mind was muddled, like the crush of lime and mint at the bottom of a cocktail glass. Nothing seemed to be making sense. "When he said make dinner, he didn't mean me, did he?"

My mother wandered over to the milky-glassed windows taking up one long wall that spanned the entryway, dining room, and living room. "Do you mean make dinner of you, or you make dinner?" she asked.

"God, I'm so confused," I said, and began opening cabinets.

"Darling, you're not making much sense." Several unframed paintings leaned against the wall. She began flipping through them.

"Gee, I wonder why," I said. The cabinets were remarkably bare, not only of food. There were a few plates of various sizes, a couple of soup bowls that did match. When I picked one up, there was a chip in the rim. As far as cooking utensils went, there was a saucepan that looked as old as me and a sauté pan barely holding onto its nonstick coating. I felt a pang of sympathy as I returned it to the cabinet.

"Darling," my mother said. "Come look at these. They're… interesting."

The paintings were similar in style, and some of them were huge. One was about seven or eight feet tall, turned on its side so we had to crane our necks to view it properly. It was a figure of a naked man, almost photorealistic, kneeling in sand with what looked like a gauzy, translucent curtain of red fire billowing over him.

I realized it was Lincoln a moment after my mind registered him as damn hot.

"It is?" my mother asked in disbelief when I told her. "I would have remembered if one of your friends was this attractive, I think."

"I'm pretty sure I would have remembered too," I said. I flipped through a few more of the canvases. There were others of Lincoln; a few of the walking, talking muscle who'd just left, similar in style; and several of a yellow lab who was dressed in various costumes: a cat burglar (ironic) climbing through a window with a flashlight clenched in his mouth; a king on a throne, crown tilted over one ear; Superman, surveying the city from a rooftop perch.

"I think I like the ones of the dog better," I said. My mother smiled and flipped back to one of Lincoln that left nothing to the imagination.

"Are you sure, darling?" she asked. Her smirk was solely for my benefit. "I wonder which of them is the artist."

"I'm assuming it's the roommate," I said. Neither he nor Lincoln struck me as the artistic type, but what did I know? My estimation of the roommate was based on his ability to flex his eyebrows. My estimation of Lincoln was based on a seventeen-year-old memory—hardly fair, but it occurred to me I didn't know much about Lincoln at all.

I went back to the kitchen, which wasn't a separate room so much as an area partitioned off by cabinets, and opened the fridge. There wasn't a lot to work with: some sad-looking potatoes shared space with two onions, some celery that had seen better days, a half gallon of milk, and a box of Velveeta.

And a six-pack.

"I don't know how that guy got so big, since it doesn't look like he eats," I said. I took one of the beers and opened it. After wondering for a few moments whether Lincoln would mind if I started making something, my stomach growled so loudly that my mother turned and looked at me. After that, I hunted around for a cutting board and started chopping the onions.

"Wouldn't ordering a pizza have been easier?" my mother asked. She joined me in the kitchen when she got tired of looking at paintings. She'd lit a cigarette, and as she leaned over my shoulder to look at what I was doing, I was tempted to shoo her away lest her ash fall in the pan. Then I remembered the ash, the smoke, and the cigarette were no more real than she was. I shooed her back anyway.

I like a kitchen challenge. It's easy to come up with

something spectacular when you have every ingredient and spice you could possibly think of at your fingertips, but working with five random ingredients is like trying to write a sonnet with a five-year-old's vocabulary: if you can do it, you're *good.*

Before long, I had a pot of potato and cheese soup simmering, and the kitchen started to smell like a real kitchen. I realized beforehand, the dominant smell had been oil paint and turpentine. I lowered the flame under the pot shortly before the front door opened, and Lincoln walked in, carrying a loaf of Italian bread and a twelve-pack of beer.

It was possible to see something of the Lincoln I recalled from high school in the person who walked in the front door. The Elvis Costello glasses were gone, and he was in better shape. He hadn't been a jock in high school, nor had he been much of a brain. He didn't hang out with the druggies, the punks, vo-tech, or the FBLA crowd either. Somehow, he'd still managed to be popular. Even after he slugged me, I hadn't warranted the sympathy vote.

The smell of the restaurant clung to him and his clothes. He gave me a hug and I breathed in the scent of cooking oil and the savory, smoked aroma of grilled meat. Underneath that was something vaguely sweet—a bit of sweat and cologne mingling in a way that made my stomach growl again. He laughed, handed me the bread, and headed for his bedroom.

"I really need a shower," he said.

His room was a mess. He sat on the corner of his bed and began untying his shoes. For a moment he bit his lip as he struggled with a knot, then gave up and pried the shoe off. He stood and shed his white button-down shirt and black trousers, which he left in a pile on the floor. He was wearing white briefs. Somehow, seeing him standing there momentarily in his underwear seemed more erotic than the paintings in which he was completely naked. He went to the closet.

Apart from the bed, there was nowhere else to sit, so I sat

on the floor. "So what have you been up to lately?" I asked, as if seventeen years could have been described as "lately." As Lincoln emerged from the closet with a clean T-shirt and jeans and headed to the bathroom, he talked about going to college for a year, dropping out, following a girl down to Boston, coming back alone, moving in with his parents for longer than he probably should have, trying to go back to school and hating it more than the first time.

The shower turned on, followed by the rustle of a curtain. From where I sat, I couldn't see into the bathroom. Lincoln raised his voice over the spray of the water.

"I did random jobs," he said, "waited tables, and saved up enough money so I could take off and head west. I don't know why. I just did."

He got as far as Chicago before his car, an old Honda Civic, got stolen from the hotel parking lot. He took the bus back to Portland and felt defeated for a while.

The water turned off. "My parents think I'm aimless and my life has no direction," he said. I wanted to tell him I knew how he felt. He emerged from the bathroom, still damp, with a towel wrapped around his waist. He slid into his jeans before dropping the towel to the floor—apparently, he still had a small amount of modesty.

"Wonders never cease," my mother said.

Ignoring her, I asked, "Do you ever think they might be right?"

"I'd be lying if I said no," Lincoln said. He retrieved a pack of cigarettes from the nightstand and offered me one. I shook my head, but my mother lit up along with him.

"Now that I think about it, maybe they were right for a while," Lincoln said. He sat on the bed close by. He still hadn't put on a shirt. "I didn't go to college—well, I didn't *graduate*, at least. Anyway, most people have a career track to follow and they feel like they're going somewhere. If you ask me, and I know you didn't but I'm going to tell you anyway—the way I see it, their direction is mostly circular. I may not always know where I'm going, but at least I'm not going in circles."

Lincoln finished dressing, and I went to check on the soup. I felt unsteady and gripped the pot handle until my dizziness subsided. I didn't know if it was from hitting my head two nights ago, the beer, or the strange time-warp effect of being around Lincoln. I lifted the lid and tasted the soup: beery, starchy, cheesy. Not bad.

Cooking in someone else's home is a curious intersection of experiences: guest, but also host. Generous, but also presumptuous. I tried to stay on the positive sides of all those contradictions as I poured the soup into bowls (they had no ladle, of course) and sliced the loaf of bread, which was still warm.

When it's done wrong, potato soup can feel like a mouthful of wet sand. At least I had avoided that. It wasn't velvet, but it wasn't gritty either. Lincoln and I sat for a few minutes in silence, bent over our bowls, and he said, "You know, it was really nice of you to go to the trouble to cook."

I shrugged. "It's what I do," I almost said "when I'm nervous," but said instead, "I've discovered lately that I'm a compulsive cooker."

"Be glad you're not fat," Lincoln said.

"Luckily, I'm not a compulsive eater."

"What do you usually do with all the food if you don't eat it yourself?"

"Invite people over," I said. "Or take the leftovers to work." I shook my head. "Not that I can do that anymore. I just quit my job."

"No way," Lincoln said. "Really?"

I nodded. "Just part of the weird month I've been having."

"That's one way to put it," my mother said.

"It sounds like you've managed to get off that merry-go-round I was talking about," Lincoln said. "It's a good feeling, isn't it?"

"Actually, it scares me shitless," I said. I got the feeling Lincoln asked not so much to reassure me but maybe to get some validation for the way he was living his own life. I couldn't believe I was confiding in him about this, but it also made sense to me he was the first person I told. Just saying the thing out loud was enough to make me feel the panic rising in my throat, which I tried to keep down by swallowing more beer. "I can't decide if I'm going crazy or if this is the dumbest thing I've ever done in my entire life."

"Or maybe both," my mother said.

Lincoln smiled. "No, dating my sister was probably the dumbest thing you ever did." He began tearing off bits of bread and dipping them in his soup. Before long, he'd torn the entire slice into crumbs. He stared at his bowl a moment, and picked up another piece. "Either way, you're doing it. That's pretty fearless."

"I'm not sure what the difference is anymore between fearless and stupid," I said. "Besides, I haven't even told you the dumbest part yet."

We took the rest of the twelve-pack into Lincoln's bedroom where I unwound the details of my mother's final request—which was, I realized, the first time I'd considered it in those terms. It was the last thing she'd ever ask me to do (her phantom presence excepted), and even if she'd never actually gotten around to asking me herself, I could at least do this.

"It doesn't sound so dumb to me," Lincoln said.

"I don't think it qualifies as fearless, though." From my perspective, I still had more than a healthy dose of the stuff. What was I going to do once I completed this errand? That thought sent my stomach plummeting toward my knees.

"Maybe fearlessness is knowing there are risks but doing it anyway."

"Maybe." I didn't want to talk about it anymore, so I asked about his roommate. It turned out Rich owned the condo and was also the artist. He'd had a few shows around town, and his work had been selling really well, including some with Lincoln as the subject. He seemed pleased by that. When he'd first moved in, shortly after coming back from Chicago, there were a few months where Lincoln had been short of his share of the rent, so he and Rich had worked it out in barter.

"Turns out to be a pretty easy way to make some money, just sitting around," he said. "Well, except for this one where I was on my knees and leaning flat on my back. I was kind of sore after that one."

"Actually," I said, "I flipped through them while I was waiting. I hope you don't mind."

"Why would I mind?" he asked. The expression I glimpsed on his face vanished before I could decipher it.

He hadn't spoken to his sister in years, he said, nor had she been back to visit their parents. He didn't say much more about her, and his tone made it clear that part of his life was closed to further inquiry.

But my impending trip captivated him. He wanted to know about the RV, how long I expected the trip to take, whether I had any idea what I'd do after that. I wanted to talk about this almost as much as he apparently wanted to talk about his sister. It made me want to get up from where I lay on the floor and run.

Lincoln, though, bounced around the room as if it could barely contain him. He leaned against the windowsill, he sat cross-legged on the floor, he got up and lit a joint. Just watching him exhausted me.

I was on my fifth beer, which I balanced on my belly while I lay on the floor. Each time it teetered on the verge of toppling over, I grabbed it at the last possible second. "The more I think about it," I said finally, "the more I think I'm out of my mind. And the more I think I'd rather not talk about this any more tonight." I looked at my watch. It was almost eleven thirty. "Do you want to go out or something?"

By this point, Lincoln had stopped pacing and was lying on the bed. He rolled onto his belly and looked down at me, then took my beer and placed it on the nightstand. He slid onto the floor, his face hovering above mine.

"How about we just stay in," he said.

"And this is where I think I'll discreetly slip out," my mother said.

CHAPTER SIX

You know how sometimes your life takes an unexpected turn and later you find yourself somewhere you never planned on going and you wonder, "How on earth did I get here?"

In my case, I knew exactly where I'd started drifting sideways: it was when I went to bed with Lincoln. In spite of the beers, regardless of the waves of grief that kept me floundering while on the outside I might have looked numb, I knew it was a bad, bad idea.

I did it anyway.

My repentance, when it came, was protracted. It started the next morning when I was jolted awake by a stream of expletives.

"Fuck! Again? Shit!"

Lincoln sat on the edge of the bed, phone pressed to his ear. He looked like he'd taken a shower—his hair was still wet—but he was also still naked. Before long he was up and pacing across the bedroom. He stopped at the dresser and pawed through the jumble of receipts, jewelry, and junk, looking for something that wasn't there. He slammed his hand flat against the surface, making the spare change and rings jangle.

I sat up and glanced at the clock. It was a little after noon. When I looked back at Lincoln, he was rearranging the loose change into stacks of dimes, quarters, and pennies while he shook his head in response to whomever was on the other end of the line.

"For how long? Yes, I need the money. But what the hell do you expect *me* to do? I can't cook." There was a pause. Lincoln's jaw stiffened—I could almost hear his teeth grinding from the other end of the room—and he banged his hand against the dresser again. The stacks of change slid back into disorder. "Can't you un-fire him? He'll sober up by dinner rush. Probably." Another pause, then Lincoln burst out, "He *what?* With a butcher knife? At Dominic? Jesus fucking Christ on a cracker."

Finally, Lincoln sighed. He leaned against the dresser, and glanced at me. Before he saw me, I think he might have forgotten I was there.

"Let me call you back." He hung up without saying good-bye.

He sat on the edge of the bed as I started hunting around for my clothes. "Sorry I woke you up," he said.

"That's okay. I didn't mean to sleep this late." *I didn't mean to do a lot of things* was what I wanted to say at that particular moment. Instead I focused on trying to find a way to extract myself from this scenario and begin my walk of shame back to the car.

"Good luck with that," my mother's voice said. She had returned and was leaning against the dresser, smoking a cigarette. "Have a good night? Or don't you remember any of it?"

I remembered plenty. I was in no position to tell her this. Nor did I exactly want to engage her on this topic. You'd think her passing beyond the veil might have spared me any further seat-squirming conversations about my sex life, but no. It seemed typical of her to bring up the subject when I was least able to respond or justify myself—if justifying myself were even possible.

I had found my underwear and was about to put it back on

when Lincoln said, "Since you're awake, I could really use your help."

In any other situation I would have laughed. The head chef at Lincoln's restaurant was found passed out behind the bar amid a bloodbath of some of the restaurant's finest reds— he'd apparently worked his way down to a bottle of the house chianti, by which point he was probably too smashed to know the difference. Luckily, he hadn't drunk himself to death. He was still drunk, however. Also, fired. And nearly arrested, since when they woke him up he went after the owner and executive chef, Dominic, with a big knife. And now they were short their head chef, and their executive chef had a big gash on his forearm.

Which was why Lincoln was asking me to help out in the kitchen that evening. It was such short notice that Dominic was planning to close the restaurant for the day, maybe tomorrow as well. This sparked a sense of alarm in Lincoln I didn't quite understand. Was he living that hand-to-mouth?

"Please, you've got to do this for me." Lincoln grabbed my hand—for a second it looked like he was about to kneel at the edge of the bed and beg. I really wanted him to let go of my hand, and I really wanted to put my underwear on. The panic rose in me to match his, and it made my head hurt. I felt some sympathy for the chef, until I realized it was really his fault I was in this predicament.

"Oh no it's not," my mother said. She brushed a stray ash off the sleeve of her nightgown.

"I've never even worked in a restaurant before," I said. "There is no way I can do this."

"You practically pulled dinner out of thin air last night. This'll be a cakewalk by comparison. And you won't have to do the dishes when you're done."

I wanted to point out I hadn't done the dishes last night either. I also wanted to point out that if I screwed up, unlike last night, when he wasn't paying for the meal, the diners who might eat and possibly wind up poisoned by my food tonight might want their money back. And he might get fired.

"Can't someone else fill in? What about the dishwasher?"

"He only speaks Portuguese. Look, I've got nothing more to lose than what I'm definitely going to lose if the place doesn't open tonight. Besides, Dominic won't let anything go out of the kitchen if it's screwed up."

This was not exactly a ringing endorsement. I said yes, even though I had a feeling I would be out of my depth.

❖

Lincoln took me to the restaurant around two in the afternoon. He led me through the back door into a room with a small row of short lockers, where Lincoln stowed his messenger bag. From another locker he pulled out a chef's jacket and a pair of checked pants.

"Put these on. They were Miguel's, but since he's been fired, I don't think he'll care if you wear them."

I looked at the pants he held out toward me. "Are those even clean?"

"Oh for Christ's sake," Lincoln muttered and sniffed the jacket. "They just smell like the kitchen. Everything back here does. You probably won't notice it after a while. Come on, Dominic's a stickler for being on time."

Dominic was the owner and executive chef. Lincoln had mentioned he was around forty or so. I thought he looked more like fifty.

He glared at Lincoln. "What are you doing in here?"

"I brought Joel in, so—"

"Out." Dominic hiked a thumb over his shoulder toward the dining room, and turned to me. He didn't even look back to make sure Lincoln left the room.

"So you've never worked in a restaurant before?" he asked.

"No, sir." I was instantly intimidated.

"That's 'no, chef.' So this is your first time working in a kitchen with other cooks?"

"Yes," I said, quickly adding, "chef."

Dominic rolled his eyes. "Well, at least you're not falling-down drunk, so I guess that's an improvement. You'll do prep work. I'd have you wash dishes, but Lincoln probably told you the dishwasher only speaks Portuguese. The rest of you"—and at that point he mercifully turned his scrutiny away from me and directed it toward the other staff caught moth-like in his glow— "that means he'll have a knife in his hands, so for God's sake watch your fingers and anything else he might be likely to chop off." The other kitchen staff laughed without any indication they found what he'd said to be the least bit humorous.

For the next seven hours, time passed in a surreal little pocket separated from the rest of reality. I was chopping celery, carrots, onions—I'd never chopped so many onions before, and apparently I didn't even know how to do that right.

"No no no," Dominic practically shouted. He'd come up behind me while I was on my second onion. "What are you doing? You *have* chopped an onion before, haven't you?"

Before I could say anything, Dominic snatched the knife from my hand, swiped my offending onion from the cutting board into the trash can, and placed a new one on the board. Although I watched, I wasn't sure exactly what Dominic did, but that poor onion certainly never saw it coming. Less than ten seconds later it had been reduced to a pile of neat, perfectly symmetrical chopped onion.

"Make your chop even and consistent. And make them this size." He grabbed a carrot next and chopped that, then similarly dispatched a rib of celery. "Got it?"

"Yes, chef." No matter that I didn't get it. At least I'd learned not to say anything besides "yes, chef."

Dinner service started promptly at five. I had no recollection of when that time arrived and passed. The work remained constantly too much, too fast. All around me was this symphony of noises—sauté pans sliding across burners, the sizzle of searing meat, the thunk and creak of oven doors opening and closing, interspersed with voices shouting out orders and responding when plates were ready. This was the pulse of the kitchen. I had been so used to working by myself, I had never realized it could beat so loudly.

Occasionally, the pulse spiked, usually because of me. Dominic didn't actually do any cooking, but every plate had to pass muster with him before it escaped from the kitchen to the dining room. The first spike was a salad plate that Dominic banged on the counter in front of me, scattering leaves of lettuce.

"Look at these mushrooms. You call these *slices*? They're crooked and chunky." Again he grabbed my knife and looked at it, testing the blade with his thumb. "There's nothing wrong with the knife, so it must be you. Try and get it right, will you?"

It wasn't long after that, when I was carefully slicing more mushrooms—these were going to be the most beautiful, perfectly translucent half moons of fungus I was capable of creating—when Dominic practically barreled up to me and said, "Where are those mushrooms? I've got two tables waiting for their salads, and at this pace their entrées will be ready before the fucking salads. Hurry *up*."

And the heat. I didn't realize how hot it would get. When I was ferrying chopped onion to the sauté station I passed the grill and glanced down at a meat thermometer on the counter. It read a hundred and twenty. No wonder I felt so clumsy in this place. Early on, I'd dropped a metal bowl full of carrots, shocked when it clanged on the tile floor with such gusto. Everyone looked up for an instant, and turned back to their stations as if they hadn't seen it. Or maybe they just couldn't believe they were working with such a raw amateur.

Hours passed without my marking them. All I knew was I was still chopping, slicing more vegetables for salads—red onions, mushrooms, olives, lettuce—and then I was slicing my finger. It was a good knife, one of the best I'd ever used, and it made quick work of my flesh, slicing with hardly any effort, going deep before I felt the first thin shock of pain.

I cursed and clutched my wounded digit in a white towel, which quickly bloomed with red. The grill cook grinned and tossed me something. It looked like a little condom sized to fit on a finger.

"Welcome to the kitchen," he said, and turned back to the filet he was searing. My finger stopped bleeding after a short time, but it still throbbed as I held a halved onion steady to chop.

If there was any saving grace to this mayhem that remained always a couple seconds away from being unleashed, it was this: it left me little time to think about the job I'd just quit, the dog I'd practically abandoned, the man on the other side of the Atlantic I now wanted to get back to so much that I was ignoring him as hard as I could. Nor did I think about the man here I'd stupidly fucked, or my freshly dead mother, who remained mercifully invisible and silent while I raced to keep up with the pulse of the kitchen.

"Okay, Joel, that's enough," Dominic finally said. I set my knife down. He then surprised the hell out of me by patting my shoulder briefly and muttering, "Good job," before vanishing into the dining room.

I wandered out the back door. Lincoln was standing there, smoking a cigarette. I leaned against the door frame and looked up. Steam billowed out of the kitchen vent and obscured any stars that might have been visible.

"I never want to chop an onion again," I said. My feet hurt. So did my back. In addition to the sliced finger, I'd also burned my left hand when the grill guy opened an oven right as I was passing. And while I hadn't bled into anyone's salad, I couldn't guarantee I hadn't sweated on someone's onions.

"You survived Dominic, which is pretty good," Lincoln said.

"Remind me why I agreed to do this again?"

Lincoln exhaled and gave me his best smile. "Because I'm irresistible?"

"More likely because I'm a pushover. How long have you worked here?"

He looked up at the sky, calculating. "Not quite two years."

"Then you're insane."

"Come on, was there really no part of it you enjoyed?"

"You mean apart from the point where I was thinking of stabbing Dominic in the eye? I'd have to say no."

"Then I guess I can't talk you into coming back tomorrow night?"

I laughed. "Oh *hell* no."

He laughed too and held out his cigarette, which was when I realized it was a joint. I took it and inhaled. I hadn't smoked pot in years, and I'd almost forgotten that neck-lengthening sense of giddiness it created.

"So when do you leave?" Lincoln asked.

I shrugged. "Whenever I want. I guess I should go pretty soon, though. Probably tomorrow or Tuesday." My plans were so indefinite, and that fact hit me with every *probably*, *maybe*, and *I guess*. I would have been glad to be gone that instant, even if I didn't know where I'd be heading once I reached the other side of the country, dropped off the RV, and had to figure out what to do with the rest of my life.

Lincoln must have picked up on that anxiety, either in the fidgety way my fingers handled the joint when he passed it back again, or in my constant shuffling from one foot to the other (although that might have had more to do with standing for seven hours nonstop). Either way, he rested his hand on my shoulder and said, "Don't back out now, kiddo."

I shrugged again and took another hit, which also served the dual purpose of dislodging Lincoln's hand from my shoulder. "I don't know why this trip seems so daunting. I've traveled by myself lots of times before." Usually, those trips were some form of escapism from my daily life. Now, though, there was nothing to escape from.

❖

"What the hell have you been doing?" Dad asked when I walked in. It had been almost twenty-four hours since I'd gone to meet Lincoln, and I felt suddenly caught. It was as if Dad had a total, embarrassing awareness of every thing I'd done with and to and on Lincoln the night before.

This made my mother laugh.

"No, darling, only your dead mother knows what you do in bed. Well, your dead mother and every boy you've been to bed with. Which is how many, exactly?"

She smirked and sat at the kitchen counter next to my dad, enjoying my inability to respond as she produced a bottle of nail polish from somewhere and began painting her nails. From the television in the other room came the muffled audience buzz of a baseball game, punctuated every so often by the rise and fall of the announcer's play-by-play.

"I mean your face," Dad said. "You look like you got too much sun."

I touched my cheek gently. It felt hot, but that could have been due to how badly I was blushing after my mother's comment. "I was helping Lincoln out at the restaurant, remember? Where you and I ate on Friday? I called?"

He nodded impatiently. "Of course I remember. What have they got in that kitchen, sun lamps?"

When I looked in the bathroom mirror upstairs, my face was a couple of shades short of lobster red. No wonder Dominic looked a decade older than he really was. He was cooking himself in the kitchen.

Once I had scrubbed off the smell of grease, I sat at the computer and began mapping my route west. I could chart any number of courses that would take me through St. Louis before heading truly west. Everything before the blue line of the Mississippi River looked and felt like a trip to the middle. If I opted to bypass St. Louis, which I didn't think I *should* do, the most direct route would take me through such thrilling places as Lincoln, Nebraska (the name was reason enough to avoid it), Salt Lake City, and Carson City, before finally reaching San Francisco. If I approached the journey like a desperate nonstop dash, it would take less than forty-eight hours to complete.

"Oh darling, no." My mother rested a hand on my shoulder as she leaned over and looked at the screen. Her nails were painted an almost indecent shade of red. "If you're going to do this, the least you can do is go through some interesting places."

"I've lived in the Midwest for thirteen years. There isn't anything interesting there."

"Well, probably not in"—she squinted—"Lincoln, Nebraska."

I clicked on a link. "I doubt the two hundred thirty-nine thousand people who live there feel the same way."

"That many people live there? By choice?"

My mother, like most coastal people I knew, had always looked down on the swath of land in the middle of the country and the people who lived there (with perhaps the exception of Chicago). My decision to move to the middle was either a vexation or an exception that proved the rule. Portland, though clinging to the ocean, was only a fifth the size of Lincoln, and it was the largest city in Maine.

"It's not like I'm planning to spend any time in Lincoln," I said.

"Then why bother going there?" She pointed at the screen. "Denver's just a little bit south and a lot more interesting, surely."

"Denver's almost five hundred miles away. It just looks close because the map is so small."

She waved a hand dismissively. Details like that didn't matter if they got in the way of her opinion. If I were honest, anything north or south of the Interstate 70 line running from St. Louis through Kansas City to Denver filled me with a little dread. Deviating from that straight and narrow path felt like entering enemy territory.

I had to get out of *this* town too. Portland no longer fit my concept of home, even with my father still here and even after spending the last four days (minus the previous night) under the same roof and in the same room where I'd grown up. I had gotten bigger, and things had gotten smaller. Nothing fit.

After Lincoln (the man, not the town), I didn't want to risk running into anyone else I might know, either. Encountering him was unsettling enough, and at least he'd had the elements of novelty and surprise in his favor. I was convinced everyone else would be married with two kids, smug and successful, or separated or divorced with one kid and a double shift at the Stop & Shop. Maybe Shaw's if they were lucky. Either way, encountering them would force me to feel either inadequate or smugly superior. I wanted to feel neither that short nor that tall.

Mostly, I just wanted to be moving.

"Don't forget that cow Sylvia said you could stay with them if you passed through Arizona," my mother said with menace. She had drifted away from the desk to look out the window and smoke. It was so dark outside; I wondered what she was looking at, what she could see.

"Did you ever go out there to visit?" I asked.

"No, but she sent pictures. She has a gorgeous house in the side of a canyon. She lives there with Gerald in a sexless sort-of-marriage and it's all very *Love, Sidney.*"

"Sounds awkward."

"No more awkward than staying in this house with your father." She didn't say anything after that, so I kept clicking the map and seeing how long a route through Arizona would take. I definitely did not ask her when she said awkward, if she were referring to me over the last few days, or her and the last few decades.

"There are a ton of spas and art galleries in Sedona, and the red rock canyons are supposed to be stunning," she said. "You can stand in the middle of the street and see breathtaking views in every direction."

"Until you get run over."

"Very funny." She returned to my shoulder and swatted me. "Hit up your dad for gas money. He's probably planning to do that anyway. Just don't make this a mad dash across the country that you won't even remember once it's over."

"Okay, okay," I said. I was beginning to worry she was a sentence or two away from uttering such profoundly empty sentiments as "You don't start a journey by standing in place" or that one about life's greatest treks starting with a single footstep.

"Oh please, give me *some* credit," she said before moving back to the window. While I outlined my route, she lit another cigarette and silently stared out at the night.

CHAPTER SEVEN

Monday, the day I started the trip, did not begin on a particularly auspicious note. After spending the previous day on my feet for seven hours straight, I woke up with cramped toes—something I had never considered possible before. I hobbled down the stairs as the phone started ringing. Dad, already awake, held it out to me.

"You know," Carrie said after I said hello, "you might think to tell me the next time you do something impetuous and spur-of-the-moment like—oh, I don't know—*quit your fucking job.*"

I was about to apologize until I remembered something. "Hey, you said you were going to stop back by my parents' house again before you left town last week. What happened?"

"That is not the point," she said, each word like a stab. I wanted to ask her what the point *was*, but I knew it wasn't a good idea. I stared at the RV through the sliding glass door while Carrie described how our boss Miranda interrogated her as soon as she got to work that morning. It was eight forty-five her time, and since work started at eight thirty, I knew Carrie was playing up the dramatic tension. She said Miranda grilled her about me and did she know anything about it and what was my state of mind was it grief but never mind all that Joel whatthehellwereyouthinking?

For a smoker, Carrie really did have remarkable lung capacity.

I still hadn't seen the inside of the RV. Out in the driveway, my mother stood in front of it, gesturing toward it with a flourish of hands and a deliberately wide smile, like a Bob Barker girl from *The Price Is Right*. When I rolled my eyes, she shrugged and came back inside.

"I've got to go," I said to Carrie, "but I'll be coming through town in a couple days and I'll tell you all about it."

When I turned away from the sink, my father was still standing in the kitchen.

"So," he said, "about your job…"

I started making coffee, which meant turning away from him and back toward the counter. Convenient.

"You mean my former job," I said.

"Well, your mother mentioned a while back that she wasn't sure you were all that happy with it. She figured this trip might give you some time to think things over. Still, I'd bet she hadn't figured you were planning to quit before you knew what you were going to do next."

She probably hadn't counted on being dead at this point either, but I kept that to myself.

"His words anyway, not mine," my mother said. I held up a finger to silence them both while I used the electric can opener on a new container of Maxwell House. What my dad said was perhaps the most polite way I'd ever heard him try to tell someone they were out of their mind. Even if he was less than convincing, I appreciated the attempt.

"I didn't figure on it either, Dad. It just sort of happened." I turned on the coffee maker. "Anyway, I have the whole trip to try to figure out what to do next."

"Maybe you want to take your time with that," Dad said. "Go slow, stop and take in some of the sights along the way."

"Well, I'm planning to stop in Las Vegas since I've never been there. And there's Mom's friend Sylvia in Sedona."

"Good, good," he said.

"Don't worry, Dad. I'm not destitute. I have enough money to get by for a while."

"Did I say I was worried?" he asked. He grabbed a cup and filled it before the coffee was finished brewing. I was pretty sure that first cup was going to be about as strong as battery acid.

"See what I used to put up with?" my mother asked. I didn't answer, but kept my eyes on the coffeepot. When it finished brewing and I'd poured myself a cup, she said, "Now's as good a time as any to inspect your chariot."

The morning had started out cold. I stood on the patio watching the steam rise from my coffee before following my mother to the door of the RV. Dad had put in the patio four years ago, the year before his bypass. To the left was Mom's garden, waiting for spring, which always came to Maine about a month later than the rest of the world. With her gone now, the garden would probably lie fallow for who knew how long.

"Darling," my mother said, "if you're waiting for a formal invitation, you're going to be waiting a while."

We had gone camping a handful of times when I was a kid. My memories of those occasions all involve a cramped contraption mounted on the back of my dad's old pickup truck. It was barely big enough for my parents; I was relegated to a two-person tent (if the two people were midgets or double amputees). The tent always smelled like a damp basement no matter how often we set it up in the backyard to air out. Mom always tried to sell me on the adventurous aspect of it—"It'll be fun!" she insisted the first time. "And you'll have it all to yourself!"—but usually it was just uncomfortably warm or painful with rocks and tree roots poking me through my sleeping bag. Once, on a beach when a massive gale nearly swept the tent away with me inside, camping was downright terrifying.

If we'd had the RV, I might have cultivated a different opinion of camping. It was palatial.

Directly in front of the doorway was a galley-style kitchen, not much smaller and a lot more stylish than the kitchen in my old apartment. The space was outfitted with a narrow oven and a glass-top range with a microwave mounted above, all of them brushed aluminum, as was the refrigerator. They even had room for a small Cuisinart and—good grief—an espresso machine.

Everything else was similarly appointed: the flat panel TV, the built-in sofa upholstered in beige canvas twill, the full-size beds with mattresses that I discovered were more comfortable than my own back in St. Louis when I sat down on them. No wonder Dad didn't want to go camping—I would have bet he thought this was *too* nice.

"So, darling, what do you think?" Mom asked. "Not bad, huh?"

"I think it's nicer than my last apartment. Why did you buy it?"

"My last failed attempt to get your father out of that recliner." She sat down on the sofa and lit a cigarette.

"You smoke too much," I said.

She exhaled and gave me the you've-got-to-be-kidding look. "Really, darling. Your concern for my health is touching."

"You realize I can smell that, right?"

"You realize it's about as substantial as I am, right? You don't need to worry about secondhand smoke from me."

I couldn't believe I was bickering with my dead mother at all, much less about her smoking. I glanced in the bathroom— chrome and glass—and opened what turned out to be the utility closet. My mother sighed—or maybe she was just exhaling; I didn't turn around to check—and she said, "So anyway, when the RV couldn't get your father to budge, along came my cancer and that turned out to be big enough to get his ass moving. Finally."

I cringed at the word *cancer*. Since my back was turned, she couldn't see me, but I forgot about her uncanny powers of perception. "It's just a word like any other. Cancer cancer cancer. See? The world hasn't ended."

I couldn't resist the urge to turn, and with a smirk, I said, "In a moment the irony of that statement will strike you."

"Darling, irony and I are on a first-name basis."

I slumped into the driver's seat. Through the expanse of windshield, the town-house windows across the street were blinded white and opaque by the morning sun. Mom slid into the passenger seat.

"Did you know you had cancer when you bought the RV?"

"Keep reading the letters," she said. "Maybe you'll find out."

I looked at her, trying to figure out if the subtext I imagined in her statement was really there. I still had my doubts about her, about whether this experience of her was real, and pointing to a clue in letters I had yet to read seemed to imply an awareness outside my own consciousness.

Maybe I hadn't conjured her up in my own head, after all.

If she knew what I was thinking, this time she kept it to herself.

"Well," she finally said, once her cigarette was finished, "hopefully your father won't do something typical like burn the house down while we're gone."

"Yeah, hopefully." I laughed at the thought of my father trying to cook for himself and winding up calling the fire department. I added, *"We?"*

"I'm afraid you're stuck with me, darling. Besides, there would be very little point in my staying here with your father. He can't see me."

"And why is that?"

"Lack of imagination?" She shrugged. "Honestly, I don't know. It may come as a disappointment to you, but the afterlife does not include an infinite supply of all-knowing."

"In that case, this is definitely going to be an interesting trip."

"Who're you talking to?"

Lincoln stood in the doorway behind us. When I looked back at him, he smiled and climbed up the stairs. He had a duffel bag in one hand and a backpack slung over his shoulder.

"Hey, sunshine," he said, leaning down and giving me a kiss. At the moment, I was too stunned to reciprocate. He handed me an envelope.

"What's this?"

"Your pay for last night's work. I told Dominic you weren't doing it out of kindness."

"Out of stupidity is more like it," my mother said. I hoped Lincoln would sit on her after that remark. I also hoped he would go away soon, though the presence of his two bags implied otherwise. This was reinforced when he set the duffel bag on the floor and let the backpack slip off his shoulder.

"Planning on moving in?" I asked. Lincoln opted not to sit up front and stretched out instead on the sofa. I tried not to let my gaze linger too long at the edge of his shirt where it rode up, exposing a trail of black hair from his navel that disappeared into his jeans. That would have only made me think of two nights ago and, possibly, trying to reenact it right here.

For a moment, he looked puzzled. "We talked about this, right?"

"Was I out of the room for that conversation?" my mother asked. I could have said the same thing, but instead asked, "So you want to come on this trip? What about your job?"

"I've got a little money saved up, so why not take a break? I can help you with the driving and chip in for gas."

"My dad's got the gas covered."

Lincoln smiled. It was the same smile he'd given me two nights ago that had landed me in this situation now.

"Even better," he said.

"Even *worse*," my mother corrected.

❖

It was after noon before we got on our way. Lincoln had to go back to his apartment to pick up "a few things" ("Probably his bong," my mother quipped). I didn't want to leave before I at least made Dad lunch.

"You know, I'm capable of feeding myself, son," he said as I slid the omelet onto his plate. He looked down at it and lifted the edge of the folded egg with his fork. "What is this stuff?"

"Brie and apple," I said, right about the same time I realized this was quite possibly the least appealing thing I could have made for him. Still, the dairy drawer in the fridge was filled with a lot of leftover cheese that was probably going to spoil while I was gone. My dad, true to form, shrugged and started eating.

"Do we have any ketchup?" he asked.

❖

Lincoln said he'd drive first. I sat in the passenger seat and was promptly unable to keep my eyes open. I would say I suddenly felt tired, except that exhaustion had been a constant companion since the end of my vacation.

I showed Lincoln the route I'd plotted, how it would take us down and across to St. Louis, over to Las Vegas, dip down and backtrack a short ways to Sedona, then over and up again to San Francisco. The course outlined in red looked like a sagging clothesline strung across the country.

Lincoln folded the MapQuest printout and stuck it in a dashboard groove where he could see it clearly. "How far did you want to get today?" he asked. It hadn't occurred to me. In my planning, I'd just figured on driving for however long I could stand it, then finding the nearest Motel 6. Now, of course, there was someone else to consider, and maybe that was why the trip now seemed less adventure and more chore.

"Halfway there," I said.

"To St. Louis."

"You got it."

He smiled and leaned over to kiss me. Even sober, his kiss was still charged, but that's what Lincoln was like. He was the live wire you knew you shouldn't touch, even as your hand was reaching out toward the bare end of it. The shock could be a thrill, or it could get you killed.

"Go ahead and lie down in back," Lincoln said, once our lips parted and the lightning storm had passed. "I'll wake you up when it's dinnertime or something."

As soon as my head hit the pillow, of course, I was awake. Sleeping through the beginning of what was supposed to be a cross-country adventure seemed as wrong as trying to look forward to it, given the circumstances. My mother, after all, was along for the ride only as a byproduct of her recent demise.

"Oh, don't be so gloomy," she said. "I'm having the time of my—"

"Don't say it."

I lifted the box of letters from the shelf above the bed and removed the lid. I didn't look inside as I shuffled through the envelopes, divining again by feel which one I should read next.

Dear Derek,

I'm going to have a baby. Arthur, as you can imagine, is over the moon. Although maybe you can't imagine that, since you've never met him. I wonder what you'd make of each other—you have so little in common.

I'm getting off track, as usual. My mother tells me I'm going to have a boy. A Colby woman's first child is always a boy, she told me. Of course, I'm an only child, and when I pointed this out to her, she fell quiet. This is how I found out about her miscarriage, which I'm sure is not how either of us imagined she would tell me this. A boy, of course. My older sibling an idea presented and revoked at the same time. I didn't feel like I had a right to be sad about something that was clearly still very painful for her, and I wasn't used to seeing that sort of distress on her face.

I want so much to be happy now, and I am, but this just colors things.

All the same, I think I'm having a girl. I don't know why, but I just feel that is the case. It doesn't matter—I'll be just as happy if she turns out to be a boy—but a girl would be simply perfect. We'll find out in six months...

From the doorway to the sleeping area, my mother stood staring at me when I lowered the letter.

"It's funny, but I don't think I fully realized my mother was human until that point." She sat on the edge of the bed. "And don't give me any lip about how my wanting a girl made you turn out gay. I gave myself enough grief over that when you came out, thank you very much."

"I don't think it works like that," I said, adding, "I thought you didn't have a problem with it?"

"Well, of course I didn't, but as your mother, it was my duty to fret over every little thing I did that might have affected you: Did I wean you too early? Should I have used cloth instead of disposables? Not to mention all the things we didn't even know we should have been doing when you were born, like getting folic acid."

"Mom, don't spend the afterlife giving yourself a guilt trip. It's too late to do any good, anyway."

She smiled and patted my knee. "Darling, you should realize it's never too late for a good guilt trip."

From the front of the RV, Lincoln called, "Did you say something?"

My mother held a finger to her lips and got off the bed. "No," I replied. I lay back and looked through the window above the bed. I probably wasn't missing much. The scenery would have changed only marginally, so there was no point in sitting up to watch it go by now. And from my perspective, the sunlight flickering through the branches of trees as we passed reminded me of a fluttering movie projector. If I reached out my hand, I wondered if I could grab one of those phantom images and see if maybe it had something to show me.

I closed my eyes and, watching the sunlight pulse through my eyelids, told myself I was just resting them for a minute.

In my dream, I was lying in bed with Dudley sprawled on top of the covers next to me. It was our usual Sunday routine: the dog, the bed, and me, with the Sunday *New York Times* spread out around us. Only this time the bed was huge, impossibly large, filling the entire room and stretching beyond it. Everywhere I looked I could see nothing but the mattress and a blanket of newspaper pages.

Dudley got up and began walking across the paper, and when he couldn't find the edge of the bed he started running, his hind legs kicking up broadsheets of newsprint. They sailed up and around me like autumn leaves until I couldn't make out Dudley receding in the distance.

I stood up to chase after him, and running across the bed was like playing in one of those inflatable moon bounce attractions at the county fair, except that each step sent me soaring high above the bed. From up there, the pages of the newspaper looked like farmland patterns. When I came back down, I landed near my mother, who was still dressed in her peach nightgown and robe. She was reading the obituary section.

"How come I'm not in here?" she asked me.

"I don't know. Have you seen Dudley?"

"You're headed in the wrong direction. You do realize this, don't you?"

She looked past me, and I turned to follow her gaze. In the distance was a man who waved at us and started running in our direction. From where I stood, I couldn't tell if it was Philip or Lincoln, but it had to be one of them. Even though he was too far off to see clearly, each footfall rippled through the bed, making my mother and me bob up and down as if we were in a rowboat.

When I woke up, the bobbing continued, accompanied by a slapping sound like the sole of a shoe that had come unglued.

"Is that what I think it sounds like?" I asked, wobbling my way to the front.

"If you think it sounds like a flat, then yes," Lincoln said. He was already steering the RV to the side of the road. "If you think it sounds like anything else, then I couldn't say."

It was the right front tire. I stood staring at it for a moment and listening to the occasional whiplash of passing traffic. The light was already starting to fade, and it occurred to me, perhaps now that I was fully awake, that I had no idea where we were.

"Where are we, anyway?"

"Ohio. Somewhere between the middle of nowhere and nowhere's left ankle."

"Naturally. These things never happen right around the corner from the gas station."

"They do, but only when the gas station's closed."

I fished the manual out of the glove box. The spare was stowed on the rear of the RV, and the jack was behind the passenger seat. Which made perfect sense, didn't it? To keep items always used together on opposite ends of the damn thing? I wrestled the spare out of the clamshell, the rubber of the tire giving way disturbingly under my fingers. I dropped it, and it landed with a thud and no trace of a bounce.

"You are not going to believe this," I said. "The spare's flat too."

I got out my cell phone, though I wasn't sure whom I wanted to call first: AAA to come get us, or my dad to ask him why the hell he kept a flat spare on the RV.

"That's right," my mother said. "Berate the grieving widower. *So* sensitive." She lit a cigarette about the same time Lincoln fired up a joint.

"Do you have to smoke pot out here on the side of a major interstate in broad—twilight?" I asked. He shrugged and moved closer to the shoulder side of the RV. I opened my cell phone to a display with no bars and the message "No Service." We were in a dead zone.

"How appropriate," my mother said. I turned to tell her she wasn't helping, until I remembered Lincoln was standing within earshot. Anyway, dusk was sliding to dark so quickly that the only detail of her I could see with any clarity was the glowing tip of her cigarette. Like a carcinogenic Cheshire cat.

"Can you get a signal?" I asked Lincoln.

"Well, that would require a phone, and I didn't bring mine with me," he said.

"You didn't bring your phone." It wasn't a question so much as an expression of my simultaneous disbelief yet total lack of surprise. At the moment, I resisted the urge to fling my own phone across the highway. With my luck, I'd go to retrieve it only to stand up and find a pair of headlights bearing down on me at seventy miles an hour. Like my mother, I could tell where Lincoln was standing by the flare of his joint each time he inhaled.

"I guess we can stand here and hope someone stops," I said, "or we can go ahead and start walking."

We decided to walk. Lincoln said we were about two miles from a rest area, where I hoped we'd find a pay phone or at least a better signal. A half-hour walk, tops, Lincoln said.

The fading light only lasted ten more minutes. Soon I could barely see the ground in front of us, lit only by the headlights of the occasional passing car. We should have brought a flashlight. There was probably one in the RV somewhere—though the batteries were probably dead.

We walked as far away from the roadway as possible without tumbling off the shoulder. Pausing once while Lincoln lit another joint—I wondered how much weed he'd brought with him—he asked me, "How long do you think we've been walking?" I looked down at my watch, which of course I couldn't see in the dark. I flipped open my cell phone and ignored the "No service" message, which was like an accusation.

"About ten minutes," I said.

We started walking again. The gravel crunched monotonously beneath our feet. Lincoln stuck out his thumb the next time a car passed, to no avail. The voice in my head—the one that was not my mother—told me I should have checked the spare before we left Portland, I should have grabbed the flashlight before we left the RV, I should have politely let Lincoln down this morning, and none of this was turning out the way my mother had probably hoped.

Walking just on the other side of Lincoln, her glowing cigarette tip bobbing in sync with his joint, my mother said, "It's always best to go into something like this with very few expectations. Why don't I keep you entertained by reading one of my letters?"

We paused while Lincoln put out his joint and tucked the roach in his shirt pocket. In that interlude, the sound of paper rasping in my mother's fingers as she opened an envelope seemed amplified by the dark and the silence.

"Hey," Lincoln said before my mother started reading, "look up."

I'd never seen so many stars, certainly not so bright. In the middle of St. Louis, looking up while waiting for Dudley to do his business at the other end of the leash, I could only see a handful of the brightest stars that pierced the city haze. Here, the stars made a haze of their own, a blurring gray band bisecting the sky. It was the galaxy, clearer than I'd ever seen, bigger than I could conceive, indifferent in its vastness to the minuscule existence of any one thing.

"Kind of puts things in perspective, doesn't it?" Lincoln asked.

It did, but not in any comforting way. The casual apathy of the cosmos was easier to ignore when I'd had a full-time job. And a mother.

"How unique," my mother said. "A pothead philosopher. My dear, you really know how to pick them. Now, where was I?" The letter rustled and, before she started reading, she said, "This is one you won't actually find in the box, darling. This was the last letter I wrote to him, and I sent it.

"'Dear Derek,

"'I know it will come as a surprise to you, hearing from me after all these years. It will probably also come as a shock to learn that I'm writing you because I'm afraid my health has taken a bit of a turn'—how's that for understatement, darling?—'and I don't think I have much time left. It would mean a great deal to me if, when the time comes'—now honestly, what was I thinking using such an insipid euphemism? 'When the time comes'? I make it sound like I'm catching a bus.—'if you would come to the service and perhaps say a few words. Or just be there. I would like my son to meet you, and I think you might like to meet him.

"'Love,

"'Rachel.'"

I stared hard at her while she read, the glowing end of her cigarette hopping around in the dark. When she finished, I heard her slip the letter back into the envelope, and she took a drag. It had been a few minutes since a car had passed on our side, and it was quiet.

I wanted to ask her why she had written the letter, why the hell she was reading it to me now, but of course with Lincoln there I couldn't say a word or else he'd realize what a crackpot I was. It dawned on me that she had just given me proof that could be verified. If Derek confirmed that yes, my mother *had* sent him a letter, then the peach-swathed specter was, in fact, the ghost of my mother and not a manifestation of my disturbed psyche.

If the answer was no, then I really had lost my mind.

"Darling," she pointed out, "you do realize it's possible for me to be real and for you to have lost your mind anyway, yes? But I don't think you're crazy. Neurotic, yes, but then who isn't these days?"

"So are we not going to say a word all the way to the rest stop?" Lincoln asked. I was irritated with him for interrupting, but of course he couldn't hear the monologue my mother was performing. I was wishing right then that I had cell phone reception; I'd call Derek before I even bothered with the tow truck. The question I'd ask him felt as if it was looming behind everything else I might do until I could finally call.

"Sorry," I said to Lincoln. "I've just been going over things in my head."

"I figured as much. I was wondering how many times you'd chased your tail in circles in your head over the last half hour."

I was tempted to tell him to never mind about my tail, but that thought was interrupted by an approaching pair of headlights, followed by the blare of an air horn. A semi surged past us, kicking up a cloud of dust and gravel before its brake lights brightened and it ground to a halt on the shoulder several yards ahead.

"You guys need a lift?" the driver asked, once we had caught up to him. He wore a baseball cap, and a cigarette dangled from below his mustache. Leaning over the steering column, his face green in the dashboard lights, he looked like a potter at a wheel. We climbed in.

"Just to the rest area up ahead," I said. "Thanks."

"No problem." He didn't give us a second look, or ask for our names—and didn't offer his, either—before we started lurching forward. For a moment, we sat in uncomfortable silence, staring out the windshield at the pavement that seemed a long way down from up here. We must have looked like kids to him when we were walking along the side of the road.

"That your RV back a ways?" the driver asked suddenly.

"Yeah," I said. "Well, I'm driving it. It belongs to my parents, but they're selling it. I'm delivering it for them."

"What about you?" he asked, looking over at Lincoln.

"I'm here to make sure he doesn't fall asleep at the wheel."

"Wish I had someone to do that for me sometimes. So, what's wrong with it?"

It took me a moment to realize he meant the RV. "Flat tire. Flat spare."

"That sucks." The trucker flicked his cigarette in the general direction of the ashtray. The engine got quieter once it was up to speed, and it was possible to hear the low murmur of the radio on a country station, a woman singing about walking away.

"Are we close to a town where we can get a new tire?" Lincoln asked.

The trucker reached forward and plucked a GPS unit off its dashboard perch. "That's why I never travel without this anymore." He handed it to me, and I fumbled through the menus until I found what I was looking for.

"There's a town with a Dobbs about five miles past the rest area," I said.

"If you want, I can drive you all the way there," he said.

"Thanks," I said, genuinely surprised.

"See? Chivalry isn't dead yet," my mother said. She was reclining on the bed in the back of the cab.

"No big deal," the trucker said, as if contradicting my mother. "It's on my way."

"Where are you headed?"

"Indianapolis. You?"

"We're dropping the RV in San Francisco. Ever been there?"

The trucker shook his head. "Not the easiest place to get around in a rig. Too many hills. Too many queers."

I didn't respond, but I think I felt Lincoln tense up next to me. Maybe the trucker had figured out that not only were there too many queers in San Francisco, there were too many in his semi as well.

"Pull over," Lincoln said.

"What?" I asked at the same time as the trucker—and my mother.

"Pull over," he repeated. He had one hand on the door handle as he unbuckled his seat belt with the other.

"We ain't even at the rest stop," the trucker said, "and it's another five miles to—"

"I said pull the fuck over, or so help me, I'm opening this God damn door right now and getting out."

He did open it, in fact, and I caught a glimpse of the shoulder paint stripe whipping past. At that, the trucker began throwing gears and stomped on the brakes. I braced myself against the dashboard and hoped I didn't slide onto the floor or into the windshield. That scared me more than the idea that the trucker might have a baseball bat or a tire iron in easy reach and might not be opposed to a little gay bashing.

Through clenched teeth, I asked Lincoln, "What the hell's the matter with you?"

"Are you gonna be sick or something?" the trucker asked.

"My Lord," mother said, "how remarkably clueless."

"I'm sick of listening to that kind of crap," Lincoln said. The semi was still rolling a little, but Lincoln opened the door and hopped down anyway, landed on his feet, and began walking without a backward glance.

I sat for a second in silence, then the trucker said, "I didn't mean to offend your friend, but he's kind of hotheaded, ain't he?"

My first instinct was to say, *Yeah, well, you did offend*, and point out that Lincoln wasn't the only one offended. I knew there was a right thing to say here, but I couldn't come up with it. Instead, I muttered, "He's not my friend, but thanks for the lift."

"It's about another half mile to the rest stop. They got pay phones, I think." I couldn't tell if he was tipping his baseball cap or just tugging it lower. "You all be careful out here."

I watched the truck pull back into the freeway lane, its headlights briefly illuminating Lincoln's back before we were plunged into darkness again. When I caught up to Lincoln, I could see the glow of another joint. I touched his shoulder, and he knocked my hand away.

"Were you just going to let that slide?" he asked. His tone wasn't accusatory so much as incredulous.

"I wouldn't expect him to change his opinion based on anything I might say or do," I said.

"Well, not as long as everyone's looking the other way."

Now his tone *was* accusatory. I knew exactly what he meant. I wasn't in the mood, and lacked the energy for a fight. Instead, I just put my hands in my pockets, hunched my shoulders, kept walking, and tried to ignore the feeling that I should be walking in the other direction away from him.

CHAPTER EIGHT

The next afternoon, two tires and several hundred dollars later, we were back on the road. I drove. We'd wasted most of the day waiting for Dobbs to get replacements for the old tires, which had not only holes, but dry rot. We didn't get very far down the road before dark. We were finally headed in a straight line west, though. In a way, it felt like heading home.

A home I was going to pack and close up before heading west again. Maybe that wasn't necessary, but it made sense to me. I no longer had a job to keep me tethered to St. Louis, so there seemed little reason to stay—no family, no relationship, only a handful of friends, and my dog.

It wasn't a very compelling case.

For two nights in a row, we stayed in motels and ordered pizza for dinner. Even though we were rolling across the country in what was basically a mobile apartment with its own fully outfitted kitchen, I was in no hurry to spend the night with tires under my back. It didn't feel like my space to use. We were just delivering it, after all.

Lincoln didn't seem to mind—or if he did, he kept it to himself. We hadn't said much to each other since Ohio. If one of us was driving, the other one slept. We probably could have driven straight through, but I was in no hurry at the moment to be finished with this errand. It was like an intermission between acts of my life.

And once I was done with it, I had to figure out what I was going to do next.

Lincoln seemed content to let me set the pace on the highway. Once we were done driving for the day, though, he got behind the wheel and steered our bodies in whichever direction he felt like going. He was like this two nights in a row. After the second night, it felt like he was trying to prove something—to me or himself, I wasn't sure.

If this trip was an intermission for him, he hadn't shared with me what was in store for him on the other side of it. If he really adhered to his philosophy of going in any direction as long as he wasn't going in circles, Lincoln might have been just as clueless about his future as I was.

Lincoln was driving early Wednesday evening when we got to St. Louis. Afraid Lincoln might get lost once we got closer, I tried to keep my eyes open for a while in the afternoon. But the glare from the sun got to be too much, and I closed my eyes.

When I woke up, I caught the last glimpse of sunset through the windshield. It was the golden hour again, that time of day at home when evening often got away from me, when I lost track of the hours until the street lights came on and I'd look at my watch wondering how another evening had disappeared.

I'd been reading another one of my mother's letters before I'd nodded off. She'd written it when I was around twenty years old, the year my grandmother died.

Dear Derek,

I don't know why you were the first person I thought of when 75 State Street called to tell me that my mother had passed away. I almost dialed your number, but then Arthur turned on the kitchen light and asked who had called at three in the morning. I'd already been up for a couple hours, but he never asks why I'm still awake anymore. Most nights for a few hours while he's in bed, I get up and wander the house. I've been doing this ever since Joel left for college. Sometimes I'll read or watch TV if there's anything still on, though most of the time I sit on the porch or in the living room and stare at the street. I feel like the world is all mine at times like that.

My mother didn't recognize me the last time I visited her. Over the past year her lucid moments had become shorter and less frequent. I'd always hoped she or my father would tell me something, give me some nugget of wisdom that would help me make sense of the world and my life. But my father died too suddenly and my mother just seemed to disappear behind this curtain of fog, and all I could see was her smile on occasion. I remember thinking how unfortunate it was when you lost both your parents so young, but if I had the choice, I think I would want to go quickly like my father and perhaps not know what was about to happen. At the very least, I think it would be a mercy to Arthur and Joel.

I had stopped reading at that point. The sheets had slid from my lap onto the floor after I nodded off. As I leaned forward to pick them up, it was hard to resist interpreting clairvoyance into her words. In a way she had gotten her wish, hadn't she? My father and I had been blissfully ignorant of her impending oblivion, even if she had been forced to stare it in the face for who knew how long before the end. It had been her decision to face that alone. She had made her choice. Regardless of what she had written in the letter, I suspected I could have been reading her grocery list and been able to find insights in its words.

"Oh darling, as if I ever wrote a grocery list," she said.

Lincoln glanced over at me and smiled. He had the radio turned on, its murmur low enough that it hadn't woken me.

"Hey, it's alive."

I pulled myself up in my seat. "Where are we?"

"Hang on," he said. We were approaching a rise in the

highway. We crested the hill and the St. Louis skyline spread out before us, the Arch glittering in the distance like the Emerald City. This was the best view of downtown, and the irony was you had to leave Missouri and go to Illinois to see it.

I rolled down the window as we crossed the Mississippi River, hoping to catch the scent of hops from the Anheuser-Busch brewery near downtown. Instead, I inhaled a face full of humidity and the heavy brown funk of the muddy river oozing by beneath us.

"Oh, gag," Lincoln said, wrinkling his entire face. "What's that smell?"

"The Mississippi," I said before I rolled the window back up. *The past*, I wanted to add. Summer felt like it was paying St. Louis an early visit. Summer was my least favorite season in this city—the warm, wet slap of humidity, stagnant air you could slice and chew squatting over the river valley and making every breath an effort. There was never even a faint hope of a breeze.

The apartment smelled like dust burning on a hot radiator when we walked in. In the bedroom, the dirty clothes from my trip to London were still piled where I'd dumped them on the floor. I had nothing clean to wear; I really did have to do laundry. I turned on the air conditioner and opened the living room windows for a minute to let the place air out. From the sofa, I was able to see the RV parked at the corner. That seemed important to me, like I was being responsible.

Lincoln sprawled in the corner chair and propped his feet on the ottoman. I resisted the urge to tell him to take his shoes off. After I looked at him, he kicked them off. I glanced around at the shelves of books, the TV, the mirror on the wall meant to make the room look bigger.

What the hell was I going to do with all this stuff?

I called Matt and Carrie to let them know I was back in town and I was planning to break my lease. When Carrie asked what my plans were (which in her case amounted to thundering, "What the *hell* are you thinking?"), I told her I was planning to spend some time with my father. It could even have been the truth.

Matt asked if I needed any help. Although I probably did, I told him I had a bigger favor to ask.

"Can you look after Dudley a little while longer?"

"Of course I can." He didn't even hesitate. "How much longer do you think the trip is going to take?"

"Maybe another week? I don't really know."

"Take as much time as you need," he said. "It's no big deal."

It took two days to pack up everything. Mainly, I worked at night after Lincoln had gone to bed and gotten out of my way. It was easier to do this by myself. My mother, perched on the arm of the sofa while I packed, was another story.

"Why are you saving all of this?" she asked, turning a CD case over in her hands, but waving her arm to take in the stacks of boxes. "Do you really need it?"

"The afterlife has turned you into a minimalist, hasn't it?" I asked.

She shrugged and put down the CD. It was an old Erasure album. I couldn't remember the last time I'd listened to it—years, probably. Even though it was midnight and Lincoln was sleeping in the other room, I turned the stereo down low and put it on random play. Soon, Mom stood up from the sofa and picked up the case again. She was tapping her foot. "I rather like this. Who's the girl singing?"

"Andy Bell," I said. "As in 'Andrew.'"

She stopped tapping. "Well, how very pretty. What's the song called?"

"'Save Me, Darling,'" I said.

"If only I could." She sighed and began tapping her foot again. Pretty soon, she was twirling around my living room, the hem of her dressing gown fluttering around her ankles. Seeing her look so lively made me laugh, and she stepped a little higher. By the time the disc switched over to the next song, she had collapsed, breathless, onto the sofa and was staring out the window, her cigarette burning down almost to her fingers. She made no move to flick the ash or toss away the butt. I wondered, when the ember burned low enough, whether she'd feel the heat.

"What are you staring at?" I asked her while I took more books down from the shelves.

"Hmm?" She looked back at me. For an instant, it seemed as if she'd grown transparent, but maybe it was just a trick of the light coming in from the street lamp outside the window. "Oh, you'd be amazed what I can see. Let's see, it's"—she looked at her wrist, which was bare—"five a.m. in London and Philip has just woken up, but he hasn't dragged himself out of bed yet." She smiled. "He still hasn't put the pillowcase you slept on in the laundry yet. Isn't that the sweetest thing?"

I went back to packing. "I think I've lost my chance with Philip," I said.

"What makes you think that? If I had to guess, he'd still love to hear from you."

"How do you know that, Mom? I mean, really, how?" I sat back on my heels. I had a stack of books in my hands—paperbacks mostly, novels I hadn't read in ages either. I put them in the box anyway.

"I honestly haven't the foggiest idea, darling. I don't even have to close my eyes but I can see him, and somehow I know I'm seeing what's really happening, not just something in my imagination." She sat up straight and held her cigarette hand out stiffly, like she was about to give a dramatic recitation. "He's gotten up now and he's making coffee." She smirked mischievously. "Apparently the man does not own a bathrobe. Does he always sleep naked?"

"How do you *do* that?" Perhaps for the first time in my life, I was jealous of my mother. If Philip owned a robe, it never made an appearance while I was there. Clothing had been optional inside his flat.

"If I knew, I'd tell you." She stood up and moved toward the bookshelves. Picking up a hardback, she examined the cover and flipped it over. "Really, are you going to ever read any of these again? Why not get rid of them and give someone else a chance?"

She handed me the book—*On the Road*—and I placed it in a box. "This from the woman who kept a box full of letters for four decades. Oh, and let's not forget the shoe collection that would have made Imelda Marcos jealous."

She waved her newly lit cigarette in dismissal. "Darling, your father and I didn't move once in all those years, so why would I get rid of anything? There was no need."

She picked another book from the shelf. She frowned and opened it. The cover was blank, but the pages inside made her smile.

"Oh look," she said, and handed it to me.

Amid all the books, she found the one that wasn't a novel or cookbook or guide to understanding your dog. It was a journal. I hadn't written anything in it for years. I was almost afraid to open it and be confronted by whatever arrogance of youth I had chosen to commemorate in writing.

I opened it and flipped through a lot of empty pages at the back to the last entry, which was dated June 13, 1995. I'd graduated from college that May and was about to move to St. Louis for my first job. It wasn't exactly my dream job, but at the time I remember thinking it was as good a place as any for a start.

"Maybe for a couple years," I'd written. "Then I'll move on to New York or Chicago, maybe even London if I'm lucky. In the meantime, it'll do for now."

Showed what I knew. Two years lengthened into fifteen, much the same way the distance from St. Louis to Chicago became an impassable frontier. I hadn't even visited Chicago that much. In spite of my profound indifference, somehow St. Louis had a hold on me.

"And anyway," she said, resuming her seat on the sofa, "my letters should be enough to keep you entertained for at least a while longer."

Once the bookshelves were cleared, I sat down with a glass of water and the box of letters. Since there were no postmarks on the envelopes—letters never sent, after all—I couldn't easily tell in what order I should be reading them. Reading them chronologically seemed the obvious thing, but dipping my hand in and pulling one out at random felt a little like opening a fortune cookie, which seemed appropriate at the moment also.

> *My mother always said boys were easier to raise than girls—though I don't know how she could possibly know this for certain, since I was an only child—but I think she would have a hard time making sense of my son. It's not that Joel is difficult or prone to tantrums, quite the opposite, in fact. Sometimes I'll find him sitting at the kitchen table with his school books spread out in front of him, and he's just staring out the window or off into space. I very nearly have to yell sometimes in order to bring him back to the world. And I can't help but wonder, where does he go?*

After I handed over the keys to the landlord and closed the front door for the last time, we piled into the RV and headed for Matt's condo. Though he had agreed to keep looking after Dudley while I completed this errand, I wasn't about to leave town again without seeing my dog. Matt suggested Lincoln and I spend our last night in town at his place.

"Right, because *that* won't be awkward, not at all," my mother said. She was kneeling between the two front seats as we drove from the Central West End to Clayton. For once, neither she nor Lincoln were smoking anything.

The RV barely fit in Matt's driveway. It was another warm

evening—it should have only been scraping the sixties this time of year, but the forecasters talked of beating the record high tomorrow.

"Nice place," Lincoln said, staring up at the front of Matt's corner unit. The living room light was on, and Matt had opened the front door by the time we were halfway up the steps. He wasn't there long before another silhouette peered around the door at knee level.

Dudley stayed where he was—*Good boy*, I thought. He wagged his tail, thumping Matt in the calf, and pretty soon he was shaking his entire hind end.

"Did you miss me?" I asked. I knelt down and wrapped my arms around Dudley's neck, burying my nose in the fur at his collar. Dudley leaned into me the way he always did when he was happy to see someone.

"He missed you, all right," Matt said. "Every time I came in the front door he looked around me to see if you were coming in behind me. Whenever I parked out back and came in through the kitchen, I'd find him sitting in the living room looking out the window."

"I missed him too." I gave Matt a hug and introduced him to Lincoln, who patted Dudley absentmindedly while he submitted to the dog's customary initial sniff test. He at least passed that.

Matt was a little harder to read. His expression had settled into an almost frown while Lincoln looked around the living room.

"I thought dogs were supposed to be good judges of character," my mother said. She had taken up a perch on the corner of the sofa. Together, we all watched as Dudley, apparently satisfied with Lincoln, curled up on his bed in the corner, rested his chin on his paws, and closed his eyes. Before long, his snore buzzed through the air.

Lincoln laughed and yawned. "I think I'm going to turn in too."

He took both our bags and followed Matt up the stairs to the guest bedroom. I sat on the opposite corner of the sofa from my mother and glared at her. She was lighting a cigarette and ignored me for a moment. When I finally caught her eye, she exhaled and asked, "What's with the look?"

"What've you got against Lincoln?"

She laughed. "Darling, I don't have a dog in that race. The better question would be what have you got to feel defensive about?"

"I'm not defensive."

"Of course you're not. That statement might be more convincing if you hadn't just crossed your arms."

I looked down and uncrossed my arms. "I couldn't have just told him not to come with me."

"I don't see why you couldn't have done exactly that."

"Well, it sure as hell wouldn't have worked with *you*, would it?"

I wanted to take it back as soon as I said it. She lowered her cigarette at the same time she raised her other hand to her chest, as if to ward off a blow. For a moment, she looked as if she might tear up. I was about to apologize when Matt came back downstairs.

"Were you talking to yourself just now?" he asked.

"Bad habit. Thanks again for letting us stay here."

"You know you're always welcome," he said. I wondered briefly whether he meant that singular or plural. Before I could ask, he said he was going to bed himself. He gave me another hug and said, "It is good to see you again," with extra emphasis on the "is," like I needed to be convinced.

My mother didn't reappear after Matt was gone. At some point, I would have to apologize—to a ghost.

I doubted my life could get any stranger.

I stretched out on the sofa and looked over at Dudley. If I kept staring at him, eventually he would open his eyes and, seeing me watching him, start to wag his tail. I would only need a little patience before he got up and joined me on the sofa. He didn't disappoint. I patted the cushion and he gamely jumped up, settling with his chin resting on my thigh. Before long, he began to snore again.

Some days, that was all it took for things to get better.

Chapter Nine

I wished I could have slept as easily as Dudley. I spent most of the night staring at the ceiling, listening to Lincoln breathing next to me, or Dudley snoring downstairs. When I finally drifted off sometime after one, in my dreams I was still lying in bed trying to fall asleep. Meanwhile in the dark, an unseen and vaguely sinister animal circled the bed. I didn't dare close my eyes.

When I woke up after that, I thought it might be preferable to give up on sleep.

An alarm clock went off somewhere in the house. At first it was hard for me to tell whether the noise was real or a residual part of the dream. Out of instinct I flailed for the nightstand and the clock that wasn't there. I finally remembered this wasn't my house.

I managed to slip out of bed without waking Lincoln and reached the head of the stairs in time to hear the jangle of Dudley's collar, followed by the front door opening and Matt whispering, "Let's go, boy."

As I stood there waiting to hear the front door shut, guilt and jealousy jockeyed for top billing in my mind. I should have been able to drag myself out of bed, nightmare or not, in time to walk my own dog while we were in the same house. The petty, caffeine-deprived part of my brain thought Dudley should have been able to communicate to Matt his preference for me.

Neither thought made me feel very good.

I waited until the front door shut before I went to the kitchen to start making coffee. By the time Matt and Dudley returned, I had finished half my cup, poured one for Matt, and filled Dudley's food bowl. It felt quaint and domestic, until I remembered the man still asleep upstairs was the man I was sleeping with at the moment. The most Matt and I had shared in the years since our breakup was friendship and that one awkward, poorly timed kiss before my mother's funeral—and that could have been caused by stress, grief, lack of sleep, or all of the above. Things had changed—a lot—since my trip to Maine. Or they had changed long ago and I hadn't been paying attention.

I found out just how much the landscape had shifted later that afternoon. Carrie wanted to come by for lunch before Lincoln and I headed west. I had been dreading seeing her in person, so I put it off as long as I could. Since we were seeing her at eleven and Lincoln and I wanted to hit the road by three, I'd done a stellar job of procrastinating.

Even though I hadn't told her anything about Lincoln except that he was an old friend from high school, I knew she would take one look at him and see "fuck buddy" written all over him. And she would tell me I was out of my fucking mind. I wouldn't have necessarily disagreed with her. Nor would I have been able to explain myself. I had thought letting Lincoln come on this trip was the path of least resistance, but the more time we were together, the less true that seemed.

Before she arrived, I started flipping through Matt's recipe box. I wanted to make something nice for lunch, something requiring effort, to make up for avoiding Carrie the brief time I'd been in town.

If my mom was around, she probably would have told me that my phone received calls just as well as it made them. But I hadn't seen her since the night before. I tried not to let her absence get to me, but I hadn't considered the possibility that she might not come back. What then? I wouldn't have believed the thought of her ghost departing could have filled me with even more despair than her death had.

"What are you planning on making?" Matt asked. He'd gone into work to open the nursery. By the time he came home at ten, he'd managed to get thoroughly filthy. Lincoln was stretched out in an Adirondack chair on the deck, trying to make the best of the heat wave and the rapidly brightening sun. He had on dark glasses and might have been asleep.

I kept pulling out recipe cards, flipping them over and putting them back. Nothing seemed right. "I don't know. I thought I should make something nice," I said. "You don't mind if I take over the kitchen for a while, do you?"

"I never mind when someone else does the cooking," Matt said.

The next card in the box made me smile. It was one I'd written down for Matt years ago, a recipe for manicotti. It had a dark red half-moon stain obscuring some of the writing. It had been our second date, and at some point that evening Matt had used the card as a coaster for his wine glass.

"Remember this?" I held up the card. Matt was sitting at the kitchen table taking off his shoes. "I could make manicotti."

Matt smiled, unknotting his shoelace. "Actually, I made that last week. How about something else?"

I slipped the card back into the box. "It's probably too warm for this anyway."

I settled on a cold pasta salad and gazpacho. Matt offered to go to the store for fresh tomatoes after he took a shower. Only after he left did it occur to me to wonder *for whom had Matt made manicotti?* He didn't cook often because it was a hassle to cook for one, and he didn't think he was very good at it, anyway.

If he made manicotti for someone, it must have been a special occasion.

The doorbell rang at ten forty-five. Maybe Carrie was early, but she'd never been early for anything. Five minutes late would be surprisingly punctual for her.

It wasn't Carrie. The man on the porch was a little shorter than me. He was wearing a white button-down shirt, jeans, and a faltering smile. We stood staring at each other for just long enough to start feeling awkward.

"I'm sorry," I said, and laughed a little. "I was expecting you to be someone else."

"Me too. I mean, is Matt here?"

"He'll be back in a bit." Still wondering who the hell he was, I opened the door wider. "I'm Joel, by the way."

Before the man could answer, Dudley managed to wedge himself between us and looked up. Typical. If someone other than Dudley was getting attention—well, that couldn't be allowed.

The man smiled. "Hey, Dudley." He knelt down and stroked Dudley's head for a moment. "How you doing, bud?"

"You've met already?" I wasn't sure if I was asking the man or the dog. Or both.

"Yeah, the last time I was over. He's great, isn't he?" The man stood up and shook my hand. "I'm Jacob, by the way."

And Dudley is MY dog, I wanted to say. Instead, I asked if I could get him something to drink.

He stood by the front door and slid out of his shoes. "You're sure it's not too early?" he asked as I poured champagne and orange juice into glasses. I wanted to have something special for Carrie; hopefully she wouldn't mind if we got started a little early without her.

Hopefully, Matt wouldn't mind that I'd gone into his champagne stash.

"Early? Mimosas are a breakfast drink," I said.

"Silly boy," my mother said. She was leaning against the counter when I returned the juice to the refrigerator. "It's never too early. Though it can sometimes be too late."

I was wondering when she was going to show up. While my back was to Jacob, I silently mouthed the words *I'm sorry* to her.

Smiling sadly, she reached out and patted my cheek—thankfully, with the hand not holding a cigarette.

"It's not like it was going to kill me, darling," she said.

I closed the refrigerator and stood there a moment, basking in the rapidly fading bubble of cold air. Lincoln still looked unconscious outside. His skin was darkening and on its way to red. He glistened from sweat more than sunblock. I wondered if I should pour him a mimosa.

"If he wants one," my mother said, "let him get off his lazy, perfectly formed ass and get it himself."

It seemed poor timing to point out how uncharitable that sounded, especially since I'd just apologized. Jacob's presence made it impossible to speak to her directly, anyway. I handed Jacob his glass and leaned against the counter opposite my mother.

"I didn't know Matt had a roommate," Jacob said.

"He doesn't. I'm just an old friend." My mother raised an eyebrow, but remained silent. I had opted for the simplest, if incomplete story. Jacob and I both sipped from our mimosas, looking at each other in that way you do when you're being civil while secretly sizing up the other person and deciding who could take whom in a fight. Not that we had anything to fight about, of course. He seemed perfectly nice. Short, but nice.

I thought I could take him if I had to.

"Darling, please," my mother said. "Your one and only fistfight was in high school, and your own fist wasn't even involved."

While I concentrated on projecting peevish thoughts toward my mother, Lincoln came in from the deck, shirtless and sweaty. He was still wearing his sunglasses and smelled of Coppertone.

"Is that your boyfriend?" Jacob asked, after introductions were made and Lincoln went upstairs to take a shower.

"Not really," I said. "Kind of complicated."

"Kind of hot." I had to smile at that. When Lincoln walked through a room, it was like the prickly feeling in the air before a thunderstorm. He was exciting to watch, and if you happened to be in danger of getting struck by lightning, well, the risk was worth the thrill.

At least, I'd thought so at one point.

"So," I asked, "how did you and Matt meet?" While he told me about going to the nursery and asking for flowers that someone with the blackest thumb couldn't kill, I tried not to wonder whether they'd had sex yet. And while we talked about the hardiness of geraniums, and how all Matt had to do was look at something and it started growing, I could only picture them in the broom closet of an office Matt kept at the nursery, the papers and invoices and receipts scattered across the battered wooden desk sticking to their asses as they sprawled across the surface. The paper would have been the only thing to keep them from getting splinters. I opened the fridge to top up my champagne glass.

The doorbell rang before I could say anything embarrassing. Carrie was putting out her cigarette in a flowerpot beside the entryway when I opened the door.

"Hey, classy," I said. I handed her my mimosa.

"Just don't tell Matt, okay?"

"That you're using his flowers for ashtrays or that you've started smoking again?"

"He knows I'm smoking again." She gave me a long hug. Her hair smelled like cigarettes, sweat, and perfume. "Why does it feel like you've been gone a year?" she asked.

"I think a year's worth of shit has happened. To both of us."

We went inside and I headed for the fridge again to replace my drink. Carrie squared her shoulders and extended her hand to Jacob.

"You must be Lincoln," she said.

Jacob smirked. "Then I have to disappoint you. But pleased to meet you just the same."

As Jacob shook Carrie's hand, she turned to me with her eyebrows suspended higher than normal. Just for a moment, but long enough for me to take a little reassurance in not being the only one for whom this was news. Jacob laughed, his smirk turned into a real smile, and he introduced himself. My mother, apparently disappointed that fur wasn't going to fly at this encounter, wandered off toward the deck. To my surprise, Dudley followed her.

"Lincoln's upstairs in the shower," I said. "Jacob is Matt's—" Matt's what? I didn't know how to finish the sentence. The longer the silence stretched out, the more I wanted to stick my head in the fridge.

Or maybe the oven.

"Friend," Jacob said finally.

"Well, pleased to meet you," Carrie said, drained her glass, and held it out to me. I opened another bottle, wondering why Matt had so much champagne in the house.

My mother turned from the sliding glass door, a mimosa suddenly in her hand. "There's something worth celebrating in every day, darling. Sometimes you have to dig a little to find it, but it's good to have supplies on hand when you do." She lifted her glass, sipped, turning back to the deck and the yard. She reached down and stroked the fur between Dudley's ears. I shivered.

My dead mother was petting my very much alive dog.

"You going to let me actually drink that?" Carrie took her glass from me; I was still standing in front of the open fridge. Before she drank, she asked, "Are you okay? You look like you've seen—"

"Don't say it," I said. My mother started to guffaw. She even slapped her knee and held her glass out to avoid spilling anything.

Lincoln finally came downstairs. He had changed into a white T-shirt and jeans. His hair was still damp from the shower, and looked jet-black and slick. His face was red, either from the sun or the shower. He looked at my glass and asked, "Is there one of those for me?"

As I poured him one, Carrie held out her hand again and said, her tone almost a question, "You must be Lincoln?"

"Someone has to be," he said and shook her hand.

I gave Lincoln his drink, and the four of us clinked glasses.

The last time I'd had a mimosa was on my vacation. One morning, Philip and I actually put on clothes and dragged ourselves away from his bed and his flat. We'd gone out for brunch. It was the day before I was due to leave, and our sense of happiness seemed to have taken on a desperate edge as its expiration date approached. To blunt that edge, Philip ordered champagne and was mock-appalled (I think) when I poured some in my half-empty glass of orange juice.

"It's a crime to do that to Bollinger," he said. I dipped my finger in the glass and flicked a few drops at his face. He grinned and wiped them off his nose before I could give in to the temptation to lean across the table and lick them off.

"The only crime would be not finishing the bottle," I said. So we did. Then we raced back to his flat, breathless and giddy from the champagne, to have sex again.

We drank, and stood in a momentarily awkward silence. Everyone here was new to someone else, and the one who might tie us all together was still at the store. On a humid day like this, soaking in champagne besides, everything seemed in danger of dissolving into mush.

Carrie seemed sharp and brittle. She was wearing a black dress with electric blue and red designs crisscrossing it like lightning. It was cut like Marilyn Monroe's white dress—a good look for Carrie's figure, but it also exposed enough high-contrast flesh to enhance how pale she was by comparison to the newly tanned Lincoln or Matt's habitual bronze. She'd also gotten a new haircut since my mother's funeral; a short, severe style that played up the angles of her cheekbones and made her look like a new woman altogether.

A new, angry, about-to-be-divorced woman.

"I almost forgot," Carrie said, apropos of nothing. "Philip called the office this week."

"Philip who?" I asked, about half a second before I realized she meant Philip from London.

"Philip from London, you idiot," she snapped before draining her glass. She held it out to me like a threat, and I grabbed it to refill before it occurred to me she'd just called me an idiot.

"I really like this girl," my mother said. She held out her glass too.

"Get your own," I muttered to her as softly as possible.

"Who's Philip?" Lincoln asked. This, of course, was the question I was hoping wouldn't get asked by the person I was hoping wouldn't ask it. As I handed Carrie her now-full glass, I wanted to stab her with it.

"Someone I met on a trip last month," I said, and hoped he would leave it at that. Meanwhile, I gave Carrie such a look that she raised her eyebrows in surprise. I don't know what the hell she was surprised about. The look had the desired effect, though. She didn't say another word, just slipped me Philip's number on a Post-it note later.

We were alone in the kitchen; Lincoln had stepped out onto the deck to smoke, and Jacob had followed with Dudley, who he thought needed to go out. With a pang of regret, I watched my dog clamber back up the steps from the yard and approach Jacob for a pat.

"He sounded like he really wanted to talk to you," she whispered. I didn't know why she was whispering. I took Philip's phone number into the bathroom and shut the door.

For a while I stared at the number before dialing. Maybe I was wishing the figures to rearrange themselves into a message, a secret code or a guide of what I should say to him when—if—he picked up on the other end.

"Try telling him the truth," my mother said. "Tell him you miss him."

"You're even following me into the bathroom now?" I asked.

She shrugged. At least for once she wasn't smoking. "Just us girls, I guess. Now call."

In the moments between dialing and waiting for him to answer, I mentally calculated the time difference and momentarily panicked that I was calling at five in the morning. About the same time I realized it was five in the evening, not morning, the line clicked.

"Joel?"

It would have been so much easier if he hadn't picked up. I wouldn't have felt quite so ridiculous then, hiding in my ex-boyfriend's bathroom, sitting on the lid of the toilet, hoping the man I was sleeping with wouldn't come find me while I talked with the man I'd been sleeping with just before him. I was buzzing strongly from the champagne. If I wasn't careful, the afternoon would find me stumbling around as if I were wearing clown shoes, and the next morning I'd wake up with a head full of cottony memories.

And the fear I'd done something really dumb.

"That's practically a sure thing, darling," my mother said.

I shushed her and said to Philip, "I'm sorry I didn't call sooner."

There was a clatter, and Philip muttered, "Crap. Hang on, I just dropped the shopping."

"I could call back later—"

"No!" he said, sounding like he'd just mainlined a triple espresso with extra anxiety. I heard a rustle of shopping bags and some clanking—maybe wine, maybe canned goods. "No," he said, a little calmer. "I've got it sorted. It's good to hear your voice again."

I closed my eyes. "Yours too."

"So, your friend Carrie told me there was some sort of family emergency back home?"

I didn't really want to tell him about my mother dying, but

I couldn't see a way around it. The phrase had hardly left my mouth when Philip sucked in a breath through his teeth and said, "Oh Christ, love, I'm so sorry."

I stumbled on through the details of her illness and how she hadn't told either my father or me anything. As I spoke, I was still back at that word he'd just called me. Maybe it hadn't meant anything. Everyone from the barmaids to your grandmother was "love" over there, weren't they?

In order to avoid addressing that one word, I piled on more words, burying it beneath a rambling narrative as I kept going headlong through the rest of the story. I told him about the funeral and the RV, Carrie's divorce, and Lincoln tagging along for the ride. I didn't tell him I'd been sleeping with Lincoln.

Perhaps later I would need to, but not now.

The air-conditioning clicked on. The vent close to floor level sent a cold breeze across my knees. I leaned forward and flicked the louvers shut. When I sat up again, my mother was frowning at me.

"That omission will come back to bite you in the ass if you're not careful," she said. I silently mouthed the words "I know." I couldn't imagine confessing to him now that I'd slept with Lincoln. Not after he'd just used the L word. Philip and I didn't have a commitment—*not after four days*, my champagne-fizzed brain reminded me. So why did I feel guilty? I'm not sure if it was toward Philip, or toward Lincoln. Maybe toward myself.

What the hell was I doing?

"Joel?" Philip asked from four thousand miles away. "Are you still there?"

"Yeah." I'd been staring at the frayed edge of the toilet paper roll in front of me. I stood up and leaned against the vanity. "Sorry, my head's still a blur."

"That's to be expected. How long before you think you'll be in San Francisco?"

I did a mental calculation. "Maybe three or four days."

"Fuck, I won't be there until the week after."

"I'll wait," I said.

"Seriously?"

I almost said, "It's not like I've got anywhere else I need to be," but that would sound like I didn't have anything better to do, making it seem insignificant. I figured this was going to require considerable effort on my part. I would have to explain to Lincoln that we were no longer going to sleep together. By the time we got to San Francisco, I had to make sure that he had found his own direction and was following it.

A direction that would hopefully not intersect in any way with Philip.

"Good luck with that," my mother said.

❖

By the time Matt finally returned with the tomatoes, we all were well on our way to getting fairly tipsy. I finished making the gazpacho, and no one was in any condition to tell if it was good or not. I briefly considered pouring vodka into it and calling it Bloody Mary soup. But after all the champagne, it seemed like overkill. We ran out of champagne after the fifth bottle and switched to chardonnay. Late morning became early afternoon, lengthening into suppertime. We ate and drank more.

Thoughts of getting on the road receded into tomorrow.

I mentioned our next stop was Las Vegas, and Jacob said he could get us a good deal on a hotel room. He was a travel agent, specializing in group bookings and package tours, and said he had a knack for getting people where they wanted to go.

"Can he get Lincoln on a bus back to Portland?" my mother asked.

While Matt helped me load plates and bowls into the dishwasher, I asked, "So, did it work?"

"Did what work?"

I rolled my eyes in the direction of the living room. If Matt cooked for somebody, it meant he was trying to impress them or get lucky.

Or both.

"Did the manicotti work? You made it for Jacob, right?"

Matt looked at me a little sideways. "Yeah, how'd you figure that out?"

"Call it a hunch."

"Well, I hate to disappoint you, but that night wasn't the greatest date ever."

Matt had made dinner on their second date. Even though the meal had turned out fine, something about the evening had been off. He wasn't sure if it was their moods, but the date had seemed awkward and forced. By the time they got to dessert and moved to the living room sofa, the rhythm of the evening had smoothed out from its earlier bumps and potholes—until, right in the middle of what Matt said was a really damn good kiss that was probably going to lead to the removal of clothing, Dudley decided he needed to be on the sofa with them.

"He's lucky he didn't hurt himself," Matt said, "but he knocked over the coffee table. There was cheesecake everywhere, and Dudley couldn't decide if he was going to be in trouble or if he should try to lick up some of the cake anyway."

I laughed, louder than I should have or the story deserved, perhaps. I blamed it on the champagne.

"Jacob ended up wearing most of his coffee on his shirt—"

"Ah, see?" I said. "Dudley was just trying to help get him out of his clothes for you."

"Nice try, I'll give him credit for that, but it didn't work. I sent Jacob home in a clean shirt and figured I'd never see him again."

"Which obviously turned out not to be the case."

Matt liked to say he had no trouble getting dates. It was second and third dates that were the problems. Sometimes he blamed his past as a lawyer ("You were a *lawyer*?" he'd been asked on more than one occasion). Other times, it was his present as a glorified gardener ("Entrepreneur," I insisted; "Non-migrant manual laborer," he countered). Really, it was his inability to show up on time anywhere but the nursery.

"So what happened?" I asked.

Jacob stopped by the nursery a few days later to return Matt's shirt. "And, well, one thing sort of led to another."

Even with his tan, Matt's face flushed as if suddenly sunburned. He glanced back toward the living room to see if anyone could hear what we were talking about, but Carrie had Jacob and Lincoln enthralled about—something. I couldn't hear what she was saying.

I leaned closer to Matt and lowered my voice. "You mean, right there?" I asked. "At work. In your *office*?"

"Hey, the door locks! It's not like we fucked right in the middle of the bedding plants!"

"Darling," my mother said—even she was whispering, "I'll have to give you credit for calling this one. I would never have guessed he could be such a dog."

Matt was embarrassed, but from the turn of his smile I could tell he was also a little pleased with himself for shocking me.

I took a pile of forks and knives and began lining them up in the silverware rack. "I hope it was a slow day at the nursery."

Matt shrugged. "We were really quiet."

"Please," I said. "You were never quiet."

He did turn a little thoughtful at that point. "And all he'd come in for was to give me back the shirt and look at some shrubs."

I was tempted to ask if he'd given Jacob a good discount for laying the owner. Given my own circumstances, though, I figured it best just to let it go.

Once the dishwasher was loaded, Matt started serving up dessert. He'd picked up ice cream while he was out getting the tomatoes. I made coffee—I figured we could all use it. Jacob, looking in the fridge for the half and half, rested his arm at Matt's waist. A few times earlier, I noticed Matt passing his hand across Jacob's shoulder as he walked by. That awkward familiarity of initial infatuation was sweet.

It was early, but I had a feeling it could last.

❖

I woke up on Sunday morning surprised not to have a hangover, so I decided I'd go for a run before we hit the road.

The first few minutes were painful as I pushed through an already humid morning. The effects of the previous afternoon became evident. I ran down Hanley Road and turned onto Wydown, which was lined with big, shady trees and even bigger houses. I saw other joggers running down the grassy, sun-filled median, but I stayed to the side of the road facing the few oncoming cars. Instead of focusing on how miserable I felt and how slow I was going, I concentrated on my breath and just putting one foot in front of the other. Eventually, I sank into the rhythm and was able to forget about the discomfort as my feet ate up the miles.

Forest Park was one of my favorite places in the city. I crossed Skinker on the west edge of the park. I took up the trail running around the park's perimeter. When I wasn't working, I'd spent a lot of my time running this trail. There was the summer I was unemployed and the only way I could cope with the stress was to run it off every afternoon at the height of the heat. This was also where I first ran into Matt, or rather, he ran into me. We both were wearing headphones—he was on rollerblades, and neither of us heard or saw the other one coming. In the resulting collision, I skinned my knee and wound up with bits of gravel in my palm. Matt broke his ankle. While we waited for his ankle to be set, I asked him out. He said yes.

Though it didn't stop me, I wondered if the painkillers had been a factor in his answer.

Whenever I ran around the park, I felt like each mile, each landmark was something I was picking up and putting away until the next run. This time I was picking them up and putting them away for good.

Matt and Lincoln were both up by the time I returned. Jacob had headed home while I was out. Lincoln's bag was already packed and waiting by the front door. Showered and dressed, Lincoln sat on the sofa.

"Ready when you are," he said. He seemed almost eager. Exhausted and hungover, I felt barely alive. A shower helped slightly. What helped more was the text message waiting on my phone, from Philip: *Check your e-mail.*

When I logged in from Matt's computer, Philip's message contained two photos: the first was of me, lying on my side in Philip's bed in that blue light, my hair a mess, a drunken-looking smile on my face. In the other, Philip was lying beside me, one arm outstretched and holding the camera. The angle was odd, like a funhouse mirror. It made his chin look huge and his forehead seem miles away. My face was a barely visible blur. If I remembered right, it was from the second-to-last day, sometime after brunch. The blur was because I flipped him over on his back shortly after he snapped the picture and made him put down the camera.

I'm counting the days, the message said. *Love, Philip.*

I hit the reply button and typed: *Me too.*

CHAPTER TEN

In all the time I lived in St. Louis, I rarely drove very far west. (Driving north or south were out of the question—the state quickly devolves to roadside fireworks stands, double-wides with cars on blocks in front, and shops with signs like "Liquor, Guns, & Ammo Sold Here.") Apart from a few trips with friends out to wineries in the Missouri River valley, where the wines were German in style and sweet enough to make my teeth hurt, I stuck mainly to the city. I'd only been to Kansas City once—and never gone farther west than that.

Kansas was the visual equivalent of white noise. After we crossed the Missouri state line, the landscape became even flatter. I'd never thought such a thing was possible. There were massive storm clouds forming miles ahead of us. We passed exit signs for towns with names like Grinnell, Grainfield, and Goodland, with population counts that barely registered above five hundred. With few landmarks to differentiate one stretch of highway from the next, sometimes it felt as if we weren't even moving.

"Kansas," my mother said at one point, "is proof either that God has a sense of humor or that the devil managed to make a little piece of hell on Earth." Even she looked bored. Lincoln was asleep. Her statement was the first thing any of us had said for hours.

We stopped for gas at a Walmart in Colby, population 5,450 according to the sign. Walmart seemed to be the one thing all the small towns we passed had in common. I couldn't begin to imagine what reason these towns had for existing in the first place. The idea of living in one of them filled me with dread. Portland was by no means a big city, and I had heard St. Louis often described as the biggest small town you'd ever visit.

This was a completely different level of small.

"Where are we?" Lincoln asked after I cut the engine.

"In the middle of nowhere," I said. "Otherwise known as Kansas."

He looked at his watch, then out the window toward the front of the Walmart across the parking lot. "I'm going to get a soda or something," he said. "You want anything?"

I want to be heading in the other direction, and I want you gone. "If you want to grab me a Diet Coke, that'd be good."

It was windy when I climbed out of the driver's seat. The sun had started to set, and I was facing east watching the darkness slide across the flat fields toward us. The monotony of the landscape was somehow enthralling, just as it was boring. This almost trancelike state I had fallen into was probably why I didn't hear the man who'd pulled up at one of the other pumps until he was standing almost directly behind me.

"'Scuse me," he said. I must have jumped when I turned around, because he stepped back a little. Behind him was a pickup truck with a sign on the side advertising a landscaping business. I wasn't sure at first what it was about him that was unsettling. His eyes didn't seem able to focus on the same target at once. When he spoke, I could see he was missing some teeth.

"You ex-military?" he asked. He dropped the "r" so the word sounded incomprehensible at first. He looked like he hadn't shaved in at least a couple of days.

"Darling," my mother said, "is he high?"

"Am I—?" I asked, and it dawned on me what he'd actually said. What on earth made him think *I* might be ex-military? Was there a base around here somewhere? Did I look like I belonged in combat? "No, no, I'm not."

"Well, how do you feel about helping out a veteran who's down on his luck?"

I looked at him blankly for a moment, his question not registering at first. When I realized what he was asking, though, I wondered if I was getting dumber the longer I stood in this place.

"I don't know if I have anything," I said. Even though I knew I was probably being played and he most likely wasn't a veteran at all, something made me reach into my pockets and fish around to see what was there. I came up with a couple dollar bills and a few quarters.

"I wish I had more," I said, realizing the banality of those words after they were out. "I'm driving this"—I hitched my thumb over my shoulder—"across country for my dad because I don't have a job right now." So it was an incomplete truth—it wasn't a lie. I was using a credit card my father gave me to pay for the gas.

"Yes," my mother said, "because it makes perfect sense to panhandle from people at the Walmart gas station. That's where the rich people shop, isn't it?"

The man stared at the bills for a couple seconds, then reached out and folded my own fingers back over them, giving my closed fist a pat. "Sounds like you need 'em more'n I do," he said, and started shuffling back to his truck.

"Who was that?" Lincoln asked. He handed me a plastic Diet Coke bottle and a bag of Fritos. He'd gotten himself a Mountain Dew and a box of Fig Newtons.

The gas pump had long since shut itself off. I put the hose back and punched the No button when it asked me if I wanted a receipt.

"Some panhandler," I said.

"Who panhandles while driving a heavy-duty pickup truck hauling a trailer full of landscaping equipment?" Lincoln asked.

"I have no idea. Maybe that's just how they do things here in

Podunk, Kansas." I walked over to the passenger side door. "You mind driving for a while?"

He climbed behind the wheel and steered us toward the highway on-ramp. "How much farther do you want to go today?" he asked. "I think we're going to run out of light soon."

"Shows what he knows," my mother said. "It's been dark for a while already."

❖

The rest areas and truck stops all began to look alike. Logos changed, but the convenience store shelves blurred into one long aisle stretching across state lines. Same with the people. The family I saw the next morning near the Kansas/Colorado border could have been the same family I had seen the day before at a truck stop outside Kansas City. The same mother herded the same pair of children—why did they look like they would feel tacky to the touch, like spilled grape soda? The father was undoubtedly waiting behind the wheel of an RV like ours or some SUV. Mother always looked harried and tired, on the verge of tears if one more thing went wrong. I pictured the family as—not exactly poor, but not terribly well off either. If they could have afforded it, they would have flown wherever they were going, instead of joining the caravan on the interstate.

Las Vegas seemed built in part for families like that. I'd have sworn that family from Missouri was standing in front of us at the Aladdin reception desk. The kids coughed and wrinkled their noses. For once, I couldn't blame them. A toxic fog drifted into the non-smoking lobby from the adjacent casino, where it hovered like a storm front. It was one of three gaming floors in the hotel, and lay on the other side of a broad archway festooned with flashing lights.

I felt a headache coming on.

Our room was decorated in various shades of gold, more garish than palatial. The windows unspectacularly overlooked the heating and air-conditioning units on a lower roof. Beyond that was the back of the Paris hotel next door. From the right angle I could glimpse the big balloon and a leg of the fake Eiffel Tower.

Jacob had helped make our reservations, though, so at least the rate was dirt-cheap. I'd make the best of it.

I heard water running in the bathroom. Lincoln leaned over the bathtub, which crouched in the center of the room.

"This makes me want to take a bath for the first time in years," he said. "No wonder Las Vegas has a water shortage."

"Well, why not?" my mother asked. "They clearly have shortages of a lot of things: common sense, good taste." The entire bathroom was tan and brown marble, giving the room an echo chamber effect. The lighting, indirect and tasteful, was just about the only thing that wasn't overdone.

I didn't have anything else to say, so I repeated what my mother had said. She frowned, but Lincoln laughed and pulled his shirt over his head. "I feel filthy after driving for so long," he said. I ducked back out and said something about checking out the casino floor.

"While we're here," he called after me, "there's a show I wouldn't mind seeing."

In the elevator, my mother asked, "The casino floor? Darling, you don't even like gambling."

We were alone. My mother had finally changed out of her peach nightgown and now wore a sleeveless blue cocktail dress with a high neck, her hair up, and her cigarette in a long holder. Noticing me appraising her outfit, she took a little spin.

"You like it?"

"Very fancy," I said. "So why the costume change? Expecting to run into anyone you know?"

"Hardly, darling. Though if any town would have its share of ghosts, this one would be it. Mind you, most of them are probably wearing cement shoes, so I don't know if I'd want to meet them."

"Now that you mention it, have you seen any other ghosts?" I was beginning to hope that maybe I'd successfully distracted her from her original line of questioning.

"Strangely, no. And don't think I've forgotten what I asked. Why do you want to go to the casino floor?"

"Take a wild guess, Mom." She may have been dead, but it didn't take a genius—or in her case, a pulse—to figure out being in the room while Lincoln got undressed made me uncomfortable. He'd pretty much taken it in stride two days earlier when I'd told him I didn't think it was a good idea for us to keep sleeping together. When he asked why, of course I lied. Still, he bought my excuse that this was a very awkward time for me emotionally. Standing in the elevator, staring at my dead mother, I realized my excuse was truer than maybe I wanted to admit.

We walked through the lobby toward the casino floor. A constant, bright tinkling of notes from the slot machines bled together into a wall of sound piercing the fog of cigarette smoke. I bought fifty dollars' worth of chips, netting me two green-rimmed plastic discs with gold lettering on them and the words "no cash value."

My mother stared down at the chips in my hand. "Fifty? That's it?"

I would have pointed out to her I was unemployed, but we were standing in the middle of a busy gaming floor a few feet to the side of the cashiers' cages with a steady stream of people going by. My mother said, "Oh, please. Do you honestly think you'd be the first person in this casino to be talking to himself?"

"Well, fifty dollars is all I can afford," I said, which got me a startled glance from a young woman walking by. She glanced away as quickly as she could and put her arm around the man with her before I could explain at least I was aware how crazy I looked talking to myself.

This was probably, I reflected, one of those cases where explaining things would only have made things worse.

"What are you going to bet?" my mother asked. We'd decided on roulette since it seemed a safe medium between the leaden repetition of the slot machines and the murky strategy of poker. When I got to the table and sat down, I stared at the grid of red and black numbers and the gold-finialed wheel and realized I was not going to figure this out intuitively.

"I have no idea what the hell I'm doing," I said to my mother sotto voce, but not so sotto the woman sitting next to me didn't hear.

"That's the story of most people's lives," she said. She was smoking a cigarette—was I the only person left in the world with an aversion to lighting up? She wore her hair in a loose ponytail. It was gray turning silver. Her face was unlined. It was hard to pin down her age. She was wearing a gold pantsuit. She smiled and held out the hand that wasn't holding the cigarette. "Rhonda."

"Joel," I said.

"So, you've never played?"

When I said no, she started pointing out the differences between inside and outside bets, and the odds on each, and she took one of my $25 chips and gave me five $5 ones from her considerable stacks.

"Minimum bet's five dollars, hon," she said. "Bet with one of those twenty-fives and the fun's over real quick."

As it was, the fun lasted about three minutes. I won once on red, then lost and lost and lost. As I watched the dealer slide my chips across the table toward him, my mother said, "Remember this is not a metaphor for anything. It's just money won and lost."

Rhonda laughed in a way I could tell was meant to be kindly, but the smoke in her voice made it sound more than a little jaded. "Maybe roulette just isn't your game."

"Maybe not," I said and slid off the stool.

❖

I had no idea why Lincoln wanted to see this show. It was away from the strip on Fremont Street, at a casino that looked like it had about as much luck as me. My misgivings began when I saw the posters in the casino lobby, which could be summed up as a combination of glitz and tits. Now that I wasn't putting out, was Lincoln getting nostalgic for something less manly?

"I could make a joke," my mother said as we took our seats, "but it's too easy, so let's just take it as given." We were at a small bistro-type table near the front. Our drink order was taken, and before I could ask Lincoln why he wanted to see this particular show, the lights dimmed and the music started.

The set looked like something out of an old song-and-dance movie, with sweeping staircases up either side of the stage toward an opening through which the dancers emerged: tall, leggy women in costumes that consisted of a lot of feathers, sequins, an elaborate headdress at least half as tall as the shortest girl, and not much else except high heels. The headdress, while stunning, tended to limit their abilities as dancers, but I doubted that mattered much to the rest of the audience.

They did manage to twirl and kick and high-step once they descended the stairs and reached the stage. Interlocking arms, they twisted one way then the other like a racier version of the Rockettes. They moved toward the edge of the stage as the headliner, whom I still didn't recognize, emerged at the top of the stairs and began singing—not badly, but not well, either.

Hopefully there would at least be some witty banter later on, I hoped.

I turned my attention to the down-market Rockettes, and I realized one of the dancers was Lincoln's sister, Linda.

Like her brother, she'd hardened in the years since I'd last seen her. Her costume left no doubt of that. Just like her brother, her presence was a lightning bolt that set me on edge waiting for the subsequent crack of thunder. I wondered if she could see us through the glare of the footlights.

She was barely ten feet away when she looked right at us.

Recognition fluttered across her face, and her obviously practiced smile faltered at the corners for a moment. She directed her eyes elsewhere and turned the smile back on.

"If looks could kill," my mother said, "there'd be a white, you-shaped outline on the floor."

I looked over at Lincoln. He stared directly at his sister, a sort of nostalgic smile on his face, as if he were seeing her not as the showgirl strutting across the stage but as she'd been in high school.

Or maybe that was just my imagination.

We had to sit there for over an hour, through a handful of costume changes and different routines, but none of the breaks was long enough to give me the chance to ask Lincoln about his sister. No matter how many times I looked over, hoping to catch his eye, he kept looking up at the stage, ignoring me. What game was he playing?

"Lincoln, what the hell?" I asked when the show finally ended and the house lights came up.

The look on his face was almost manic. "Let's go backstage."

The backstage door was unlocked. Lincoln told the first person we ran into, a guy wearing a headset, that he was Linda's brother. We were waved in the direction of the dancers' dressing room.

"Be sure to knock first," Headset Guy said before rushing off to do something ostensibly more important.

Standing in front of the dressing room door, I asked him, "When was the last time you talked to your sister?"

"Let's just say it's been a while." Lincoln knocked.

Linda opened the door. She had taken off her headdress. Up close, I could now see that parts of the costume I thought were nonexistent were actually flesh colored. Even without the extra height from the headdress, in four-inch heels and six-foot attitude, she looked like an Amazon.

She hit like an Amazon too. Before anyone could say

anything, Linda slapped Lincoln hard across the face. The peal of it reverberated in time to the swaying of her costume's tassels. Lincoln's hand whipped up to his face reflexively, cupping the offended cheek.

"I like her already," my mother said. Her cigarette was burning down, and she took that opportunity to grind it out on the back of Lincoln's head.

Linda looked like she was about to haul off and wallop me as well, but she paused with her hand in the air. She lowered her hand, but still didn't look happy.

"Joel?"

I didn't have time to give her a proper greeting before she started laying into her brother again. This time the pummeling was verbal. I took a few steps back. If I could, I would have melted into the wall.

I was also hoping not to get hit myself.

Linda paused in her tirade. She looked at me and asked, "Would you mind if my brother and I continued this conversation in private?" She took my arm before I could answer, opened the dressing room door, and propelled me inside. Half a dozen dancers were still in various states of undress.

"They won't bite," she said to me. To the dancers, she added, "Don't worry, girls. He's gay." She shut the door behind her. I faced a rack of costumes, a row of tables with makeup lights, mirrors, and chairs. The dancers didn't pay me much mind. I sat in a free chair at one of the tables. The mirror in front of me reflected quite possibly the worst version of my face I'd ever seen.

The dancer sitting at the next table must have noticed my grimace, because she said to me, "Don't worry. It's the lights. They make everyone look like a hag. I think it's supposed to inspire us to really lay on the foundation." With her eyes she gestured toward the door. "Who's she talking to, ex-boyfriend?"

"Brother."

She momentarily stopped fussing with her hair. "Oh, shit. No wonder she's so pissed."

Even with the door closed, we could still hear Linda's tirade. The one break in her monologue was short, punctuated by a rise in her voice and a shrill, "I am *not* done talking here!" Unabated, she continued.

"So what did he do that she's so angry about?" I asked. I wondered if everyone knew but me.

She shook her head. "Oh no. That's Linda's story to tell. Believe me, though, he fucked up big-time. She still hasn't forgiven him after twelve years."

"And you're not even going to give me a hint?"

The dancer smiled at me briefly, gave her hair a shake, and started brushing it. The sound was like wind blowing through straw. "You afraid to ask her yourself?"

I glanced toward the door. Linda was still shouting. She apparently had a lot to say, and all of it loudly. I looked back at the dancer. "Maybe a little," I said.

"Smart boy. That's exactly why I'm going to let her tell you instead of giving you the story myself."

We both looked toward the door. It had grown suddenly quiet outside, and I wondered if we'd open it to find one of them out on the floor and bleeding. A few moments later, though, we heard the tap of high heels growing louder as they stabbed the concrete floor. Linda flung open the dressing room door. The dancer took that as a cue to get up and find someplace else to be.

"I had to go outside and have a smoke," Linda said. "And make sure he left the fucking building." She sat down at the makeup table the other woman had recently vacated. Her hair, which had been the color of wheat in high school, was now dyed blond, a trace of darker roots visible as she unpinned it. Before I could ask what the deal was between her and her brother, she turned from the mirror to look at me.

"So," she said. "Hi."

"Hi. Wow, you look great."

My mother scoffed. "Darling, she looks like a hooker."

"Really great," I added.

Mom threw up her hands. "Fine, a really great hooker. But still."

I ignored my mother, and Linda turned back to the mirror. "So what the hell are you doing in Vegas with my brother?"

"A question all of us would like answered," my mother said.

I should have expected an interrogation. It was a way Linda had, I remembered now, to deflect any questions.

"Honestly? Trying to get rid of him," I said. Linda wasn't any more surprised to hear Lincoln had invited himself along for the ride than she was surprised I'd caved into him ("You are *still* such a doormat," she said). And she was only a little surprised that I'd slept with him. ("Yeah, you and half our high school class.")

I got the impression nothing surprised her where her brother was concerned.

"Sorry about your mother," she said. "And that you got stuck with Lincoln's unsightly baggage."

"Thanks."

Linda started taking off her makeup. As she swiped a cloth across her face, she uncovered something of the girl I remembered from high school. Now, though, that girl looked older–a lot older.

"So what the hell did he do?"

"You mean he didn't tell you? Why am I not surprised?" She stood and stripped off her costume and was completely naked for a moment. Before I could turn away she slipped on underwear and a T-shirt. She sat back down to start struggling into a pair of jeans. "He got me kicked out of UMaine for selling my English term papers. The idiot actually sold one to a guy taking the same class with the same professor the semester after I did. Naturally, he denied it, and our parents actually believed him. I have no idea what *they* were thinking."

"UMaine?" I asked. "Whatever happened to Juilliard?"

"Money happened. Or didn't happen. I couldn't afford to live in New York, and I couldn't ask my parents to foot the bill. So I had to settle for Maine until I got kicked out." She finally succeeded in tugging the jeans over her hips and buttoning them. She slipped on some shoes—flats, in contrast to the high heels she wore onstage. "So it was either go to community college or try to get a dancing job, which is basically how I ended up here. Getting a part in a show isn't easy, even when it's a rinky-dink one like this. The competition for these jobs is brutal. Luckily, I met a guy. Unfortunately, I also married him."

"You're married?"

"Divorced. We had a kid before we split up too." She looked at her watch. "And I am about five minutes away from being late to pick him up from the sitter."

There were a dozen questions I'd have liked to ask her—whether she ever got home to Maine, would she ever forgive her brother, what happened to Darren the football player—but she made it clear she had no time for questions, or for me. Her cell phone, wallet, and keys were scattered across the makeup table. She swept them into her purse and stood up.

"Some free advice? Ditch him. I don't know what he wants, but I'm sure he wants something. He always wants something. And it probably won't be good for you."

I couldn't imagine what Lincoln might want that I could possibly offer. If he wanted something of value, he could have picked a better target. I'm sure Linda would think me naïve. But she hadn't seen or spoken to her brother in over ten years. Was it possible for him to change?

I doubted it.

"Take it or don't. It didn't cost me anything."

She stopped with her hand on the door. "Wait, do me one

favor: get out of town first, *then* ditch him. I don't want him in the same city as me."

❖

"So what did she tell you?" Lincoln leaned against a bank of slot machines just outside the theater. It was hard to stand anywhere in a Vegas hotel that wasn't close to a slot machine.

"What were you two fighting about?" I countered. I hated when people answered a question with a question, but I figured Lincoln was the one who had some explaining to do.

Lincoln pushed off from the slots and headed toward the exits. "She probably told you about the paper of hers I sold in college to a term paper service and how she got kicked out of school. And if she didn't leave anything out, then she also told you I told our parents she was the one who sold the paper, effectively ruining her college career and life and ruining her relationship with our parents. Did I miss anything?"

"I think that was pretty much it," my mother said. "I'll at least give him points for candor. Finally."

"Did you really expect her to react any differently by just showing up without warning her?"

"I figured if I called her in advance, she would have hung up on me."

"Though she probably would have told him to go to hell before she hung up," my mother said.

"So what the hell did you hope to accomplish?" I asked. "And why the hell didn't you tell me?"

"Because I *knew* you would have said 'hell no.'"

"Could you blame me?"

We emerged into the dry, hot night at the front of the hotel. We'd parked in back. Instead of cutting through the casino again, we circled around. As with most casino hotels here, walking around to the back was like walking around the outside of a shopping mall. We were barely halfway around before my shirt was drenched in sweat.

"You didn't answer my original question," I said. "What did you hope to accomplish?"

"I don't *know*." A tone of frustration crept into his voice for the first time since the incident with the truck driver in Ohio. I was beginning to wonder if his policy of traveling through life without a definite direction was leaving him stranded.

"Uh, Lincoln," I asked when we reached the back of the hotel, "where's the RV?"

We had walked past the spot where it had been parked before I realized it. For a second I couldn't remember if we'd parked on the other side of the street. Regardless, it was nowhere to be seen.

"Uh-oh," Lincoln said. A slow burn crept up my neck. Soon my face would be flushed and my sweat would come from panic instead of the heat. Had Lincoln told me to park here, or had I just found the spot myself? It felt really important, all of a sudden, to know the answer to that question.

And find a way to blame Lincoln for this.

"I can't believe this," I said. It was a lie. I could completely believe it. Why not screw this up royally, after all? It went with my batting average. "This is so typical. Why am I not surprised?" As I paced in front of the parking spot, I finally noticed the "No Parking Any Time" sign at the curb. How I'd missed it earlier was beyond me.

"We'll get it back," Lincoln said. "It's probably been towed."

"Really? Towed? Thank you so much," I snapped. "I figured it was just temporarily invisible."

Lincoln put his hands up. "Hey, calm down."

"Calm down?" I stopped pacing and glared at Lincoln, now the picture of calm. He was scrutinizing me right back. It felt like he was looking into my head.

"Yes, calm down. Is getting worked up going to do anything to help resolve the problem?"

"Here's a news flash for you. People don't get upset because they think it's productive. They get upset because something fucked-up has happened."

Lincoln shook his head, a maddening smile playing across his lips. "You always were tightly wound, you know."

"Not another word," I said before I turned and started walking back up the sidewalk. I was past caring whether Lincoln followed or not.

"I don't know why I'm not surprised that you haven't changed much since high school. The way you react to things is so predictable."

"Why are you even still talking?" I asked.

"Because he has no common sense?" my mother offered. Lincoln ignored my question.

"You've got to lighten up, Joel. You've finally started breaking out of your circular pattern, but if you seize up now, you're just going to fall right back into it. This is just a little setback. I know you hate when you let yourself slip just a little—"

"When I let myself slip," I said, "I apparently do stupid things like park in a no-parking zone or let you come along on this trip."

We had just passed a line of newspaper racks displaying free circulars, entertainment guides, and ads for escorts. Lincoln walked up to the first one. I knew what he was going to do, but made no move to stop him. He picked it up and flung it end first through the passenger window of the nearest parked car—ironically, a Lincoln Town Car. The window shattered, the rack wedged halfway in, and the alarm started going off.

He stood in front of me then. He was breathing a little heavier from the exertion, or maybe from adrenaline. I was certainly feeling it.

And he still managed to look smug.

My mother crossed her arms and shook her head. "Oh, this is not going to end well, darling."

"So," he asked, "how are you going to slip up now?"

I punched him.

It seemed like I was watching someone else who looked just like me land a punch on Lincoln's jaw.

He went down with an unexpected swiftness, like a fast pitch.

It surprised me how much my hand hurt, and how hard it was to resist the urge to kick Lincoln before he got up.

"Lincoln, you are a fucking idiot," I said. He stayed on the ground, looking stunned from the punch and maybe a little worried I might go after him again. He didn't look surprised at my reaction, though, and that disappointed me the most.

It had taken fifteen years, but it felt like we were even now.

I didn't wait to hear what he had to say next. From behind me, Lincoln called, "Well, at least it made you do *something*!"

It was a long walk back to the Strip. For the moment I decided not to worry about the RV. I just wanted to get back to the room and shut the door. As long as I could see the Stratosphere in the distance I figured I was headed in the right direction.

It was a little after one by the time I wove into the crowd flowing along the Strip's sidewalks. With the lights and the people, it still managed to feel like daytime. It seemed wrong that it was past midnight and the temperature was still in the eighties. As far as I could tell, things in Las Vegas seemed designed to fool the senses and trick you into believing the opposite of what was real was reality.

We hadn't eaten dinner. Cooking would have taken my mind off things, but the only kitchen I'd had access to had probably been impounded. Back at the hotel, I ordered room service and started filling the tub. It was still only halfway full when dinner arrived: a twenty-five-dollar hamburger, fries, and beer. I sat in the tub anyway, turned on the bathroom TV, and started eating.

By the time I climbed out, it was two thirty, my fingers and toes were wrinkled, and the last of my fries were cold. Lincoln still hadn't returned.

To her credit, my mother had been equally scarce.

My cell phone woke me up around eight. I'd fallen asleep on the sofa, and the sunlight streaming through the window above it was harsh and disorienting. I fumbled for the phone before I was fully awake. It was my father.

"Son, is there something about the RV you want to tell me?"

"RV?" I was trying to make sense of his question at the same time I was registering that Lincoln hadn't returned last night.

"Did I wake you up?" my father asked.

"He's probably wondering how you managed to lose something as big as an RV," my mother said. She was seated on the edge of the unmade bed, back in her peach nightgown and robe, and was sipping a cup of hot coffee.

"Yeah, sorry Dad," I said. "Listen, about the RV—"

"It's at the impound lot, and I've paid the towing fee, so go get the damn thing. And next time, try not to park in a tow-away zone."

"Okay, Dad," I said, and hung up before it occurred to me to ask him how he was doing. Considering he still had the presence of mind to make me feel about six inches tall, I figured he was doing better than I was.

CHAPTER ELEVEN

A cab ride and a couple hours later, I was behind the wheel of the RV again and driving it off the impound lot. When I returned to the hotel this time, I parked it in the garage. I figured it was better to pay the thirty dollars a day for parking than chance the street and wind up spending another five hundred dollars of my father's money.

I expected to see Lincoln when I got back to the room. Everything looked the same as it had when I'd left for the impound lot, but the air felt disturbed. I then noticed the small changes: Lincoln's keycard lying on the desk, his toothbrush missing from the bathroom. I didn't have to open the wardrobe to know that Lincoln's duffel bag was no longer in there, but looked anyway.

There was no note. Lincoln had removed himself from the room.

"Not like I couldn't see this coming," Linda said when I called to let her know. "I told you he was up to something."

"I have no idea what, though," I said. I was sitting in the hotel lobby. Here the steady seashell roar of the slot machines faded a little, until it sounded like a swarm of bees somewhere in the distance.

Her shrug was almost audible in her voice. "If he tries to call me, I'll get an unlisted number. And I've already told them at work to throw him out if he comes around."

"You still think he could cause you more trouble?"

"Joel, the last thing you saw him do was throw a magazine rack through a windshield. Does a normal person pull shit like that?" She sighed. "I wish I knew why my brother did half the stuff he does. No, wait. I don't."

On her end of the line, I heard a boy's voice in the background saying, "Mom!" in the unique way children have of extending a single-syllable word into ten or more.

"I have to go," Linda said.

"Is that your son?"

I could hear Linda smiling. "Yeah. Ever since he turned five he never seems to run out of questions. If I had to pick one good thing that came out of getting kicked out of college, thrown out by my family, moving here, and getting divorced, he'd be it. So I guess things even out in the end."

"Well, congratulations."

"Thanks. If you hear from my brother, tell him I moved to Alaska."

❖

It was at some point on my way out of Las Vegas that I realized I was starting to feel invisible. If it was a formula, it would have been anonymity times dislocation plus silence. This discovery occurred after Lincoln had left, when I walked through the hotel's casino without once running into someone, speaking to someone, or turning to make sure Lincoln was still with me. I didn't realize my discovery until its spell was broken, when I went into the Starbucks (every hotel had one, it seemed) and had to speak to the girl behind the counter. Once the interaction ended and I'd stirred half and half into my venti dark roast, I drifted back into the flow of people and was invisible again.

I remained invisible the entire time I was leaving the city. I checked out of the hotel from a menu on the TV screen, left the parking garage by swiping my ticket and my credit card, and didn't speak to anyone as I found the highway that would take me to Sedona.

Even though I was more than a little relieved he was gone, I found myself missing Lincoln a little bit on the drive down to Sedona. It was at the point when I finally felt the exhaustion rising up in me like the shimmering mirage of heat waving up from the pavement at the horizon. The spot where I'd hit the back of my head on the oven two weeks ago had started to ache again, and I felt as if I'd woken up with the longest hangover in history. Maybe it was from the constant squinting. Everything beyond the windshield seemed excessively bright, and I wished for an instant—too long to take back—that Lincoln was here to spell me while I lay down in the back.

"Bite your tongue," my mother said. She sat in the passenger seat with the road atlas spread open on her lap. Though she said she was helping me navigate, she wasn't giving much direction.

"I didn't say anything," I said.

"You thought it, though. Which is almost as bad."

"I thought we agreed you were going to stop that." The more time my mother spent picking up on what I was thinking, the more I felt like I was losing my grip. Having Lincoln around also had served as a buffer for that. He kept me tethered more securely to reality. That tether seemed to be slipping now.

"It's a hard habit to break, darling," she said. "It's kind of like seeing in color. It's impossible to make yourself see the world in black and white."

"Well, for my sake, try."

Maybe it was the combination of her presence and the monotony of the road, but I was having a harder time identifying my thoughts as my own. It was more like they were received over the air, like a station on the radio, and my mother was the deejay.

"Anyway," I continued, "I just want someone else to do the driving for a while."

She looked down at the atlas. "Not much longer, darling."

❖

It was a relief when Carrie called. I needed company of a corporeal variety, even if it was just a voice hundreds of miles away. I hated it when other people talked on the phone while driving, but I did it anyway.

"You didn't," she said after I told her about punching Lincoln.

"I did," I said.

"And he didn't even fight back?" she asked. She didn't sound all that disappointed to learn that I'd decked him.

"Well," my mother said, "speaking as someone who was there, it *was* rather satisfying to witness."

"I think he was too surprised to do much of anything," I said.

"Well, it must have felt good to get a little even after all his crap."

"I guess." I didn't believe it. Lashing out at Lincoln felt like just one more way he'd manipulated me. In retrospect, I wasn't even surprised by it. He'd been steering me around like a game piece since we left Portland, and I'd known it. I'd let him do it.

What did that say about me?

"I guess that's one less thing for you to worry about," Carrie said. "He never came back after that?"

"Only while I was out of the room getting the RV out of hock. He took his stuff and got lost."

"Well, that was good timing."

His timing *had* been pretty convenient. I wondered whether he'd been waiting for me to leave the room so he could collect his stuff without a confrontation. On the one hand, that would have meant I'd succeeded in making him at least a little scared of me. It also meant he'd been watching me, which was creepy.

While I pondered that, Carrie covered the mouthpiece of her phone and said something.

"What was that?"

"Sorry, I had to tell the movers something."

"Movers? You're moving?"

"Well, I'm not exactly enthused at the prospect of staying in this house, so I'm putting my stuff in storage until I decide where to go next. Sound familiar?"

I smiled. "A little. I guess it just seems a little sudden."

"Well, that's because it is." She paused, her silence interrupted by the flick of a lighter, and punctuated by a loud exhale. "But then it didn't take you long to decide you weren't coming back."

"True." I wanted to tell her it was different, but that would have antagonized her. I wasn't sure the difference in our reasons mattered. Either way, neither of us was going back to our old lives. "Where are you moving?"

"Short term? The Chase. And yes, I'm making Doug pay for it. Long term, any place where I don't stand a chance of running into him."

"Has that been a problem?"

She laughed, or maybe just exhaled again. "You could say that. It's all Matt's fault too."

Somehow, Matt had persuaded her she should go out. Sitting at home was not doing anything to improve her mood or her state of mind, and of course he knew someone she might like. Figuring our call might last a while, I pulled over.

Matt set Carrie up with Rich, a guy who works at the nursery. I remembered him vaguely: younger, on the short side, dark hair, perpetual tan, used to work at Boeing before he got downsized. I didn't think he was Carrie's type, but I'd thought Doug was her perfect match, so what did I know?

"Wait," I said. "How old is Rich?"

She hesitated before answering. "Twenty-nine, and don't

you fucking dare call me a cougar. I'm barely in my mid-thirties."

"If that's what you like to tell yourself, kitten," I said as deadpan as possible.

"Just be glad you're not here, otherwise I'd be putting my cigarette out on your arm."

My mother leaned over. "You can tell her that if she wants me to do that for her, I'll be happy to oblige."

I narrowed my eyes at my mother, turned on the emergency flashers, and cut the engine.

"So you went out with him?" I asked Carrie.

They met for dinner at Ricardo's in Lafayette Square, a nice little Italian place she'd never gone to with Doug. Rich knew she was just beginning the process of getting a divorce. Even as she told me how the evening got off to a nice start and Rich seemed like a perfect gentleman even if he was a little young, I was waiting for the thing that would send their evening into a skid.

I didn't have to wait long.

"Rich was telling me how much he enjoys working in landscaping after having to sit at a desk all day when he was at Boeing, and I'm glad he was the one talking because I'd have started tripping over my tongue when Doug and his bitch walked in."

"You're kidding. How is it he picked that restaurant the same night as you?"

"I'm just a lucky girl, I guess. Maybe he was trying to avoid going to the places he and I used to go together."

"Did he see you?"

"No, thank God. We were back in a corner, and he sat down across the room with his back to me."

She paused again. Each time there was a hesitation on the line, I was afraid she was about to start crying. Instead, I heard the sound of breaking glass.

"What was that?"

"That was a crystal wedding goblet. They don't make as much noise as I'd hoped. Maybe I'll have better luck with the wedding china."

I had to laugh. "Don't get crazy. You could hock all that stuff on eBay or something."

"I think I get more pleasure this way." There was another tinkle. "Besides, I'm going to get enough of a settlement from Doug that I won't have to worry about things for a while.

"So anyway, there we were, sitting at a table in the corner, and this charming, nice-looking man was talking to me, and all I could do was watch Doug kiss her."

I had no clue what to say. In the space of a few seconds, she'd gone from cynical black humor to deflated. I needed some air. I went out the cabin door in back, stood on the shoulder, and leaned against the side of the RV. I was in a flat area off Highway 93, the horizon awash in heat haze. The sun was relentless, and the breeze kicked up sand and offered no relief. It was like standing in front of an open oven with a fan blasting the heat in your face.

"God, I don't know what to say," I finally said.

"Hang on," she said, maybe to me or to one of the movers. "That stays...No, wait, it goes." To me, she asked, "I should take the flat screen, yeah?"

I smiled. Maybe she wasn't beaten down completely by this. "I say you should take anything that isn't bolted down."

"I'm leaving a few things. I left his bowling trophies, although apparently the movers accidentally broke some of the figures off them. I can't decide if I'm going to throw them away or put them in the microwave."

"Only if you want to risk burning down the house."

"Don't tempt me. I really wish you were here. A pity party would be so much more fun with some company. Breaking all these glasses would go a lot faster too."

"Where are you doing all this breakage?" I pictured her in the middle of the street in their upscale, wooded subdivision, casually causing mayhem and havoc for the neighbors.

"I'm in the driveway. I've already moved my car out onto the street."

"So you're going to leave all that glass for Doug to discover the next time he pulls into the driveway?"

Carrie laughed. "I thought about it, but I don't want the mailman or someone walking over it by accident. Where are you now?"

"On the way to Sedona. Well, actually, I'm standing on the side of the road. In the middle of the desert. There's not much to see except sand. So I guess things didn't go all that great with Rich after that?"

"Well, not that evening, but we're going out again next weekend. I'm not going to make a big deal out of it one way or another. And neither should you."

We hung up with promises to touch base later. I didn't get back in the RV right away. Instead I stared out at the short, spindly shrubs dotting the sandy landscape, and the jagged hills in the distance. I inhaled deeply and the air burned. It felt hot enough to singe the hair in my nostrils. There was little traffic. What few vehicles passed were usually semis, which set the RV rocking against my back a little.

After a while, my mother came out and stood beside me. She lit a cigarette.

"Sometimes you have to see something before you'll believe it's true," she said. "I don't think I would have really believed it if someone had told me Mark was the reason Derek left me. I had to see it for myself."

"Did that make it any easier?" I asked.

"Oh, good heavens no, darling. It was like shoving the knife in myself. I suppose in my case it gave those feelings a clean kill, though."

"I don't think it's had the same effect on Carrie."

"I suspect it's different when your fiancé leaves you for another man instead of your husband leaving you for another woman." She took another drag and flicked the cigarette away only half-smoked. It vanished before it hit the ground, and she looked pleased at that little trick.

"Shall we, darling? We're burning daylight."

❖

Once I passed Kingman, I was headed almost straight east toward Sedona. After all the time I'd spent feeling as if I were heading in the wrong direction, now I actually was.

Driving through the desert was a lot like running. I settled into a rhythm metered out by the stripes in the middle of the road and the hum of the tires over pavement. It wasn't until the mountains started rising up in the distance as I got closer to Sedona that I realized how many miles had passed without my marking them.

When she came out of the house to greet me, Sylvia was wearing a peach dress that looked like it could have come out of my mother's closet. The splash of color on her surprised me; maybe because the last time I'd seen her, she'd been dressed in black.

"Don't even get me started on that outfit," my mother said.

Sylvia rested her hands on my forearms and appraised me. "I was beginning to wonder if I'd imagined it back in Portland, how much you look like your mother," Sylvia said. "You can just tell you're her boy." Her voice must have sounded coquettish at some point in her youth. Now it just sounded nervous and high.

"I can't believe how much you look like my mom," I said, and tried to ignore the gagging noise my mother made.

Sylvia smiled. "Oh, do you think so?" She looked surprised, and I could tell she considered it a compliment. She touched her hair as if to make sure it was still in place. My mother, always considered the beautiful one, must have easily outshone Sylvia. My mother's face was more angular and refined than Sylvia's round, friendly features.

She looked over my shoulder toward the RV. "Where's your friend you were traveling with?"

"Oh. Lincoln decided to stay in Las Vegas."

"My, how impetuous."

"Well, his sister lives there."

She took my arm and led me toward the house. "So, how *was* Las Vegas? I haven't been there in years."

"More like decades," said Gerald. With one hand he leaned heavily against his gnarled wooden cane and shook my hand limply with the other.

Sylvia gave Gerald a matronly scowl and ushered me through the doorway, apparently forgetting her previous question. "Let's get inside out of this heat, and you can see the place where we've chosen to descend into the fog of our dotage."

"If you can't tell, Sylvia was a poetry major," Gerald said.

"Whatever you do, don't be a poetry major," she said to me. "It's almost the most useless thing I ever did."

"Sylvia, I think he's past the point where he would be choosing a major," Gerald said.

"If that was *almost* the most useless thing you ever did, what was the most useless?" I asked

"Getting married," she said, and closed the door behind us.

The house was cool and cave-like with the heat of the desert shut outside. The floors were slate, and the walls of the entryway looked like white plastic. I reached out to touch one; it *was* plastic, and lit from behind by what looked like fluorescent lights. It reminded me a little of Moonbase Alpha, but I resisted the temptation to point this out.

They took me down a flight of wide slate stairs into the living room, which looked like it really had been carved out of the canyon. Three walls were made of rock. In front of us was nothing but windows, two stories high, looking over the edge of a ravine and a wide expanse of dusty red rock. It was what I imagined looking across Mars might be like.

Gerald actually had a fire going and was using a poker in the fireplace to rearrange the glowing logs. The sofa was a low, tan sectional that hugged a glass-topped coffee table with a base of petrified wood. The colors of the throw pillows, the rug, and the massive terra cotta vases near the fireplace were varying shades of rusty oranges and reds. Combined with the rock walls, the austere decor made it seem as if the room was merely an extension of the alien landscape outside, and enclosing it had been an afterthought.

Sylvia watched me take in the room. The way her wrinkles were gathered at the corners of her mouth made her look as if she was always about to smile.

"Welcome to life on Mars," Sylvia said. "Well, the view's about the same as Mars, but at least the atmosphere's breathable."

"That's if you can stand the heat," Gerald grumbled.

"Says the man who's stoking the fire," Sylvia said.

"It gets cold in here," Gerald said, waving the poker to indicate the room, "with these rock walls, especially as the sun goes down. And we're old, so we're always cold."

"If you want real heat, you go down to Phoenix," Sylvia said, "which is miserable."

"How did you know I was thinking of Mars when I saw this place?" I asked.

"I've lived here for thirty years, Joel. Almost everyone who comes here tells me that. I think it's the red."

She made her way slowly to the bar, jutting from the rock wall next to the windows. It looked better stocked than some actual bars I'd been to. "Would you like something to drink, darling?"

"I'll have whatever you're having," I said, and wondered whether the habit of calling people "darling" was something Sylvia acquired from my mother, or vice versa.

"She never had an original thought in her life, darling," my mother said, then added, "Oh, sorry. I'm doing it again, aren't I?"

Sylvia reached under the bar and took out a wine bottle. "I'm having merlot. Is that okay?"

"Thank you, I'd love a glass," Gerald said. He finally raised himself up from his stooped position over the fire and shuffled to the bar. Sylvia pursed her lips but still managed to look on the edge of smiling as she took down three glasses. She looked at me again, and paused in her pouring. "You look so much like her. It's uncanny."

"When was the last time we saw Rachel, Sylvia?" Gerald asked.

"Was it the thirty-year reunion? Did we go to that?"

"I don't know," Gerald said. "Were you already divorced by that point?"

"Oh, before the tenth, honey." Sylvia handed me my glass and slid another toward Gerald. "Henry never met any of the old gang except you. Thank heavens," she added, and smiled at me. "But we don't want to bore you with this dusty old nostalgia, do we?"

"I don't mind," I said. "Maybe I'll find out something about my mother that I never knew."

Sitting on Sylvia and Gerald's sofa, listening to them talk about things that had happened thirty or more years ago, I felt like I was vanishing again like I had that morning. I was sitting there, and that was enough reason for them to unwind one old story after another, things that had nothing to do with me. I was there and yet felt like I was not there, even as Sylvia refilled my glass and opened another bottle an hour later and filled our glasses again. Their housekeeper, Celeste, returned from the grocery store. She set another place for dinner, and said something about hoping I liked pork chops.

"I almost didn't recognize him," Sylvia said of Gerald. She'd been talking of how they'd reconnected at their twenty-year high school reunion. By that time she was divorced and rich. ("Marry well, divorce even better, then invest wisely," she said.) He was single, gay, and poor. As Sylvia talked, she mixed a pitcher of something alcoholic, maybe martinis. I had decided to switch to water, but she pressed a glass into my hand anyway. "He had changed so much. Lost all that young adult softness. He looked handsome, but so hard."

"New York will do that," Gerald said. "Or at least it did back then, when it was a real city. These days, you go back to Times Square and you don't see a single hooker. It's lost all its character. Anyway, I knew who Sylvia was right away. She hadn't changed a bit in all those years. Still looked gorgeous, still in the middle of a group of admirers, still pissing off those admirers' girlfriends."

"Wives, at that point," Sylvia said. "I wasn't doing anything wrong, you know. I was just being myself."

"That's dangerous enough," Gerald said.

"You senile old queen," my mother said. "That was *me*."

After her divorce, Sylvia had spent most of her time traveling, going to every continent ("except Antarctica!") and doing things like traveling by train across China and hiking in Peru when single women didn't do those sorts of things.

"I think that's why I did them, just to show that I could," she said.

She'd kept in touch with Gerald, mostly via postcards. Reconnecting with him in person at their high school reunion, she'd instantly suggested he come live with her.

"Were my parents at that reunion?" I asked. Apart from "yes please" and "Thank you" when Sylvia refilled my glass, I hadn't said much. The conversation was more of a dialogue between Sylvia and Gerald performed for my benefit.

Sylvia looked like she was trying to remember. "Well, they must have been," she said.

"Don't we have a photo of us from that reunion?" Gerald asked, gesturing toward the piano.

Celeste came out of the kitchen to announce dinner. As we moved into the dining room, Gerald's mention of the photo slipped my mind. I was concentrating too much on where I was putting my feet. I'd had way too much to drink.

I stared at the plate Celeste placed in front of me. It looked like a pork chop, but it was...gray. The same could be said of the sad little pile of spinach clustered next to it. The potatoes were not roasted so much as singed. I was stinking drunk—maybe that was how Sylvia and Gerald managed to stomach the cooking.

Across the table, Gerald sawed away at his chop. Eventually, he managed to carve off a piece, which he put in his mouth and chewed.

And chewed.

And chewed.

He took a gulp from his wineglass and managed to force it down. Like a lumberjack, he went back at the chop. Sylvia had begun slicing the charred bits off a potato, leaving barely a mouthful of unburned core. She ate it and began staring vaguely out the windows at the canyon.

"Is it always this bad?" I asked Gerald.

"Keep your voice down," he hissed in a loudly audible whisper. "She's probably getting dessert ready." He said it like dessert was a threat. He lowered his voice and said, "Sometimes it's worse. Be glad you weren't here when she made risotto. I thought I was going to lose a filling."

"How do you manage not to starve?" I asked.

"Cereal later, after she leaves. Sometimes we order pizza in."

We both looked over at Sylvia, who was twirling her lump of spinach with her fork. She glanced up.

"I vote for pepperoni and mushroom," she said.

We waited until Celeste had cleared away the dessert (apple pie with a crust made of, if I had to guess, plaster) and got ready to leave for the evening. Gerald took the phone into the den to call the pizza place.

"Why do you still keep her if her cooking's so bad?" I asked Sylvia.

She sighed. "I just can't bring myself to let her go. She's almost as old as we are, you know, and I don't know what else she would do."

"Something besides cooking, I hope," I said. I leaned closer. The table was a wide expanse of black lacquered wood. Seated at the head of it, she seemed dwarfed and far away. "If you like, you can give her tomorrow night off and I'll do the cooking."

"Oh, you don't have to go to that trouble, darling."

Thinking of the pork chop I'd just tried to eat, I said, "Believe me, I don't mind."

Chapter Twelve

That night I dreamed about food.

An eight-burner range was in front of me, a pot or a sauté pan going on each burner. Sylvia and Gerald would have a feast. One of the pots in back started bubbling over. When I reached for it, the pot seemed to recede no matter how hard I tried to grasp it. As the overflow crackled and blackened on the range, I stretched as far as I could, until it felt like I was flying over the pots in front, the heat prickling my belly. If only I could reach a little farther, I'd be able to grab it.

The pain when I woke up was unimaginable. I was sort of lying on my side, although my waist and legs were twisted so they were lying flat. Around my abdomen a belt of pure agony cinched tight. I couldn't move.

There was a knock on the door. It was Sylvia. "Joel, we're having crepes for breakfast. Shall I have Celeste make you up a plate?"

I tried to reply, but the pain squeezed all the breath out of me in a barely audible hiss. I would have tried to move, but breathing caused enough pain. Moving seemed foolish—not to mention impossible.

When I didn't answer immediately, Sylvia asked, "Joel, are you awake?" Then in a lower voice, she added, "Her breakfast cooking is usually much better than her supper."

I sneezed, and the pain that followed—I wished for

unconsciousness, because that would have been preferable to the hot knife that was twisting somewhere in my lower back while someone simultaneously yanked on my nether bits. It felt like my back was trying to tear itself apart, and the resulting spasm sent me over the edge of the bed onto the floor. The sound I made was somewhere between a moan, a groan, and a hiss, only much louder. At first I couldn't believe the noise came from me. It sounded like something dying.

Sylvia opened the door and gasped. "Oh my goodness, what happened?"

"My back," I managed to say between quick, shallow breaths while I prayed for darkness to descend.

It didn't.

Sylvia hesitated, started to move toward me, and hurried out the door instead. "I'll get Gerald. Gerald! Come help me!"

Together, they managed to maneuver me back onto the bed. I lay on my side, knees pulled up to my chest, which seemed to reduce the pain enough to make breathing possible.

"I'm calling Dr. Wilson," Gerald said, and left the room.

"No, I'll be fine," I said, but Sylvia shushed me.

"Fine? You're practically immobile. What on earth happened?"

"I don't know," I said. "If I had to guess, I'd say it was from sitting behind the wheel for so long."

A half hour later, Gerald came back to the room with another man behind him. Dr. Wilson was older than both Gerald and Sylvia, his white hair trimmed close to frame his overly tanned face. He wore a white jacket over a polo shirt and plaid pants and carried a black bag.

Dr. Wilson sat gently on the edge of the bed and rested a hand on my shoulder. "So I understand you've got some back pain, son?"

"You could call it that," I managed to say through clenched teeth.

"I'm going to see if I can't figure out what the problem is. Let me know if anything hurts."

As his gnarled hands gingerly felt their way along my back, I said to Gerald, "I didn't know doctors still made house calls."

"We don't. I'm retired. Now hold still."

"He makes exceptions for his old patients sometimes," Sylvia said.

"And we're pretty damn old," Gerald added.

I would have asked if he worried about getting sued, but his arthritic hands found the source of the pain, and I howled.

"You've got one hell of a knot here. What have you been doing, hauling bricks?"

"Driving across country."

"Amazing how much trouble sitting on your ass can cause," he muttered. "You probably have a torn muscle," he went on, "so you won't be going anyplace soon." He left prescriptions for muscle relaxants and painkillers, along with instructions that I wasn't to stay on my back for longer than two days.

"If he doesn't want to get out of bed after that, make him," the doctor said to Sylvia.

"Yes, because two old septuagenarians can be really persuasive," Gerald muttered.

"Threatening him with Celeste's cooking might do the trick," Wilson said. "You might want to get a heating pad too. A stiff drink or two couldn't hurt either, just not while you're taking the painkillers. Or the muscle relaxants. You'll turn to Jell-O and fall down the stairs or something."

Gerald left the room to see the doctor out. Sylvia sat at the edge of the bed. "You poor thing. If your mother knew how much this errand was taking a toll on you, she would regret having asked."

Carefully, I rolled onto my side. The pain seemed more bearable. My mother leaned against the dresser and spread her hands as if to say, *How was I to know?*

"I'll be okay," I said to Sylvia, though I was looking at my mother.

Sylvia leaned over, placed a finger in the small of my back, and barely pressed. I winced and, embarrassingly, whimpered.

"Sure you will, darling," she said. Judging from the look on my mother's face, if she could have, at that moment she would have ripped Sylvia's hair out.

❖

For three days I did nothing but lie in bed or shuffle to the bathroom. Sometimes even that required help from Gerald or Sylvia. I couldn't believe I was in one of the most beautiful places in the country and I could barely move, much less see and experience it. Sightseeing was replaced with magazines, the TV remote, and painkillers. Gerald and Sylvia tried to help me down the stairs for dinner the first evening, but we didn't get beyond the second step before I asked them to help me back to my room. Periodically one of them (or, if both were out, Celeste) came in with a fresh ice pack and a tray of something to eat—if Celeste brought it in, it was usually something inedible. Mercifully, Gerald and Sylvia brought cereal or yogurt, and on one occasion, Chinese takeout.

At least there was the view. At first Sylvia drew the curtains against the sun's glare. After the second day, I asked her to leave them open. Hours bled away as I watched the changing angle of the sun and the shadows shifting and lengthening along the canyon. The midday sun bleached the sky white, stark against the red rock walls. As the sun fell below the canyon wall, the rocks darkened to rust and black, and the sky flared orange and purple.

The muscle relaxants and painkillers gave me enough relief so I could sleep. Once I was out, my dreams were bizarre. In one, I was still in Vegas, standing on a sidewalk, the curb lined with cars. Lincoln approached from a distance, picking up newspaper racks and flinging them through windshields. When he had no more racks to throw, he picked up the cars themselves and heaved them end over end down the street. He did this effortlessly and without rancor. He even had a smile on his face.

The dreams with my mother in them were more disorienting. It was hard to tell, sometimes, whether I was asleep or awake. Little things gave it away—the clouds moving too quickly across the sky or, once, my mother spoke without moving her lips. Still unsure if I was dreaming, when I asked if this was a new trick of hers, she just smiled and shook her head. She had also taken to referring to herself in the third person.

"Your mother no longer walks in this world, Joel." She looked out the window. "She can only do so much."

"I didn't ask for her help," I said. Even in my dream, my back hurt too much to get out of bed.

"Didn't you? Who's to say you're not here to help her?"

I didn't know what to make of that even after I'd woken up. My immobility was maddening, and it occurred to me I hadn't made all that much progress in moving my life forward on this trip even before my back betrayed me. Saying that grief had stalled me felt like an excuse more than a reason.

Besides, I was still waiting for the grief to settle on me.

"Oh, I don't know, darling," my mother said. "I think you've made a lot of progress." This was a waking comment, not a dream. "You've done a fantastic job of deconstructing your life. Now you just have to decide what you're going to rebuild it to be."

❖

The morning after my third day of bed rest, before Sylvia had a chance to bring up a tray, I dressed and carefully hobbled down the stairs to the dining room. Gerald was already seated at the table with his coffee and the paper. Sylvia was making tea while Celeste prepared French toast in the kitchen.

"What a lovely surprise. Are you sure you're up to it?"

Sylvia left the teapot to pull out a chair. I braced my arms against the table and lowered myself into the seat.

"I'm feeling much better, really," I said, hoping I meant it.

"You don't look it," Gerald said, not unkindly, as he looked over the top of the paper. "Coffee?"

"Please." Celeste brought a mug and the coffee carafe, and had to rush back to the kitchen. The smoke alarm was going off.

"Open a window, dear," Sylvia said. She brought her teacup to her lips and sighed. "I don't know why she keeps trying. She's never had luck with French toast."

Pulling my chair up to the table was a process of tiny slides and lifts that took about fifteen seconds. After each motion, I paused and waited for pain to knife up my back, but it mercifully stayed at bay. Once situated, I leaned forward slightly, grasped the coffee cup, and raised it to my lips. Sylvia and Gerald both watched intently.

"Perhaps today you might want to try out the whirlpool, dear," Sylvia said.

"I think that sounds like a great idea," I said.

"We should send him down to the spa," Gerald said, snapping the newspaper as if to punctuate his statement.

"You don't think it's too soon?" Sylvia asked.

"They can work miracles there."

I spent the afternoon at a day spa named Divine Sunrise. Sylvia's treat, she insisted. When I asked if she was sure about that, Gerald said she had more money than she knew what to do with. Once inside the cathedral-like silence of the low, cool adobe building, I traded my regular clothes for a white robe that made me look like an acolyte. I moved through a series of devotions that included a soak in a whirlpool, a massage, acupuncture, and, because Sylvia insisted, a seaweed wrap and a facial. I may have felt better after all that, but I was too exhausted to notice.

Sylvia was mixing a pitcher of martinis when I returned. For two people in their seventies, I was pretty sure they could drink me under the table and through the floor.

"Did you enjoy your day at the spa, darling?" she asked.

"If she calls you 'darling' one more time..." my mother grumbled. She went up to Sylvia and blew smoke directly into her smiling face. I looked at her and wondered what she had against Sylvia.

"A story for another time," my mother said.

"It was great," I said, "but for some reason I feel exhausted now."

"Oh, I always come back feeling like I've walked a hundred miles," she said. "All that pummeling and twisting just flush out tons of toxins. Martini, darling?"

I took the glass from her and settled in the chair opposite Gerald's perch on the sofa. He was still reading the paper. "I think I'll be able to hit the road tomorrow," I said.

"So soon?" Sylvia asked. "Are you sure?"

"For Christ's sake, Sylvia," Gerald said. "He's been here for four days already. We've held him up long enough."

"Ooh, snappish," my mother said. "You know, he's always been like this. He was the most curmudgeonly teenager you could have ever met."

Sylvia shrugged off the vehemence of his outburst. "There's no need to bite my head off now, Gerald," she said in the same tone she would take with a cranky five-year-old. She sat down on the sofa next to him and said to me, "I almost forgot to mention, darling. You had a phone call while you were out."

"A phone call?" I couldn't imagine who would know to call me at their house, besides my father. About the same time that I realized my cell phone was not in my pocket, Sylvia had retrieved it from the breakfast table and handed it to me.

"You must have left it here before you left for the spa, and it's the same model as mine. See?" She took her own from her pocket, and sure enough, they were the same shiny black blocks. "I picked it up before I even realized it wasn't mine."

"Nice," my mother said. "You have the same cell phone as a little old lady."

I shot my mother a look before I started pulling up the call history and asked Sylvia, "Do you remember who it was that called?"

"At first I thought it was the boy who was traveling with you who stayed in Las Vegas, but then it turned out to be someone with an English accent. I wasn't sure if it was a wrong number at first, but he used your name, so I guess I was just confused. We had the loveliest conversation."

I swallowed a lump I assumed was my heart. "I ought to call him back, then."

"Oh yes, he did want me to ask you to do that."

I took my phone back upstairs and shut myself in the bathroom. Sitting on the closed toilet lid put me in a direct line with the vanity mirror. I looked like crap. The messed-up brown hair that was starting to go gray over my ears. The unnatural flush from the scraping and the exfoliating my face had just been subjected to. The frown lines that stayed there even when I wasn't frowning. Maybe it's a mercy we can only see ourselves through a reflection.

"Joel?" Philip's voice sounded sleepy. I could tell I'd woken him up.

"I'm sorry, you were asleep, weren't you?" I asked. "I don't think I'll ever figure out these time differences. What is it there, two in the morning?"

"You know," my mother said, "you wouldn't have to worry about time differences if you were both in the same place." She sat on the edge of the tub and ashed over the drain.

"Two a.m.?" he asked. "No, it's six in the evening."

"Six? Where are you?"

"I'm in New York already, actually."

"You are?" My heart suddenly felt overheated. We were on the same continent. Now all I had to do was not screw things up.

"Yeah, I was just lying down for a little while before dinner."

"Jet lagged?"

"And pretty much meeting'd out."

"So, you talked to my mother's friend Sylvia."

"Yeah, she seemed a bit confused. Thought I was your friend Lincoln? Is he not traveling with you any more, then?"

"No, he stayed with his sister in Vegas. Well, not *with* his sister. She doesn't want to see him again. Neither do I, for that matter."

"You and he had a falling-out?"

"More like a blowing up. Followed by a meltdown."

"Well, I'm sorry to hear that, but for purely selfish reasons I'm not sorry to hear he's gone. I was starting to wonder if I had anything to worry about from that one," he said, his tone obviously trying to keep the comment light. I wanted to play along, I really did. Something made me pause a little too long before I laughed in response, and he asked, "Did I?"

"Philip…" I trailed off. I avoided my mother's gaze. I didn't want to know if it was sympathetic or disappointed.

"Oh," he said, as if I'd confessed everything. I suppose I had. "He's gone now, though. Right?"

"Yeah, he's definitely gone."

"And he's not coming back?"

"No."

"I don't suppose I should ask how it happened in the first place, should I?"

"I wouldn't know what to say." I at least knew better than to say I was sorry. Anything else I could think to say would have sounded like I was making excuses, which would have been even worse than saying sorry. "When do you leave New York?"

"Day after tomorrow."

"You're still coming to San Francisco, right?" *Please say yes please say yes*, I repeated over and over in my head. My mother covered her ears.

After a second's pause, Philip said, "Yes, I'm still coming." If he didn't sound as enthusiastic as I might have hoped, I couldn't necessarily blame him.

❖

"Is everything all right, darling?" Sylvia asked when I returned to the living room. She had topped up my martini glass. The pitcher, now on the coffee table, was nearly empty. I sat down and finished it in three swallows, not so much enjoying the burn as it went down, but feeling like I deserved it.

"I'm fine," I said. "Like I was saying before, though, I ought to get going tomorrow."

Sylvia got up to mix another pitcher. How was it, I wondered, that neither of them slurred their words or seemed in any way tipsy?

"Decades of practice," my mother said. She was lying on top of the piano, behind the array of framed photographs displayed there.

"In that case," Sylvia said, "I was thinking of someone you might want to visit. He's very entertaining."

"Don't oversell Walter," Gerald said to her. "He's over seventy like the rest of us and surrounded by all those dusty antiques."

"Walter was at my mother's funeral, wasn't he?" I asked. "I think I remember meeting him."

Sylvia nodded. "You know, I think there's a picture of us with him over there on the piano." She waved the swizzle stick over toward where the baby grand crouched in the afternoon sun.

"Sylvia, that picture must be fifty years old if it's a day," Gerald said.

Sylvia ignored Gerald's comment and, when it was clear that he wasn't budging from the sofa, she went to the piano—Mom flicked her cigarette at her—and picked up a small silver frame. She moved her finger across the photo.

"Oh, it *is* old, isn't it?" She held it out to show me, and I got up to take a closer look. "We all look so young. That's me, that's

Gerald—oh, there's Walter, in the back! And that's your mother, and that's your father."

I peered closer at the picture. It was in color, but the colors had faded and flattened so much that it might as well have been in black and white. I recognized my mother instantly: hand on hip, her stance tilted slightly backward to show the bottom of her chin. Though she wore dark glasses, I could tell her even smile didn't reach her eyes. But the man was not my father, and I said so.

"Isn't it?" Sylvia asked.

"No."

Gerald got up then and looked at the photo. He took it and held it closer to his nose, squinting. "Let's see, that's me," he said, pointing as he listed off the people, "that's Sylvia, that's Walter, that's your mother, and that's—Sylvia, that's Derek, not Arthur."

Sylvia slipped off her glasses and slipped one temple into her mouth, looking puzzled. "Arthur? Didn't Rachel marry Derek?"

"Good heavens, Sylvia. Has your memory gotten that bad?"

She frowned at him. "You're a fine one to talk, Gerald. How many times have you locked the keys in the car?" Gerald didn't respond, and she went back to her musing. "Do I know an Arthur?" Sylvia asked. She still had the temple of her glasses in her mouth. She looked like she might chew the end off. "He didn't go to school with us, did he?"

Though her lapse in memory alarmed me, Gerald just rolled his eyes.

"No, but you went to the wedding," he said. "Don't you remember that?"

She looked like she needed to sit down. "And that wasn't Derek?"

Gerald gently suggested to Sylvia it was time for her

afternoon siesta. She glided off toward her bedroom and Gerald headed to the bar. "Would you care for another drink?" he asked.

"Please."

Gerald's hands were slow but steady as he picked up the pitcher and finished where Sylvia had left off. "You'll have to excuse Sylvia," he said, swirling some vermouth around the pitcher. "Her recollection of certain memories is inexact at times. I don't think it's Alzheimer's, really, so much as she's just slowing down a bit. I'll bet you that when she wakes up from her nap, she'll have remembered everything about Derek and Arthur and your mother."

"Although there are a few things she might omit," my mother said. She'd gotten down from the top of the piano and now leaned against it. "Let's see if the grumpy old queen knows about them."

I took a sip from my martini, grateful Gerald had served it in a highball glass. Between my back and the kneading at the spa, my grip was hardly what you could call steady. "Will she remember why she seemed so angry at Derek when she saw him at the funeral? I had wondered about that."

"Oh, that." With his drink in one hand and his cane in the other, Gerald hobbled back to the sofa. To his credit, he gained his seat without spilling a drop. "I'm not even sure what to call it. A little bruised ego, some sour grapes, and a bit of transference for good measure. As far as I can remember, Sylvia made a pass at Derek and when she got the brush-off, she demanded to know why."

"While he was engaged to my mother?" This surprised me. Judging by the look on my mother's face, it didn't surprise her in the least.

Gerald sipped from his martini, giving himself time to draw up the memory while he also reached for his glasses. "Let's just say your mother was a good girl and Sylvia was what we used to call 'fast' in those days. Now we'd just call her a slut, if we bothered to be bothered by it at all."

"Well, there goes my reputation for being glamorous and worldly," my mother said.

"And he told her why?" I asked.

"Sylvia can be pretty insistent. Naturally, the first thing she did was go and tell your mother. After she got over the initial shock, your mother asked how Sylvia learned this. Unfortunately for her, Sylvia is not very quick on her feet when it comes to making excuses. She and Rachel didn't talk for, oh, a year, I think it was."

"It would have been longer," my mother said, "but your father insisted that I bury the hatchet with her. He wasn't amused when I suggested burying it in her back, either."

Gerald reached again for his paper. He folded it in fourths so that he could hold it in one hand and his drink in the other. "Derek was quite handsome, back in the day. He still is, I suppose."

With a sip from his drink, Gerald turned his attention to the newspaper and I returned the photo to its place on the piano. There had been regret in Gerald's voice when he talked about Derek. I wondered if he'd been as envious of my mother's relationship with Derek as Sylvia had been. The more I wondered about my mother's relationships, of course, meant the less I worried about seeing Philip in two days, and I hoped to heaven I wouldn't find some other way to screw things up even more.

Chapter Thirteen

After we left Sedona, my mother grew more and more taciturn. Most of the drive to San Francisco passed in silence. Whenever she wasn't talking or looking at me, she really was becoming transparent, her edges softening until she looked only slightly more substantial than her cigarette smoke.

In San Francisco, I felt like I was always on the verge of falling. The city seemed to cling to the edge of the continent, its streets sloping toward the bay as if they might slide in. One misstep and I could trip over myself, or fall in and drown.

Walter's house was in the middle of one of those sloping blocks. It was sunny and the sky was postcard blue, but the town houses on either side of the street encased the block in shade. A steady breeze swept up from the bay, and I thought of going back to the RV for my jacket. Instead, I knocked on the door, which was a big oak slab painted a somber shade of purple.

A minute passed. I wondered if anyone was home and whether they could even hear anyone knocking from the other side. Off to the side of the front steps, smoking a cigarette, my mother waited.

Philip should have already been in San Francisco too. He hadn't called, though he'd said he would. Maybe he'd just gone back home once his work in New York was over. The desire to call him was negated by the fear I'd get sent straight to his voicemail.

I looked over at my mother. When I brooded over things like this, I'd gotten used to her being ready with a snappy remark wrapped in a smirk that at least managed to take my mind off whatever was bothering me. Now, though, she seemed to have her own brooding to do.

"You okay?" I asked before I knocked again.

She looked back at me as if she'd forgotten I was there. Rolling her cigarette between her fingers, she said, "Never felt better in my life, darling. Why?"

Before I could answer, the door opened and Walter practically pulled me inside. He shut the door behind us faster than I would have expected a man his age to be able to shift something that big. It slammed shut with a resounding thunk as Walter shouted his hellos before disappearing into the darkness.

"I'm this close"—he held his hand above his shoulder, thumb and index finger nearly touching—"to being outbid on an amazing Queen Anne table."

"I thought he was retired," I said to my mother.

She ran her finger along a mahogany secretary in the entryway. "Walter never could resist a deal. The only thing he liked better than new and shiny was old and dusty." She smirked. "Which explained his late wife. She was fifteen years older than him."

"Nice, Mom."

"Well, it's true!" She peered into a darkened room to the right of the entryway. "We always wondered what he saw in her. I guess she matched his taste for vintage decor."

Everything about Walter's house was shrouded in darkness and shadows. The old chandelier in the foyer, converted from gas to electric, gave off a sallow glow that bathed the room in sepia.

"Come on in," Walter called from somewhere in the back of the house. "I'm almost done here."

I followed his voice through some rooms encased in darkness until I found him in a parlor the size of a ballroom that blazed with light. It was packed with stuff, as were most of the rooms I'd passed through. Walter sat behind a desk that faced French doors looking out over the backyard. In front of him was a flat-panel monitor that appeared to be the only concession to modern life in the room.

Maybe even in the whole house.

"Sorry there isn't more of a welcoming committee," Walter said as he got up and shook my hand. His grip was surprisingly strong. "I'm afraid it's just me." He had a hard time holding on to housekeepers, he said. The dusting always proved too much for them in the end.

I wanted to get a move on—my mother did too, judging from her too-forceful exhales. The process of Walter showing me to the guest room he'd prepared was cluttered with digressions: a statue on the second-floor landing he and his late wife had picked up in Venice; a bookshelf full of first editions in languages he didn't even read; a table identical to the one he'd just bought on eBay. Everything seemed worth collecting to him. Even when we got to the guest room, there were shelves and tabletops lined with porcelain milkmaid figurines. He'd bought his first one in Switzerland when he was in the Army, and he'd collected them ever since.

"Do you collect anything?" he asked.

"I think he means besides bad decisions, darling," my mother said.

"I used to collect baseball cards," I said, "but I got rid of them when I was a kid." I didn't mention that I stopped collecting when I realized I hated baseball and trying to like it was not going to make me straight. Nor did I mention that the ones I liked were the handsome guys with the nice hair who didn't have the crazy '70s mustaches.

"I had a co-worker who collected snow globes from all around the world," I said. "Whenever people went on vacation, she'd ask them to bring her one back. Most of her collection was from places she'd never even visited. Said it was just like being there."

Walter turned over a milkmaid figurine in his hands before returning it to the shelf. "I think it's good to collect something," he said.

"Who'd have guessed?" my mother asked.

"It keeps you always looking for something," he continued. "I think you tend to notice things more, be more observant. And they've managed to last. I guess I admire that too, their ability to endure. Certainly, they'll outlast me."

When we finally left that cave of a house, squinting into the daylight, it felt like emerging from a movie theater into the middle of the afternoon.

It was *really* that dark in there.

"It was more like a funeral home," my mother said, and shivered. "I've already spent all the time in those I care to, thank you."

"Well, we still have to go back there after this," I said. We were on our way to drop off the RV. The Millers, as it happened, were out of town. I'd been instructed to park it in the driveway and slide the keys through the mail slot. It was close to Walter's house; he said it would be a nice walk back on a day like this.

"Maybe you should call Philip," she said.

"He was supposed to call me, Mom."

"Oh honestly, who cares?" She threw her cigarette out the passenger window before I could tell her not to litter. "You're going to let him get away because of who was supposed to call whom first? Really?"

"I don't know if he even wants to hear from me after Lincoln."

"You'll never know if you don't call him, now will you?"

"Mother, how can you be so sure that falling for Philip is not just another way for me to run away?"

"Darling, consider the fact that you don't really seem to be running *toward* him at the moment, then ask me again what you're running from."

"God damn it, Mom." I missed our turn. We circled the block

in silence and came back to the Millers' street. The driveway was so narrow I couldn't get out from the driver's side. I slid sideways out the back door and scooted, nose-to-nose with the neighbor's fence, until I was clear.

I dropped the keys through the mail slot and waited to hear them hit the floor on the other side. They fell soundlessly. I lifted the flap and peered through the narrow hole, imagining the keys falling forever downward until they emerged on the other side of the world.

The reality was just carpeting on the foyer floor.

My journey had ended with neither a bang nor a rattle.

Before we left, we stood in front of the RV for a long, silent moment, listening to the engine tick off the last of its heat.

"I feel like we should say a few words to commemorate the moment," my mother said.

"Like what? 'Thank God that's over'?" I put my hands in my pockets, which was when I realized I didn't have my cell phone on me—because it was in my backpack, which was still on the floor next to the driver's seat in the now-locked RV.

"Oh, shit," I muttered.

"Not exactly what I had in mind as words for the occasion," my mother said, "but okay."

I'd never broken into anything before. I picked up one of the decorative stones bordering the flowerbed by their front walk, and scooted between the RV and the fence again. When I was at the back of the camper, relatively shielded from view, I lifted the brick to my shoulder, like a shot put, and heaved.

The shattering glass wasn't nearly as loud as I'd expected. It sounded like a lot of bubbles popping at once, and like a heavy book dropped, open, onto a bare floor—that was the rock landing inside. I reached through the jagged opening gingerly, flipped the catch, and slid what was left of the window open. I climbed through, then shut the window behind me—which was of course pointless. I opened it again. More shards of glass fell out.

After I retrieved the bag, I headed back to the broken window and realized I could just as easily go out the side door again. My mother stood waiting for me at the end of the driveway.

"Right," I said. "Now we can really leave."

She lit a cigarette and we began walking. The Millers' house, like Walter's, was perched midway along a steeply sloping street. Thankfully, we were heading downhill. It was once we were halfway down another street that I realized we'd made a wrong turn. I stopped for a second, looked behind us at the hill we'd come down, and didn't have the energy to try going back up. We turned again, and before too long, we were completely lost. Eventually, we wandered long enough that we left North Beach and came within smelling distance of Fisherman's Wharf.

"Maybe we should stop and ask for directions," my mother suggested.

"How the hell did we get here?" I muttered.

"I know you're not really asking *me* that question," my mother said.

"No, I'm not." I refused to look at her. Instead I got out my phone and wished I had a fancier one, with GPS or some way to find out where I was and where I should have been going. I tried to remember Walter's phone number, which of course I hadn't saved.

"You could just call—"

"Jesus Christ, mother, would you knock it off? I'm not calling him." I put the phone away and started walking toward the smell of fish and water. I didn't care that I had no idea where I was going, and I didn't look behind to see if she was following. Of course, she was.

"Darling, if you would only listen to reason."

I stopped and turned on her. "Why would I want to do that? Haven't I been listening to your reason all along? And for God's sake, would you stop smoking all the God damned time?" I snatched the cigarette from her mouth and flung it to the sidewalk, where it let loose a burst of embers before it bounced into the gutter. I stared for a long time at the place where it had landed, its fire slowly going out.

"How did I do that?" I asked, almost at the same time my mother asked, "How did you do that?"

She frowned. "I don't know. Maybe for a minute you forgot so strongly I was dead it didn't make a difference."

"Forgot you were dead? How can I forget when you're always here reminding me of it?"

"Maybe that's the problem." She sighed and stared down the street toward the water, like she might find the answer to what was bothering her in the bay. "When someone dies, they're gone. I'm not."

I couldn't ignore the brief, startled looks from passersby as they heard me talking to someone they couldn't see. My mother noticed it too, and she looked even more disturbed by it than I did.

"These people, they think you're crazy. Aren't you even the least bit bothered by that, darling?"

"Who cares? The streets in this city are packed with loons. What's one more?"

She shook her head and pulled another cigarette from her pack. "It may not matter to you, but I'm your mother. It matters to me. And heaven knows, it really should matter to you."

"Fine," I said while she lit her cigarette. "If you'll stop talking to me when we're in public, no one will think I'm nuts."

"If only it were that simple."

My mother never got angry if I misbehaved or did something wrong as a kid. Worse than that was disappointing her. She could reduce me to tears in an instant with this expression she had, a cross between a smile and a frown as she shook her head slowly. *How could you saddle me with this?* it seemed to say.

Facing that expression now, I realized she was preparing to leave.

"It's time for you to get on with things without me following you like a second shadow and holding you back," she said.

"You're not. I never would have made this trip if it weren't for you," I said. "I've changed so many things in my life in such a short time, and you're a big part of the reason for it."

"Let's not be *too* dramatic, my dear. I think those changes would just as surely have taken place if I weren't here."

Panic swelled in my throat as I realized what she wasn't saying. "Mom, you can't go. We don't even know why you're still here yet."

She stared down at the sidewalk. "I thought it might be because I was too selfish, but I think it's because you haven't learned to let go." Anxiety flickered across her face. It was gone before I could offer any reassurance. She straightened up and smiled. "Time to learn, then." She leaned in and, holding her cigarette away from us, kissed my cheek. "Love you, darling."

When she started walking away, I was too numb to move. I stared at her receding back as she literally passed through the crowd, heading toward the bay. When I tried to call after her, it came out like a strangled whisper.

"Mom, please."

A woman at my elbow did a double take, which was enough to jolt me out of my paralysis. I started running.

I could just see the back of her head. She was over a block away when the light changed in front of me. I kept going, drawing a blaze of car horn and some shouting, along with a generous dose of profanity. By the time I got to the other side of the intersection, she was gone.

"Joel?"

Behind me, on the other side of the intersection I'd just crossed, Philip stood waiting for the light to change. I looked up and realized one of the buildings I'd run past was his hotel. It was as if my mother had intended to deliver me to the spot where running into him was a certainty. I wouldn't have put it past her.

When the light turned green, Philip jogged across the street and stood in front of me. He was wearing a green windbreaker, jeans, and a white T-shirt. It took me a moment to realize it was the same outfit he'd been wearing the first day I met him, under Waterloo Bridge.

"Hi," I said.

"Hi."

"You're here."

"I said I would be, didn't I?" He was still a bit breathless from running. "Who were you chasing after?"

"My mother," I said.

"Your mum?" His forehead wrinkled in concern, he put his hands on my shoulders. "Love, your mum's gone. You know that, right?"

I nodded. "I know." I said it again. "I know." I kept saying it over and over, like a mantra, until the words and the tears bled into an incomprehensible sob.

The less said about the ensuing cloudburst, the better. Like a violent storm that can't maintain its fury, though, mercifully it was over fast. We were sitting on a bench—I didn't remember how we'd gotten there, but Philip must have steered us toward it—and he used his thumbs to swipe away the tears from under my eyes.

"I'm sorry," I said.

"There's nothing to apologize for, love. You're in mourning. It's what's done."

Why was that such a revelation for me? "I'm so tired," I said.

"You're bound to be, love." He pulled me close again.

I tried to breathe normally. There was a painful tightening across my chest, and I wondered if I'd cried so hard I'd broken something.

"What do we do now?" I asked.

We went to Philip's room.

My original plan had been to go get coffee—there was a Starbucks in the lobby of his hotel—but when we got to the front door I yawned and Philip asked if I wanted to lie down for a bit and get coffee later. I nodded, and he steered us toward the elevator.

Of course, we didn't sleep.

Sheets have always been my favorite thing about hotels: white, flat, and smooth, softened by countless washings. Sliding into them the first time is like gliding across a plane of glass.

An hour after he unlocked the door to his room, that plane of glass lay in shards at the foot of the bed. I lay on my back, Philip still straddling me with his head hanging forward as he tried to catch his breath. He rolled off and sprawled beside me, staring at the ceiling.

"Wow," Philip said.

"Welcome to America," I said.

"That was definitely worth crossing an ocean for."

I rolled onto my side and looked over Philip's profile at the window. The sheers were pulled shut, but the curtains were open. I could only make out vague shapes outside. We were on the seventeenth floor, and the room could have been floating in limbo.

"What?" Philip had turned and caught me staring. I shook my head.

"Nothing. I haven't had a coherent thought in at least an hour."

"Mission accomplished, then." He smiled, reached down to the end of the bed, and pulled the sheet up over us. "Now what?"

I rolled onto my back and stared at the ceiling. Over by the window, the heater clicked on. I had no idea what to do next.

"When do you have to be back home?" I asked.

"Four days. You?"

"At the moment, I have no idea where home is. My dog's in St. Louis, my newly widowed dad's in Maine, my job is gone, and I'm here." If there was a way any of these things connected, I couldn't see it.

I'm not sure how much time passed before Philip said, "You're doing that thing again, aren't you?"

"What thing?"

"Where someone asks you a question and you start turning it over in your head and before you know it, you've managed to tie your brain up in knots."

I smiled. "That obvious?"

He rolled over on top of me. "That obvious."

I put my arms around him, my right hand resting in the small of his back. It was my favorite spot on him, the swooping arch between his backside and his ribs. My hand fit perfectly there. I never wanted to stop touching it. It was a place worth coming back to. We'd met in March, it was now the middle of April, and yet it felt as if a hundred years had slipped away in the meantime.

"I suppose you've got to get back to your dad now that you've finished up here, right?" he asked an hour later.

"I think I should, at least for a little while. He's all alone now. I should help him get settled." Into what, I didn't know.

"What do you want to do?" Philip asked.

What I wanted was to brush my fingers through the curls at Philip's forehead, so I did. Philip rolled onto his back and rested his head against my belly.

"You know, I've done a great job of dismantling just about every constant in my life up to now. You'd think I would have put a little effort into figuring out what I'd do after that." I closed my eyes. "Now what?"

I felt Philip roll over. When I opened my eyes, he'd rested his chin on my sternum and was staring up at me.

"Why don't you come with me back to London?"

Chapter Fourteen

Philip nodded off five minutes into the flight. As his head slid to my shoulder, I stared at the magazine in my lap without grasping a single word. The flight attendant took our drink orders. I ordered martinis for us both. If he was still asleep when they arrived, I'd drink his too.

Philip was coming with me to Portland and would stay as long as work allowed. He'd give me as much time as he could, he said. (When I'd told him I had to return to Maine and said, "Come with me," he'd smirked and replied, "I just did. Twice.") Hopefully it would be all the time I needed to decide whether to go back to London with him.

"Why do you even *need* time?" Carrie asked when I called her from our gate before the flight. Philip was in the bathroom. "He flew halfway around the world just to see you."

"He had meetings in New York."

"Oh, that's bullshit and you know it. Besides, last time I checked, New York was not in San Francisco."

Carrie wasn't waiting for the divorce to be final. After all of two days in the apartment at the Chase, she decided to pack up again and move home to Baltimore.

"You really want to go back?" I asked. She was inclined to describe her mother in somewhat totalitarian terms.

"At this point, it's really not a question of want, considering my flight leaves in an hour," she said.

"You're at the airport?"

"I know. Coincidence, right? Actually, I'm still standing outside. I've got one last cigarette before I have to check in. Anyway, don't deflect my question. What's the problem with Philip?"

"Maybe that there isn't a problem?" I kept an eye out for Philip. He hadn't returned from the bathroom yet. "Besides, I've spent a grand total of five days with him."

"I spent three years with Doug before I married him, and five more years before I discovered he was a God damn, motherfucking son of a bitch, so length of time? Not always the best gauge." She was silent for a moment; I was starting to feel the need to fill the silence when she said, "I mean, Jacob's already moving in with Matt, and it's only been, what, two months?"

"Seriously? He's moving in?" I wanted to ask her more, but Philip was heading back from the bathroom. "Our flight's about to leave. I'd better get going."

"Go to London," she said before hanging up. "I'll come visit. If you don't go, what excuse will I have?"

I watched Philip cross the concourse, his smile open and uncomplicated, and wondered over all of the things I didn't know about him: whether he liked dogs or cats; what his favorite color was; whether he'd ever been in a serious relationship before, and whether he'd fallen in love as thoroughly as I thought I had. The way he walked was like an open book, and it made me think I could ask him any of these questions and he would answer without hesitating. He was so forthright, he was almost canine.

He sat down and kissed me—he didn't care who looked—and asked, "Almost time?"

"Almost," I said. He squeezed my hand, and I asked, "Do you like dogs?"

❖

Philip's soft breathing escalated into full-on snoring. I moved my shoulder a little, which pushed his mouth shut, and all was peaceful again. The flight attendant brought the drinks, and I started on the first martini. Maybe it would help me sleep. All I could do at that point was stare over the other passengers' heads down the length of the plane. We were seated toward the rear, far back enough that when I looked toward the front, it was hard to forget I was thousands of feet in the air, in a tin can hurtling through the sky at hundreds of miles an hour. I finished the first martini in a couple gulps and started on the second.

It felt odd being alone in my head. I'd gotten used to my mother's near-constant presence, and now with her gone, I felt less tethered, as if I were miles above the ground in more ways than one.

The night before, I'd had another dream about Dudley. We were running, which was odd because Dudley was usually too busy sniffing every tree and lamppost to go faster than a brisk trot. The grass was tall, and Dudley, off his leash, was leaping high through it, clearing the top like a gazelle. It was one of those idyllic landscapes like out of the opening to *The Sound of Music*, and bore no resemblance to any place near San Francisco, St. Louis, or any place I could remember ever being.

We climbed to the top of a rise and Dudley paused there, looking out toward the Cinemascope horizon and glancing behind him while I caught up. When I got up beside him, I knelt down and wrapped my arms around him, burying my nose in the soft fur at his neck. Was this the sort of place Dudley dreamed about when he yipped in the middle of the night, when I turned on the light to see his paws paddling at the air? Did I ever make appearances in Dudley's dreams?

"Am I in your dreams?" I asked. Dudley looked at me a moment, his brown eyes inscrutable, before he looked back toward the horizon and let out an almost human sigh, as if despairing that I would ever understand.

When I awoke, it was three in the morning. I left Philip sleeping soundly and took my phone onto the balcony. Three in San Francisco meant it was five in St. Louis, and Matt would be awake.

He balked at putting Dudley on a plane to Portland, though. "They put them down in the cargo hold, and dogs aren't cargo," he said. "I've got time. I'll drive him out."

"You'd do that?" I tried not to get my hackles up at the implication that I'd been content to treat Dudley like an oversized bag that needed to be checked. It was what I'd wanted to ask Matt originally, but after all he'd done to look after Dudley while I took a wrecking ball to my life, it seemed too much to ask.

"You even have to ask?"

Leaving him alone for so long, I felt I'd let Dudley down somehow. Matt's willingness to drop everything and drive him halfway across the country to me reinforced the feeling.

❖

I ordered a third martini and hoped it might help me sleep. It didn't. But by the time Philip woke up, I was quietly and thoroughly drunk. When we landed in Portland, the drunk had worn off and I was sliding into hangover territory, which was probably the perfect condition in which to introduce him to my father.

We stood outside the front door long enough for it to feel awkward, the seconds piling up on the doormat while I stood with the key in my hand hovering a few centimeters from the lock. Dad hadn't said he'd be at the airport, but somehow I'd expected him to be there anyway. When he didn't show up, I visualized him on the living room floor, lying in his own filth and agony, a hip broken or worse.

Before I could unlock it, the door was yanked open and my dad was standing there. "Son," he grumbled, "are you going to come in or what?"

He turned around and shuffled through the foyer. "You'll never believe what happened," he said. "Some asshole threw a rock through the window of the RV after you dropped it off."

It actually cheered me that this was the first thing he said when we walked in. Not "Welcome back, son" or "You must be Philip, I'm Arthur. Pleased to meet you." His curmudgeonly self reassured me he was doing fine.

"Actually, I was the asshole who did that, Dad," I said. "Where's your cane?"

"My what?"

"Your cane." My father wasn't setting any speed records crossing the foyer into the living room, but he stood straighter and moved faster than he had before my trip, and he wasn't using his cane to hold himself up.

"It's upstairs, I think. What does that have to do with anything? And why are you an asshole?"

Once I explained to him what had happened, he sighed and said, "I'll send them a check, if I can ever figure out where your mother put the checkbook."

At that point, my father tuned into Philip's presence as if he'd forgotten we weren't alone. As they shook hands, Philip maintained an expression somewhere between "I'm terribly sorry for your recent loss" and "I'm delighted to be screwing your son." I'd never brought home anyone I was dating, much less a man, so I didn't know how my father would react. Turned out, neither did he. He shook Philip's hand, asked how the flight was, and said something noncommittal about the weather, then decided his glasses needed to be cleaned.

While my father rubbed the lenses on the hem of his shirt, I turned to Philip briefly and gave him a conspiratorial roll of the eyes. I hadn't known what to expect when I got back. I worried three weeks alone might have given him enough time to descend into doddering old man territory. I feared that I would find him unwashed, unshaven, living amid piles of dirty dishes and takeout containers.

What I found were boxes, lots of them, in almost every room of the house. Some of them were already taped shut and labeled. Others were still in the process of being filled. The rooms, because of the boxes and the once-familiar things now absent from their usual places, seemed full and empty at the same time.

"Dad, what the hell?" I asked.

He looked at me as if I were an idiot. It was obvious he was planning to move. Maybe he refrained from calling me an idiot out loud because Philip was there. My father handed me the brochure from the independent living community. It looked nice; the pictures showed smiling seniors doing active things, like playing tennis or walking briskly along sunlit paths. I wondered how much of it was just stock photography.

"It's kind of sudden, isn't it?" I asked.

"Summer's going to be here soon and I still haven't gotten around to cleaning out the gutters," he said. "Then fall's here before you know it, and I don't know that I want to have to rake up all those leaves this year."

"You could always hire someone to do that," I said.

He shook his head. "They never do it the way you want them to. Then there's the housekeeping and the cleaning. You know I'm no good at that." He put the brochure in his back pocket.

"This seems awfully sudden, Dad."

"Compared with what?" He moved with surprising briskness to the bookcase and began removing picture frames. "I'm not packing up everything right now. It's just that the realtor recommended eliminating clutter if you want to sell faster."

"You've already met with a realtor?"

"Right after you left." His answers were getting more clipped with each question I asked. "It doesn't bother you, does it?"

"No, of course not," I said. "Well, what can we do to help?"

Very little, it seemed, except stay out of the way. We both knew he wasn't planning to move because of the gutters or the raking, but neither of us said that. Between the three of us, over the next couple days, we didn't say much at all. A breathless quiet settled in the house, as if there weren't enough air to make noise. A similar silence used to fill the rooms throughout my teenage years. The weight of things unsaid—possibly, unable to be said—felt like walking through curtains. At first Philip was oblivious to it, but he too fell silent, speaking to me in hushed tones when my father wasn't around. We were like monks in our own silent order.

That is, until Philip and I crawled into bed or left the house. Unlike my fours days with him in London, when we never wanted to leave his flat, in Portland we spent most of our time away from the house. I could have said we were giving my father space, but being silent in that space with him eventually got to be too weird, even for me.

I'd lied to my father. It did bother me, the thought of him not living in our house anymore. While I took Philip down to the Old Port, or for a drive along Route 1, or down to Freeport to shop at L.L.Bean, it was like I was becoming a tourist in the place I used to consider home. Even if I never came back here, knowing my parents would be in the same house I remembered from childhood was like having a lucky stone in my pocket I could touch every so often to remind myself it was there.

It should have made my decision easier, knowing I couldn't stay in what would soon no longer be the family home. Instead, it felt like no decision at all.

The Mona Lisa was still at the art museum. Philip and I stared at her somber face staring back at us, as if we were all waiting for one of us to smile. Nobody caved. I knew how she felt. The expression on Picasso's *Tête de Femme* was even more in line with my feelings. Her colors were harsh and all over the place, her features fragmented.

"I'm not sure which one of them I feel sorrier for, her or the Mona Lisa," Philip said.

"They both look like they're having bad days," I said.

Philip moved down the gallery, but I kept staring at the

Picasso. It mystified me in a way that the Mona Lisa hadn't. Her left eye stared out of a shape that looked like a crescent moon. Her other eye was the sun. The Mona Lisa you could at least look in the eye.

"At least your eyes are both on the same side of your head, darling."

I looked to either side of me instead of behind me, where my mother's voice was coming from. Not surprisingly, the gallery was empty except for us.

I didn't want to cry, but the thing I was discovering about grief was that it battered you when you didn't see it coming. It was more like something you rounded a corner and smacked into, or like grocery carts colliding in the frozen food aisle. I lowered my head and put my hand over my eyes, thinking maybe I could hold it in.

She'd gone, she'd come back, she'd gone again, and here she was back again. It was making me dizzy.

She put her arms around me and whispered in my ear, "Just this last once, darling. I promise."

❖

Matt arrived the next morning. Until the doorbell rang while I was in the middle of making pancakes, I hadn't even realized I'd forgotten to tell Philip and my dad he was coming.

Likewise, I couldn't remember if I'd mentioned Philip's presence to Matt when I'd called him about Dudley. His reaction to Philip was subtler than surprise. On the surface, they seemed cordial; they shook hands, pleased-to-meet each other in civil though subdued tones, which could have been out of respect for the fact that my father and I were in mourning. They chatted a little about work and how Matt's drive had been. The impression I had more than anything else was of two dogs circling each other, trying to decided who outranked whom in the pecking order.

The best idea seemed to be to separate them. Philip said he

had some work to do and went off to find his BlackBerry. I told my father I was taking Dudley for a walk and asked Matt if he wanted to come along.

Dudley led the way, as usual, stopping more often than usual since every tree was a bold new frontier for his nose to explore. Every third or fourth tree, Dudley lifted his head and tried to catch a scent on the wind. I wondered what he found exotic that my diminished senses missed. I could make out the smell of Italian dressing from Mama Leoni's, which we'd just passed, but already even the saltwater smell had receded into the background for me. Dudley looked like he'd walked into a shopping mall of scents and couldn't make up his mind which one to sniff first.

"He seems happy to be back with you," Matt said, finally dispelling the awkward silence I had yet to breach.

"I was just thinking he didn't seem like he even noticed who was holding the leash," I said. Dudley had displayed little enthusiasm to see me, much to my disappointment. Who was I to blame him, though? He had hardly seen me for the last two months.

"Give him time," Matt said.

We walked a little while longer and the gulf of silence returned. As I was wondering how to bridge it, once again Matt made the first effort.

"So Philip came all the way from London to see you?"

I smiled. How was it surprising to me that he'd ask me about Philip?

"He came out to San Francisco to meet me once I'd dropped off the RV, and he said he had enough time and enough miles to come with me back to Portland to meet my dad."

"That's pretty major." Dudley stopped to scrutinize another tree. "I'm almost afraid to ask what happened to Lincoln."

"He stayed behind in Las Vegas," I said. "His sister lives there." Dudley seemed satisfied that he'd read everything there was to read about the tree, and we continued down the block. "We had a bit of a falling-out, I guess."

Matt laughed. "Thank God."

"I know. He was bad news from the start. I just didn't know how to shake him loose."

"Hey," Matt said, "it's not my place to judge."

Now it was my turn to laugh. "Right, Counselor." We crossed the street and headed back toward the house. "He's asked me to move to London."

"Are you going to?"

"I don't know."

"You're worried about how short a time you've known him, aren't you?" he asked.

"Among other things."

"He came halfway across the world just to see you. He's the real deal, Joel."

"Maybe. I'm worried about my dad, though, and I don't know what I would do with Dudley. If I took him with me, he'd have to be in quarantine for six months."

Matt sighed. There was exasperation in his voice when he spoke. "I wish you'd said something before I came all this way. You know I would have kept him with me."

"I've asked you for so much already."

"Oh, for Pete's sake, Joel. You haven't asked me for a damn thing. And I haven't done anything that I didn't want to do."

"God damn it, I'm sorry, okay?" I shook my hands in frustration, and the tremor down the leash made Dudley stop and look back at us. "Let's not argue," I said. "We're upsetting Dudley."

Before we crossed the street back to the house, Matt said, "Look, if you want me to, I'll stay for a couple days and take him back home with me." He put his hand on my arm, the one that was holding the leash. "I don't mind. Really."

Dudley scanned the street for traffic, first one way then the other, and he looked back at me as if to ask if we were ever going to cross. I tried desperately not to cry, again. When would every little thing not make me want to burst into tears?

"I'd miss him so much," I said in a whisper because if I spoke any louder, my voice would break.

"I know, hon," Matt said.

❖

Having these three men under the same roof was bound to cause friction. I shouldn't have been surprised when I walked into the kitchen that afternoon to find that trouble had arrived. Matt and Philip were already there, and I felt as if I'd missed something that bounced off the walls like the echo of a dropped pan or a fired gun. Matt stared at the coffeemaker, daring it to blink. Philip was burning a hole through the front page of the newspaper with his eyes. All the muscles in his neck were clenched tight. My first instinct was to back out of the room, but Matt looked up and saw me.

"Coffee?" he asked. It was almost a bark.

"Sure." Philip looked up before I could move toward either of them. "Anyone want lunch?"

"No," Philip and Matt responded in unison; both looked surprised that there was something they agreed on.

I took my coffee and retreated to the front porch. I listened to the hiss of the screen door hesitating shut and paused with the coffee cup at my lips. How easily I fell back into old patterns. This was where I went when I was fifteen and wanted to hide—I could lean against the railing and be invisible from the living room windows along the porch.

The street had seemed so much wider back then. It met in a Y intersection with Emery Street, and from where I stood I'd been able to see down each street for what seemed like infinity, like standing at the railing of a ship watching the ocean churn to the horizon. Anything beyond those streets had seemed just as far away.

This was where I came to escape from the tight, clipped silences of my parents' arguments—which had been few, but at the time they had loomed like thunderstorms that never broke. A short, curt answer from my mother was a flash of still-distant lightning. It had already vanished by the time you turned to look at it. The things they really meant to say were sandwiched into the silences. I couldn't bear those silences, so I came out here.

Lincoln and his sister had lived a couple blocks down Pine Street. I could have walked there now and it would hardly have taken five minutes. Farther away was the Promenade, which really was like the edge of the world, so rarely had I gone beyond it at that age.

I sat in one of the metal chairs angled toward each other beneath the living room windows. They had been brown before; at some point they'd been repainted green. It was as quiet out here as it was inside the house, but it was a much more peaceful quiet. There were no thunderclaps to tremble the air, only a calm breeze and an occasional car.

I closed my eyes, opening them only when the screen door protested moments later. Matt settled into the other chair, bringing with him a charge that crackled in the air. Matt had always been the calm one.

I wanted to deflect the storm, so I put out a lightning rod. "How's Jacob?"

"What?" I could have sworn that the anger in that one word chased the warmth from my coffee and sent clouds across the sun. "He's fine."

"I'm glad he didn't have a problem with you bringing Dudley out here to me."

Matt's brow furrowed like the drawing of a bow down between his eyes. "Why would he have a problem with it?"

"Oh, nothing. You know."

"No, I don't know." Matt set his coffee cup on the porch railing.

"I was just thinking how I'm glad you're happy, that's all."

"Thank you," Matt said. "I *am* happy."

I sipped my coffee and let the silence hang for a moment. "You really can't stand Philip, can you?"

Matt opened his mouth to say something, and closed it. I very carefully did not grin. I'd never derailed an argument of Matt's before.

"What were you two arguing about?" I asked.

"You'll think it's stupid," Matt said.

"Why?"

"Because it is. He was making the coffee, but he was doing it all wrong. I offered to help and he got a little snippy."

I couldn't imagine Matt antagonizing Philip into an argument—but he used to be a lawyer. He never did it to me, but I wondered if anyone else was fair game.

"He doesn't even drink coffee. He likes tea," I said. "He was probably just trying to be helpful."

"Well, so was I," Matt protested.

"Of course you were."

He laughed suddenly, and I decided to let it drop. What did it matter, anyway?

Behind us, the door rattled. My father opened the screen door and Dudley came outside.

"I thought you were going to make lunch," my father said to me.

"I'll be in in a minute, Dad."

"Hey, Dudley," Matt said. Dudley ambled over and sat between us. He narrowed his eyes and opened his mouth to the breeze coasting down the street. I stroked the space between his ears.

"Who's a happy boy?" I whispered.

"He really is, isn't he?" Matt asked, his voice warming to the prospect of talking about something other than Philip. "He likes it here." Before he sipped his coffee again, Matt added, "Maybe you should think about leaving him here with your dad."

❖

The rest of the day passed in more or less silent détente between Matt and Philip. At night, when we squeezed into the daybed in my old room, Philip and I did our best to have sex as quietly as possible. I don't think it was in either of our natures, but we managed. It was funny when I thought how many adolescent nights I'd spent fantasizing about doing the things that Philip was proceeding to do to me with quiet gusto, not to mention a couple things my naïve sixteen-year-old id hadn't been creative or depraved enough to conjure up.

Once we were completely exhausted, we talked and waited for sleep to overtake us. Getting comfortable was tricky. I slung my left leg over Philip's right; otherwise one of us would have fallen onto the floor. I closed my eyes and sighed.

"Feeling all right, then?" Philip asked.

"I'm doing okay," I said. Every one of my nerves was singing, but he wasn't talking about that. I shivered and pulled the covers closer to my chin.

Philip put an arm over my chest, then snaked the other underneath me, and held me close. I kept my eyes shut, preferring to float in darkness. "I think I'm still numb. I keep wondering when the rest of it's going to hit me."

"It doesn't really hit all at once," Philip said. "You think everything is going along just fine and that you've gotten over it, then you find yourself crying in the frozen foods section at Tesco because you've picked up a packet of the veggie burgers she always liked but you can't stand."

I opened my eyes then and looked at Philip. Clearly, he wasn't just making that up. "When did your mother die?"

In the darkness, I could barely make out the Cheshire-cat trace of Philip's smile. "Mum's still alive. Still giving me guilt for not providing grandchildren and continuing the family name. Among other crimes."

"So who died?"

It was Philip's turn to sigh. "Ian. My best mate. I'd known him since university. You could always count on him to have your back in a fight, or make sure you got home after a booze-up without falling down in the middle of the street."

"Sounds like the help-you-move-a-body kind of friend."

Philip laughed. "What on earth?"

"Haven't you heard the saying? A friend will help you move. A good friend will help you move a body."

"I'll have to remember that."

"So, how did he die?"

"Leukemia. Nobody was expecting it. He'd been in remission for almost twenty years. We thought we'd have more time. I thought *I'd* have more time."

"More time for what?" I asked. Philip didn't answer, and his silence gave me a moment to draw my own conclusion. "You were in love with him?"

Philip shrugged. "He was my best mate, but I don't know if I would have called it love. I guess that's the point. I never had time to figure out for sure. Actually, no, that's my point. I had time to figure out, but I always thought I would have *more* time. So I never did anything about it." He pulled me closer. "Let that be a lesson to you."

Philip fell asleep first. I lay staring at the ceiling for a while longer, listening to Philip's breathing lengthen and grow deeper, and wondered whether thinking about long-term happiness at the moment was wrong.

CHAPTER FIFTEEN

Since the day at the museum, my mother's voice had receded. The day Philip left, she made herself heard again.

I was drinking a cup of coffee in my room while Philip showered. I got up and started looking around, making sure Philip hadn't left anything unpacked. He had to be at the airport in two hours to catch his flight to Boston, where he'd connect with British Airways and fly to Heathrow.

There was a pair of Philip's underwear under the bed. They were black, square-cut boxer briefs, the material a little shiny. I looked at the tag—Marks and Spencer. I folded them and was about to put them in Philip's suitcase, but tossed them on my own pile of dirty clothes instead.

"So you've given him breakfast and now you're just sending him on his way?" she asked.

I'd made omelets for breakfast that morning. "He's already stayed longer than he planned," I said.

From the corner of my eye I saw her flit from the bedside to the window, a blur of diaphanous peach. Her lighter clicked as she lit up a cigarette.

"Remember when you first moved to St. Louis? You thought it would only be for a year or two at the most. How long did you end up staying?"

I closed Philip's suitcase and tried to latch it. It was too full. I had to sit on the lid to get the lock to finally catch.

"Fifteen years," she said when I didn't answer. "You moved there when you were twenty-two. Do you even remember twenty-two?"

I rolled off the suitcase and lay on the bed next to it. I remembered twenty-two, though I didn't think about it often. My first place had been a studio apartment in the Central West End; I moved out when I thought I heard a gunshot in the hallway one night. My car at the time was an old Ford Escort painted the color of rust. The stick shift was missing the knob and the passenger seat had no seat belt. Most of the time, after paying for gas, groceries, and student loans, I didn't have enough money left to go out. That Christmas I couldn't afford a plane ticket home, so I told my parents I had a big project looming at work and if I left town for the holidays I'd never finish it. That was my first Christmas alone. I bought a Norfolk pine that caught some sort of fungus and died before Christmas day. I celebrated Christmas Eve with a care package of cookies from my mother (store-bought, naturally) and a twelve-pack of Milwaukee's Best—I couldn't even afford Bud Light. I woke up on December twenty-fifth with a hangover.

Alone.

I got up and looked out the window. She was to my right, a vague shimmer of color. Her left hand came to rest on my shoulder.

"I'm not twenty-two anymore," I said.

"Are you talking to yourself?" Philip asked. I hadn't heard him come in. He was wearing my old pale blue bathrobe, which barely came down to his knees. It was a good look for him. He set his shaving kit on the suitcase bed and stood behind me.

"Kind of," I said. I turned back to the window. He put his arms around my waist.

"What do you see down there?" he asked.

My room overlooked the yard. "I see the spot where the RV used to be, my dad's Buick, and the flower bed that my mother used to plant. Which is now full of weeds. Which I'm trying not to interpret as a metaphor."

"Sometimes, a weed patch is just a patch of weeds." He rested his chin on my shoulder. "Are you going to replant it for your dad?"

"I hadn't really thought about it. Maybe I should."

For a long moment we both stared out the window at the unchanging view. When I was a teenager, my desk had been under this window. Afternoons when I should have been studying raced by with me staring at the patch of green lawn and the wrought-iron fence separating it from the sidewalk and the street.

"You know," Philip said, "we haven't talked yet about whether you're coming or not."

I tried to resist the temptation to parse that sentence, but writing advertising copy for the past thirteen years had taught me to think of every conceivable way every word could be misconstrued. Nor did it help that the way Philip phrased it was, I hoped, unintentionally ambiguous.

"I want to come," I said.

Philip smiled slyly. "Which is not quite the same as saying you *will* come, is it?"

"I suppose not," I said. At this point, my mother began fairly screaming.

"Have you absolutely *lost* your mind?" she shrieked. "If you don't get on the next flight after him as soon as you can, I swear to God that I will—"

I closed my eyes and, jaw clenched, thought as clearly and as loudly as I could the words *Shut. Up. Mother.* I had never yelled at my mother when she was alive—at either of my parents, for that matter. As a child, I figured doing so would have been the shortest distance to a one-way trip out of this world.

To my surprise, though, in this instance it worked. When I

opened my eyes, I saw her flit toward the door. Before she passed through it, she said, "Do *not* screw this up." I hated to think my mother could possibly be right about this.

"You all right, love?" Philip asked.

"I'm okay." I turned away from the window but stayed in Philip's embrace. The belt on the robe had come undone. "You know, if we're going to discuss *anything* seriously, you're going to have to stop distracting me."

Philip shrugged, took off the robe, and tossed it on the bed. He crossed his arms and tried to look serious, but he couldn't keep a smirk from curling at the corner of his mouth.

I wanted nothing more than to get out of my clothes right then. Not just because he was gorgeous; I wasn't above using sex as a diversion tactic to avoid a conversation I wasn't ready to have. I glanced down the length of Philip's body and said, "Obviously, your mother never told you it's impolite to point."

"She did, but I was incorrigible." Philip patted my shoulder, turning and picking up the bathrobe. He looked like he was about to put it on, but instead hung it up in the closet. "It's not like you've got to decide today. You don't even need to decide while I'm still here."

He sat on the bed next to the clothes he'd laid out and started putting on his socks. I imagined he would wait until the last possible moment to put on his underwear. I didn't mind, but it hardly seemed fair.

Philip paused with one sock in his hand. "If you want, just come over and stay for a while, to see how things go. If we end up driving each other spare, then at least we can say we gave it a go and you can come back here."

"To the house my father's about to sell." I shook my head. "I don't want that to be the reason I go with you."

"And here I thought the reason you would go with me was because I'm irresistible and English cuisine is the best to be had and our weather is always perfect."

"I'm sorry, did you say something?" I asked. "I can't seem to pay attention to anything above your waist at the moment."

"Are you insulting my intelligence or my face?" Philip grinned wickedly and lay back on the bed without bothering to put on the other sock. I lay down next to him and placed a hand on his belly. His skin was still a little damp from the shower, and the light slanting in through the window made the fine hair trailing down his abdomen warm. I would have loved to roll on top of him and spend the rest of the morning hiding from reality, but he had a flight to catch.

"Please just tell me you'll at least think about it," he said.

"I think it's safe to say that I won't be thinking about much besides that," I said.

"I just worry that once I'm on the other side of the ocean again, you'll have plenty of other things to worry about like your dad and Dudley, and I'll just fade into the background."

I worried about the same thing too, but kept it to myself. Instead, I rolled over and kissed him. "If I ever worry that I'm going to forget you, all I have to do is picture you at this moment."

I left the room so he could get dressed. I didn't trust my own ability to restrain myself if I stayed. I stood outside the door for a moment and waited for my mother to start chastising me, but the barrage never came.

❖

At the front door, Philip and my father shook hands in a manly sort of way I thought suited Philip. My father placed his hand on Philip's shoulder and, looking at me, said, "I hope I'll be seeing more of you soon, Philip."

Matt and Philip shook hands the way two children would if they'd been caught fighting and were forced to make up. Philip knelt down and patted Dudley on the head. Dudley placed his paw over Philip's arm, which made Philip laugh. He gave Dudley a hug.

My father and Matt stayed home while I drove Philip to the airport in Dad's old Buick. The idea of leaving Matt alone with my father gave me pause, but I wanted every possible moment with Philip all to myself until we finally had to say good-bye. Once he checked his bags, we only had about five minutes before he had to board his flight.

"I didn't realize we were cutting it so close," Philip said. He looked at the monitor displaying all the boarding times. The Boston flight began to blink.

"Neither did I," I said. It had been five days since I'd met up with him again in San Francisco. Up to that point, I'd already thought I'd run out of time with him, and distance had been such an obstacle that I hadn't given much thought to anything else. Now it seemed as if the hourglass had been smashed and sand was pouring out at our feet.

I was surprised when Philip drew my face to his and kissed me in the middle of the concourse. I was shocked for only a second. I didn't care if the whole world was watching.

It had all faded to gray anyway.

"How did we run out of time so fast?" I asked when he finally released me.

He smiled. "There's plenty of time back where I'm from. I'll e-mail you when I get home."

"Do you remember when the world seemed big?"

"You mean before e-mail?"

"That's why I was actually going to ask you not to e-mail when you got home, if you can believe that."

He looked a little disappointed. "I suppose."

"Yeah," I said, "well, fuck big. I want you to e-mail me, call me, send me text messages, send me dirty pictures from your phone at inappropriate times. Send me something every day until I come."

He grinned. "Only if you send me something back."

"Count on it."

We had time for one more fast and hard kiss. I thought my lips would be bruised before he was done. "You *are* going to come, aren't you?" he asked.

"It's like I'm already there."

I watched Philip walk down the hallway to the security checkpoint, and remained standing there. Apparently, Philip didn't realize I was still watching him. He snaked his way through the line, stumbled as he took his shoes off and put them in the plastic bin, walked through the X-ray machine and out of sight.

My mother said, "I hope you know what you're doing."

I hoped I did too, but I had my doubts.

❖

Matt's departure the day after Philip's was an anticlimax. He planned to make the return trip in one day so he could be at work on Tuesday. I got up to make coffee. My father was still asleep. It was not quite six o'clock.

"You know I'll come back and get Dudley if you need me to," Matt said as I pressed the travel mug into his hands. "I don't mind."

"I'm sure we'll manage," I said, "though I have to admit it's kind of funny that you're willing to drive hundreds of miles just to make it easier for me to go be with someone you can't stand."

"It's not that," he said a little too quickly. He drank some coffee, swallowed too much too fast, and winced from the burn. Served him right for lying. "Okay, it's exactly that."

"Is it because he's so different from you?" I asked.

"More that he's not so different. You always want to think you can't be replaced, but then someone comes along and does."

I filled a mug for myself. "I think that pretty much sums up how I feel about Jacob. God, how embarrassing."

"Well, I'm glad we're both petty in the same way."

I bumped my mug against his in a silent toast. "And I

appreciate your offer, but I think at this point my father would be disappointed if Dudley left."

Sometime during the previous day, Dudley seemed to understand something neither my father nor I had been able to articulate. He walked up to my father where he sat in his recliner, reading the paper, and gently pushed his nose under the edge of the page. My father lowered the paper and looked over the top of it at Dudley. Then he folded it up, set it on the end table, and waited for Dudley to do something. The dog trotted to the front door, and my father got up.

I hadn't realized I'd been holding my breath until my father caught me staring and said, "What?"

"Nothing." The leash had been passed, and without missing a beat, Dudley began looking to my father when it was time to go for a walk, time to eat, time to go to bed. The void left by my mother's absence had been filled, imperfectly perhaps, by my dog.

My father neither objected nor acknowledged the change. He simply picked up the leash and followed Dudley to the door. He left the cane behind. I never saw him use it again.

Matt and I stood at the curb next to his truck. Even outside, we kept speaking in the same hushed tones we'd used in the kitchen, as if out here we might still wake up my father. Matt rested his hand on the driver's side door handle but seemed reluctant to get behind the wheel.

"Why do I get the feeling this is the last time I'm going to see you?" he asked.

"I don't know," I said. "London's not that far away."

That felt dishonest. London really *was* that far away. Being back in Portland again, thinking of the disaster that was Lincoln reminded me of all the friends from high school who swore they'd stay in touch and who quickly drifted away with barely a struggle. Maybe I should have been mourning the incipient conclusion of Matt's friendship as well as Carrie's. I had no idea when or even if I would ever go back to St. Louis. If I went to London (*no,* when *I went to London*, I had to remind myself), who knew when I would get back to Maine to see my father and Dudley. Then there was my mother, already lost to me, and now even her phantom was receding.

Standing on the curb in the grayish yellow sunrise, everything seemed so far away, even the man in front of me, and especially the man who was by now undoubtedly home on the other side of the world.

And still hadn't called.

❖

After Matt left, I took my coffee upstairs and tried to go back to sleep. I spent an hour staring at the ceiling and wondering how Philip and I had managed to fit together in this narrow bed that now seemed too small for me alone. When I couldn't stand lying there any longer, I took my mug, the coffee now cold, and went back downstairs to fix breakfast.

I averted my eyes as I walked past the living room threshold. Whenever I looked in there, the first thing I saw was that urn. My father had placed it on top of the mantel. The big mirror hanging behind it meant at the same time I saw the urn, I saw my own reflection. The combination was not a good one. It was hard to believe a month could change someone as much as it had changed me.

I wanted to ask my father to move the urn, but I could think of no other place in the house that seemed right for it. On top of the TV: too informal. The alcove in the stairway to the second floor: dark, and too much like shoving her in a corner.

I couldn't help it; I glanced into the living room. My father stood there, in front of the mantel, staring at the urn or at himself. Maybe both. He was rubbing his chin and didn't hear me come down.

"She's not really in there," I said. He jumped, looked at me wide-eyed, then turned back to the urn. He lifted the lid and peered inside.

"Yes, she is," he said.

"That's not what I meant, Dad."

To my relief, he replaced the lid. "So what are we going to do with her?"

I didn't know, so I left the question unanswered and proceeded to make blintzes. When in doubt, cook. Eventually, though, we had to decide what we were really going to do with her. It was the one thing she hadn't specified in her will. Coming up with an answer felt like some sort of final test.

Over the next couple days, alone in an empty house where my mother's memory was the third resident, it seemed as if my father and I were the ones becoming the ghosts who haunted the place. We behaved like wraiths that barely knew of each other's presence, only aware enough to avoid colliding and passing through one another. Certainly, that would have been disastrous, feeling the cold shock of my father's lingering grief (of course it lingered, my mother had barely been gone a month) and letting him touch the clammy uncertainty of my own future.

At one point, coming downstairs early Tuesday morning to start the coffee, I stopped on the landing when I heard voices in the living room. I thought at first it must have been the TV, but then I realized there was only one voice, my father's, high-pitched but soft, like someone strangling himself.

"How could you be so heartless, Rachel, how could you leave me like this how how how?"

The only thing that kept me from running back up the stairs was the certainty that he'd hear me, and know that I'd overheard him. I'd worried so much about coming downstairs one morning to find him collapsed on the floor or lying on the stairs where he'd stumbled, I'd forgotten that he was probably falling down inside. So I carefully backtracked up the stairs, mindful to avoid the steps that squeaked, the section of the banister that rattled, all the ways that the house could accuse me.

❖

My mother wasn't around when I heard his outburst, but I knew she had to be aware of it. She made that clear later.

"I think I would have been reasonably content as a widow," my mother said. It was early in the afternoon, and I still hadn't heard from Philip. On Monday evening, I had finally given in to temptation and called him. (And why did it feel like temptation, I wondered?) I got his voicemail, but hung up rather than leave a message.

To take my mind off his silence, and to keep from calling him again, I took Dudley for a walk. If we weren't stopped at a corner already, my mother's comment would have halted me in my tracks. As it was, I looked at her aghast.

"What the hell, Mom?" I asked. I didn't even bother to look around and see if anyone was within hearing. Fortunately, we were alone.

"I'm not saying I would have been *happy* about it, darling," she clarified. "I just think I would have been able to adjust after a certain period of time. Of course I would have missed your father, but eventually…" She trailed off for a moment, and we watched Dudley, who still hadn't tired of all the new smells to be found in Portland. He finished his inspection of a fire hydrant, and we crossed the street.

"I think it's different for men," my mother said. "I'm sure your father will be all right, but I don't know if he'll be all that happy."

"What does this have to do with anything, Mom?"

"Darling, what I'm saying is don't put your own life on hold for your father. He will be fine, he just needs to cultivate interests of his own."

"If Dudley and I stay here, maybe we can help with that," I said.

She threw up her hands in exasperation. "What on earth are you saying? Didn't you just tell Philip you were coming to England as soon as you could?"

"He hasn't called me back yet—"

"Two days!" She held up two fingers in front of my nose. The tone of her voice made Dudley snap his head back to look at her. "Sometimes I don't understand you, darling, I honestly don't. You are on the verge of being happier than I've ever seen you, and you talk about folding while you're holding four aces."

"I think you're mixing your metaphors, mother."

She narrowed her eyes at me. "Do not make fun of your poor departed mother. Anyway, as far as your father is concerned, I think he has to figure out his own interests for himself."

As we walked for a while in silence, I wondered if she was mad at me. She had a point, which I hated to admit. The idea of staying here until my father got on with his life was foolish.

Unless Philip didn't call.

As we walked down the next block, my mother placed her hand on my arm and pointed across the street. "Does that look familiar, darling?"

For a moment, it didn't. I hadn't seen my grandparents' old house in years. They hadn't lived there for a long time. My grandfather died before I was out of middle school. My memories of him were indistinct, more impressions than actual memories. My grandmother died during my sophomore year of college, but by then she had been out of the house on Spring Street for years and lived in a retirement home.

Something about the house seemed different from the way I remembered it, but I couldn't put my finger on it. Maybe it was the light; it was one of those bright spring days where the sun sharpened the lines between objects and made everything seem surreal, from the yellow siding of the house to the impossibly blue sky.

"Was it painted a different color before?" I asked.

My mother shook her head. "Same color it's always been. My mother loved that shade of yellow. I always thought it looked like we were living in a huge slab of butter."

I smiled. "I don't remember it being that...colorful."

"That's just because the picture's faded, darling."

She held out a photo. It was the same photo that Sylvia and Gerald had shown me in Sedona of my mother and her friends. It hadn't occurred to me before now that the picture had been taken in front of my grandparents' house.

"My memory is playing tricks on me, I guess. I remember it being the same color it is in the photo." I handed the snapshot back to her, all the while wondering if I'd ever really held it, or if it would have vanished had I kept it for a while longer.

"My memories of the past were never sepia-toned," my mother said. "More like widescreen Technicolor, which I suppose is even less real."

She shook the snapshot as if it were a Polaroid and the colors might brighten. "This was taken the summer before our freshman year of college. I think we were all still fairly happy at that point." She placed a finger underneath one young man's chin. "That's Dwight, Sylvia's boyfriend at the time. They were both dating other people before the summer was over. I was dumb enough at the time to be smug about that. I wouldn't meet your father until, oh, months after this."

We stood there in silence for a moment, and I wondered if the current occupants would notice me and come out to see why I was staring at their house. Some part of my memory of the place still didn't match up with the reality in front of us.

"Something still looks different, though," I said.

My mother looked up from the photo and narrowed her eyes at the house, as if daring it to confess its occupants' sins. She pointed to the first-floor bays. "Oh, they replaced the windows. Those used to be stained glass. They made the living room so pretty when the sun was going down."

She pointed upstairs. "That was my room. I can't tell you the number of times I snuck out of the house after your grandmother and grandfather were asleep. Sylvia would walk down from her house, and we'd go round up the boys. Derek had a car, so we usually went downtown and saw the late show or went to Grant's and had malts. If the weather was nice, one of the boys would buy some beer and we'd go out to the beach."

I laughed. "Yeah, Mom. You were a real wild child."

"Well, if we'd been caught we probably would have been taken in to the police station and our parents called. Which may not sound like much to you, but it could kill a girl's reputation back then."

She smiled, a little wickedly. "Or *make* a girl's reputation, depending on how you looked at it."

It dawned on me, listening to my mother reminisce about her high school days, that she must have been a lot like Linda at that age: popular without having to try, beautiful without making a fuss about it, and using both of those qualities to get whatever she wanted. Except Derek.

Eventually, Dudley grew tired of our loitering and began to pull at his leash. As we walked away, my mother looked back at the house and frowned, but didn't give voice to her disappointment.

❖

Philip finally called me late on Tuesday afternoon, while I was trying to decide what to make for dinner. (When all else fails, cook.) He'd lost his BlackBerry somewhere on his way home and hadn't been able to call until he got in the front door. Although it was probably stuck under a seat cushion somewhere, I pictured the phone bobbing up and down in the middle of the ocean before it finally slipped below the waves.

When he asked if I was coming, for once, I didn't waste time.

Chapter Sixteen

My mother's presence, bordering on translucence before, had now dissolved into a hazy indistinctness. It seemed I could only see her clearly when I looked out of the corner of my eye. When I tried to conjure up a memory of her appearance, to my horror I realized that too was fading. I could picture details—the flourish of a hand waving a cigarette, the purse of her lips as she inhaled, the feathered fringe of her slipper—but when I tried to assemble them into a complete image, the pieces didn't fit right.

It was happening so fast. I felt compelled to remember her as clearly as possible, because that was how she remained alive: the recollections by people like me and my father, her friends, Derek. Each of us, I'm sure, remembered different versions of her, facsimiles that deviated from the original in either inconsequential or critical ways. The one I remembered had to be the most faithful to the original.

I was her son, after all.

"Darling, I don't think any of us can know the whole of another person," she said. I stood at the bookshelf staring at one of the pictures my father hadn't packed away yet, the one of my mother and me at the beach. I didn't turn to look at her—this had become an unspoken agreement for us since she'd reappeared at the museum. She usually placed a hand on my shoulder or, when I was lucky, I closed my eyes and she put her arms around me.

"I have to at least try," I said.

"Maybe you're trying too hard. That was always the way with you."

"But what if I forget you?"

"Son, who are you talking to?"

I turned around. My father leaned against the door frame, a mug of coffee in his hand. Unlike me, when he heard someone talking to himself or herself, he didn't try to back out quietly. I placed the picture frame back on the shelf.

"Sometimes I talk to her like she's still here," I said.

He settled into his recliner. "Me too. Does she ever answer you?"

"Sometimes. What about you?"

"Nothing yet. Which is not much different from when she was alive. She listened to me when it suited her."

"That is *so* unfair," my mother protested. To my surprise, when I looked at her she had regained her solidity. She sat on the corner of the sofa nearest his recliner, her arms crossed.

"What does she say?" he asked.

"Dad, you would not believe how long and complex that answer could get."

"I was married to her for forty-eight years, son. I have a pretty good idea."

"Oh, *fine*." My mother threw her hands in the air, and pulled out her cigarettes. "It's bash on the dead lady time."

Still looking at her, I said to my father, "Sometimes she has some really good things to say. It reminds me how much I miss her."

She paused, lighter in one hand, cigarette in the other, and smiled. "Aren't you sweet. For a change."

"So, what would you say to her now if you had the chance?" I asked.

My father rolled his coffee mug between his palms. "Well, I'd tell her I miss her. And I'd ask her where the checkbook is. I still can't find the damn thing."

I laughed. When she also stopped laughing, my mother said, "It's in the top drawer of the hutch."

"I have a feeling it'll show up." I got up from the sofa. The time suddenly seemed right. "Actually, Dad, I have something I need to show you."

When I returned with the box of letters, my mother was still sitting on the sofa near my father. He'd picked up the remote and was flipping through channels. Her cigarette burning down, she stared at him through the curl of smoke. In my absence, she'd become a little transparent again. She turned and, seeing the box in my hands, nodded her agreement.

My father hit the mute button when I placed the box in his lap. "What are these?"

"Letters I found in her closet," I said. "I wasn't sure what to do with them or when to give them to you. Right before the funeral would have been, I don't know, weird."

He put on his glasses, picked up the topmost envelope, and read Derek's address. "*She* wrote all these. Are they all addressed to him?"

"As far as I looked."

"But she never sent them?"

"I guess not. They're mostly about us. It's like she wrote to him instead of keeping a diary."

He riffled down further in the pile. "Jeez, she did this for *years*."

"Ever since she met you," I said.

He was lost in his own thoughts for a while as he slid one letter then another from its envelope. He scanned them, flipped them over, then replaced them in their envelopes and was about to put the lid back on the box.

"I don't know if it's right to be reading these, son. It feels like I'm intruding."

"Tell him it's okay," my mother said. She didn't look at me. She kept looking at him the same way she had when I'd noticed her staring out windows during our trip, the night in my apartment while I packed.

"I don't think she minds, Dad. Maybe these are her way of telling us things she never got around to saying when she was here, or that she thought we might not listen to."

"Well, maybe that's true, son." He cradled the box in his lap carefully, as if it were a baby, or a bomb. "I don't think I'll read them all at once, though. Maybe later." He placed the lid firmly on the box and stood up. "Maybe she never mentioned this, but your mom kept more than just her own letters."

Dudley followed us upstairs to my parents' bedroom, where my father pulled a scrapbook from my mother's nightstand. I sat on the edge of the bed, and he placed it in my lap. On each page were three or four postcards I'd sent them; it looked like she'd kept everything from the past fifteen years or so, ever since I'd left college. There were even a couple from the summer I'd spent backpacking through Europe my senior year of high school. The only thing was she mounted them backward, with the images face-down on the pages and my writing face-up. I slipped a couple of them free of the corner tabs and flipped them over to see from where I'd sent them, confirming what the faded postmarks didn't make clear. My handwriting seemed tentative, the precise loops and tight spacing as if the words were copied out of a manual. I'd been made to do endless drills as a child, my penmanship was so illegible. Seeing how the effects of that wore off as I turned to pages nearer in the past, I realized in some places I couldn't read my own handwriting at all.

My mother, whom before now I would have described as the most unsentimental maternal figure ever to have walked the Earth—even less sentimental than Lilith—had kept every scrap of correspondence I'd sent her.

Standing in the doorway, she held up her hands in a pose of surrender and said, "Busted."

"Your mother always thought you'd get a job in the travel business since you took so many trips," my father said as I flipped back and forth through the pages. "I think she was living vicariously through you, to be honest. She always wanted to do more traveling. I told her she should go ahead and take some trips if she wanted; sign up with a group or something. I'd still be here when she got home. But she just kind of shrugged it off."

He didn't have to tell me why they never did travel together: his work, then his bypass. I couldn't recall ever hearing him speak for this long. Typically, he and I communicated in simple sentences and, more often, monosyllables.

"Well, you couldn't shove her passport in her hand and force her onto a plane, Dad."

He laughed. "Son, no one could force your mother to do anything."

"Some things were more important to me at the time than travel," she said. She sat weightlessly on the other side of the bed and looked over my shoulder at the pages. There were postcards from a trip Matt and I took to New York. Though the picture on the front was of the Chrysler Building glittering in sunshine, the trip for us had been shrouded in fog, the skyscrapers vanishing upward into the gray emptiness. That trip was close to the end for our relationship, though Matt and I didn't know at the time how much we were in the fog as well.

On the last page were the two postcards I sent them from London last month. It was strange to see these so soon after the trip, like a friend telling you they got your postcard two days after you'd already returned home.

One of them, of the British Museum, was something of a lie. I spent so much time in Philip's flat, I never got to the museum during my trip. I bought it from a newsagent and mailed it before I got to the airport.

"Wait," my mother said. "I didn't put those in there." As discreetly as possible with my father sitting on the other side of me, I gave her a quizzical look. It was at this point, as she leaned further over the page, I noticed my mother cast no shadow.

"The postcards from London must have arrived after I was

gone," she said. I appreciated her not saying, "after I was dead," but still her words stabbed that finality into me again. If she realized what she'd said, she gave no hint of it. I braced myself for the tidal wave of grief to smash into me, but it didn't come. Instead, a swell of sadness lifted me up and gently set me down with that sickening roller-coaster feeling in my stomach.

"So, did you put these postcards in here?" I asked my father.

"They came in the mail a couple days after you got here last month. I figured I might as well keep up the scrapbook..." I could tell he almost added "for her," but stopped himself.

I closed the scrapbook. "Philip wants me to move to London."

"Oh." My father sat back. "Are you going to go?"

"It's kind of sudden," I said. "A lot of things could go wrong. I'm not even sure if this is a real thing or just an extension of a vacation fling."

"Flings don't fly halfway across the world to see you and follow you all the way across the continent to your old parents' house. You may not be sure, but I get the feeling Philip is."

"Darling," my mother said, "I can't believe I'm saying this, but listen to your father."

"Well, there's Dudley to consider," I said to them both. He had settled on the area rug at our feet, and upon hearing his name, he lifted his head. My father reached down and scratched the spot between the dog's ears, and Dudley settled again.

"You could take him with you," he said. "I hear they have dogs in England."

"They also have a six-month quarantine period, which can't be cheap, especially now that I'm unemployed."

"No, they don't," my mother said, her voice so quick and forceful that I looked up, startled. She shrugged and said, "Well, they don't. They got rid of it years ago."

"You'll have the money," my father said, oblivious. "Your

mother's left you some from the insurance. If anything keeps you from going, it won't be Dudley."

"He's almost ten years old, though," I said. "It doesn't seem fair to take him overseas when…" I let the statement hang unfinished. I couldn't bear to say, "when who knows how much longer he has left." If I tried, I knew I wouldn't have the breath to finish the sentence.

"In that case, he can stay here," my father said. "I think he likes it here, and it's not like I couldn't use the company."

He braced his hands atop his thighs and pushed himself to his feet. "In any case, it's a lot harder to figure out this thing with Philip if you're on opposite sides of the ocean. If I were you, I'd try figuring it out from over there."

"Dad, I don't have a job."

"Big deal. I haven't had a job for ten years, and being unemployed is a lot more fun than going to an office every day. So you live off the insurance money for a while. Worry about a job when that runs out.

"And while you're at it," he added, pausing in the doorway, "you can take your mother with you."

"I'd like that," she said, "but I don't think it's such a good idea."

"What else am I supposed to do with you?" I asked, but she didn't say. I had a feeling she wasn't sure either.

❖

Give or take, I've walked Dudley almost nine thousand times. Some of those walks were short—outside in the pouring rain huddled under an umbrella just long enough for him to do his business. Others were ponderous rambles where I lost track of time and direction, though with him leading the way, I never felt lost.

I knew I was leaving him in good hands with my father,

but I wanted one last walk with him. When I lived in Portland, I preferred the view from the Eastern Promenade, which overlooks Casco Bay and is a longer distance from the house than the walk to the Western Promenade, which only overlooks the railroad tracks. The Western Promenade had the stately mansions, though, which I had liked to imagine living in when I was younger. Even though the day had turned cloudy and cool, the breeze gave Dudley plenty of scents to read. The trees still looked young, their newly unfurled leaves, still an unexpectedly bright green, clutching tightly to themselves in the wind. I sat on a bench and alternated between watching runners on the path and staring at the houses while Dudley played out the length of his leash.

"You know Derek lives here, don't you?" my mother asked. She sat on the other end of the bench.

"Which house is his?"

She pointed across the street to an ornate brick mansion with a colonnade supporting a two-story porch. It stood alone on a corner and seemed to project up and outward, as if it were standing tall and jutting its chin at the same time.

When I turned back to her, she had lit a cigarette. "That's the very same porch where I stood and threw his engagement ring into the snow," she said. "So what are you going to do, march up there and demand to see the letter I might have sent him forty-odd years ago?"

I smiled, briefly. "You assume I actually have a plan." When I was stranded with Lincoln on the side of the road in the dark in Ohio, I had needed badly to see that letter. I knew he lived on the Promenade, but I no longer felt a need to seek from him any confirmation that my mother's ghost was real. She was real enough to me, and I had decided that was sufficient.

"Any regrets there?" I nodded toward the house.

She frowned. "Such as?"

"Do you ever wish you'd sent the rest of those letters to him?"

My mother leaned forward, elbow on knee, chin in hand,

The Thinker in a peach nightgown with a Marlboro Light. She exhaled. "Maybe a little. Actually, I had hoped he would be the one to feel some regret about breaking up with me. I told him his life was going to be very lonely, which was, first of all, not very kind, and secondly, not very true. I had really wanted to hate him, and maybe I did for a while. But enough time passes and you find you don't remember why you hated someone in the first place, or you just get tired of holding on to it. I knew he just didn't love me. Couldn't love me. At least, not like that."

She flicked her cigarette away. "It would be nice to think he and I could have been friends, given enough time. But there never is enough of that, is there?"

We walked as far as the hospital at the end of the Promenade, then doubled back, passing Derek's house yet again before heading back up Pine Street.

"You're sure you don't want to call on them?" she asked again after I went past without stopping.

I waited for a pair of joggers to overtake us and move out of earshot before I said, "No, I'm really not. Do you want me to?"

She looked puzzled for a moment, as if she'd forgotten something. "Not particularly, now that you ask. I used to hope that I might get a letter or a phone call from him just out of the blue, maybe that he was thinking of me or just to let me know he was still alive. It's funny, isn't it? We only lived a few blocks away from each other, but after all he and I went through together, I never saw him.

"In any case, that's my regret to live with." She smiled. "So to speak."

We started to walk back again, but my mother placed her hand on my arm. "Wait. Open your backpack."

As I did, she spread her arms out. "This is the spot. Get out my ashes."

For my trip to England, my father and I had transferred her ashes from the urn into a heavy duty Ziploc freezer bag, which I lifted carefully out of my backpack. The contents looked like gray sugar, maybe five or six pounds' worth. I cupped one hand underneath the bag and looked around. We were alone.

"This is where you want to spend eternity? In front of Derek's house? Overlooking the railroad tracks?"

She smiled. "Darling, why not right here? You were born up there"—she waved toward the hospital—"and that's also where I died. Derek's house is right there, our house is just a few streets away, and I love these trees. What better place?"

I wasn't sure where I should spread her ashes. Just tossing them in the grass seemed anticlimactic. I walked toward the trees, unzipped the bag, and checked the wind direction. A face full of my dead mother was the last thing I wanted. Carefully, I tilted the bag until the contents began to stream out. I walked along the trees, sprinkling her ashes beneath them as I went. When the bag was almost empty, I paused and turned to her.

"Are you sure you don't want me to save even a little to take with me?"

She was looking out over the railroad tracks toward the west. On a clear day, you could see mountains all the way in New Hampshire, but today the clouds kept the city close. "Not a grain, darling."

She wouldn't even let me keep the bag after I poured out all the ashes. I dropped it in a trash can, shouldered my backpack, and we headed home, Dudley leading the way. By the time we reached the house, the sun had managed to find a space between the clouds to shine dimly once we reached our own house. My mother paused outside the gate.

"I think I'm going to walk on for a while," she said. "I'm not ready to go back in." She looked faded—not transparent as she had before, but more like the coloring of the old photo of her and me on the beach in Cape Cod. She turned her face up toward the sun. "It looks like it might be a nice day after all."

She knelt down in front of Dudley and ruffled his ears. The effect was less startling than the first time she did that back in St.

Louis. I caught a hint of Chanel No. 5 when she stood and kissed me on the cheek.

"See you later, darling."

It was odd to stand there and watch her walk away and know, though she hadn't said so, that it was the last time I'd see her. Again the tidal wave stayed out at sea, and the sad feeling that settled somewhere between my chest and my stomach was more like the gentle tug of the tide heading back out. Dudley and I waited until she turned the corner out of sight.

I pushed the gate open and took him inside.

❖

Here's the thing about borders that occurred to me while I was sitting in the departure area at Kennedy, waiting for my flight to London. They may be designed to keep things separated, but they don't have any meaning until you cross them. The most important ones don't even show up on a map.

Some borders you can only cross in one direction. At least that's what I thought before my mother made her brief return. Other borders you expect to cross only a single time. When Carrie's husband breached an unforgivable line, she found herself backtracking toward home. I couldn't blame her, but I think she was disappointed her circumstances left her, in her estimation, no other decent alternative. She could have stayed in St. Louis and toughed it out as a divorcée, but maybe she needed the comfort of family more.

I knew I'd get past this. I also knew I'd never get past this.

When I thought about my mother, when I pictured her in my memory, it wasn't as the elderly woman I visited sporadically toward the end of her life, who still resisted age as best she could with the help of Olay and Nice'n Easy number 104. Nor was it the apparition draped in peach nightclothes and brandishing a cigarette like an exclamation point or a threat. Rather, I remembered the woman from when I was five years old and standing on a beach in Cape Cod, her arm around my thin shoulders to offer some protection against the wind as we waited for my father to take our picture. When I finally asked my father for something to remember my mother by, it was that photo.

Maybe it was because she was with me for so long after she died that I still had a hard time believing she was gone, even though I knew, truly knew, that it was for good this time. Every once in a while, I wondered if I was wrong and whether I'd see her again. When I came downstairs to make a last breakfast for my father before leaving, I half hoped she might be sitting at the kitchen island, drinking tea and smoking a cigarette. She wasn't. I didn't see her at the Portland airport either, or at Kennedy, where I doubted I'd get enough of a glimpse to recognize her in the crowd.

Before the flight to Heathrow I went to the Hudson News for a bottle of water and something to read. All of my books were still in storage back in St. Louis. If I decided to stay in London—and even if things didn't work out with Philip, I couldn't imagine that I'd want to come back—I'd have to figure out what to do with all of that junk. Matt would probably help with that.

I knew I was moving toward something, not just randomly drifting through the aisles, past an old man scrutinizing a shelf of chewing gum and lozenges and a woman trying to calm a little girl reaching desperately toward the shelves in the candy aisle. At that point, trying to decide between a vampire novel or the latest David Sedaris, ultimately deciding to get both, I realized I was happy, just standing there in front of the fiction wall at the Hudson News in Kennedy Airport, waiting to leave.

My mother would have found my change of mood amusing, but I think it would have made her happy too.

About the Author

Jeffrey Ricker is a writer, editor, and graphic designer. His writing has appeared in the literary magazine *Collective Fallout*, the anthologies *Paws and Reflect*, *Fool for Love: New Gay Fiction*, *Blood Sacraments*, *Men of the Mean Streets*, *Speaking Out*, and others. *Detours* is his first novel. A magna cum laude graduate of the University of Missouri School of Journalism, he is working on his second novel. Keep up with his work at www.jeffrey-ricker.com.

Books Available From Bold Strokes Books

Sheltering Dunes by Radclyffe. The seventh in the award-winning Provincetown Tales. The pasts, presents, and futures of three women collide in a single moment that will alter all their lives forever. (978-1-60282-573-4)

Holy Rollers by Rob Byrnes. Partners in life and crime Grant Lambert and Chase LaMarca assemble a team of gay and lesbian criminals to steal millions from a right-wing mega-church, but the gang's plans are complicated by an "ex-gay" conference, the FBI, and a corrupt reverend with his own plans for the cash. (978-1-60282-578-9)

History's Passion: Stories of Sex Before Stonewall, edited by Richard Labonté. Four acclaimed erotic authors re-imagine the past...Welcome to the hidden queer history of men loving men not so very long—and centuries—ago. (978-1-60282-576-5)

Lucky Loser by Yolanda Wallace. Top tennis pros Sinjin Smythe and Laure Fortescue reach Wimbledon desperate to claim tennis's crown jewel, but will their feelings for each other get in the way? (978-1-60282-575-8)

Mystery of The Tempest: A Fisher Key Adventure by Sam Cameron. Twin brothers Denny and Steven Anderson love helping people and fighting crime alongside their sheriff dad on sun-drenched Fisher Key, Florida, but Denny doesn't dare tell anyone he's gay, and Steven has secrets of his own to keep. (978-1-60282-579-6)

Better Off Red: Vampire Sorority Sisters Book 1 by Rebekah Weatherspoon. Every sorority has its secrets, and college freshman Ginger Carmichael soon discovers that her pledge is more than a bond of sisterhood—it's a lifelong pact to serve six bloodthirsty demons with a lot more than nutritional needs. (978-1-60282-574-1)

Detours by Jeffrey Ricker. Joel Patterson is heading to Maine for his mother's funeral, and his high school friend Lincoln has invited himself along on the ride—and into Joel's bed—but when the ghost of Joel's mother joins the trip, the route is likely to be anything but straight. (978-1-60282-577-2)

Three Days by L.T. Marie. In a town like Vegas where anything can happen, Shawn and Dakota find that the stakes are love at all costs, and it's a gamble neither can afford to lose. (978-1-60282-569-7)

Swimming to Chicago by David-Matthew Barnes. As the lives of the adults around them unravel, high school students Alex and Robby form an unbreakable bond, vowing to do anything to stay together—even if it means leaving everything behind. (978-1-60282-572-7)

Hostage Moon by AJ Quinn. Hunter Roswell thought she had left her past behind, until a serial killer begins stalking her. Can FBI profiler Sara Wilder help her find her connection to the killer before he strikes on blood moon? (978-1-60282-568-0)

Erotica Exotica: Tales of Sex, Magic, and the Supernatural, edited by Richard Labonté. Today's top gay erotica authors offer sexual thrills and perverse arousal, spooky chills, and magical orgasms in these stories exploring arcane mystery, supernatural seduction, and sex that haunts in a manner both weird and wondrous. (978-1-60282-570-3)

Blue by Russ Gregory. Matt and Thatcher find themselves in the crosshairs of a psychotic killer stalking gay men in the streets of Austin, and only a 103-year-old nursing home resident holds the key to solving the murders—but can she give up her secrets in time to save them? (978-1-60282-571-0)

Balance of Forces: Toujours Ici by Ali Vali. Immortal Kendal Richoux's life began during the reign of Egypt's only female pharaoh, and history has taught her the dangers of getting too close to anyone who hasn't harnessed the power of time, but as she prepares for the most important battle of her long life, can she resist her attraction to Piper Marmande? (978-1-60282-567-3)

Wings: Subversive Gay Angel Erotica, edited by Todd Gregory. A collection of powerfully written tales of passion and desire centered on the aching beauty of angels. (978-1-60282-565-9)

Contemporary Gay Romances by Felice Picano. These works of short fiction from legendary novelist and memoirist Felice Picano are as different from any standard "romances" as you can get, but they will linger in the mind and memory. (978-1-60282-639-7)

Pirate's Fortune: Supreme Constellations Book Four by Gun Brooke. Set against the backdrop of war, captured mercenary Weiss Kyakh is persuaded to work undercover with bio-android Madisyn Pimm, which foils her plans to escape, but kindles unexpected love. (978-1-60282-563-5)

Sex and Skateboards by Ashley Bartlett. Sex and skateboards and surfing on the California coast. What more could anyone want? Alden McKenna thinks that's all she needs, until she meets Weston Duvall. (978-1-60282-562-8)

Waiting in the Wings by Melissa Brayden. Jenna has spent her whole life training for the stage, but the one thing she didn't prepare for was Adrienne. Is she ready to sacrifice what she's worked so hard for in exchange for a shot at something much deeper? (978-1-60282-561-1)

Suite Nineteen by Mel Bossa. Psychic Ben Lebeau moves into Shilts Manor, where he meets seductive Lennox Van Kemp and his clan of Métis—guardians of a spiritual conspiracy dating back to Christ. But are Ben's psychic abilities strong enough to save him? (978-1-60282-564-2)

Speaking Out: LGBTQ Youth Stand Up, edited by Steve Berman. Inspiring stories written for and about LGBTQ teens of overcoming adversity (against intolerance and homophobia) and experiencing life after "coming out." (978-1-60282-566-6)

Forbidden Passions by MJ Williamz. Passion burns hotter when it's forbidden, and the fire between Katie Prentiss and Corrine Staples in antebellum Louisiana is raging out of control. (978-1-60282-641-0)

Harmony by Karis Walsh. When Brook Stanton meets a beautiful musician who threatens the security of her conventional, predetermined future, will she take a chance on finding the harmony only love creates? (978-1-60282-237-5)

nightrise by Nell Stark and Trinity Tam. In the third book in the everafter series, when Valentine Darrow loses her soul, Alexa must cross continents to find a way to save her. (978-1-60282-238-2)

Men of the Mean Streets, edited by Greg Herren and J.M. Redmann. Dark tales of amorality and criminality by some of the top authors of gay mysteries. (978-1-60282-240-5)

Women of the Mean Streets, edited by J.M. Redmann and Greg Herren. Murder, mayhem, sex, and danger—these are the stories of the women who dare to tackle the mean streets. (978-1-60282-241-2)

Firestorm by Radclyffe. Firefighter paramedic Mallory "Ice" James isn't happy when the undisciplined Jac Russo joins her command, but lust isn't something either can control—and they soon discover ice burns as fiercely as flame. (978-1-60282-232-0)

The Best Defense by Carsen Taite. When socialite Aimee Howard hires former homicide detective Skye Keaton to find her missing niece, she vows not to mix business with pleasure, but she soon finds Skye hard to resist. (978-1-60282-233-7)

After the Fall by Robin Summers. When the plague destroys most of humanity, Taylor Stone thinks there's nothing left to live for, until she meets Kate, a woman who makes her realize love is still alive and makes her dream of a future she thought was no longer possible. (978-1-60282-234-4)

Accidents Never Happen by David-Matthew Barnes. From the moment Albert and Joey meet by chance beneath a train track on a street in Chicago, a domino effect is triggered, setting off a chain reaction of murder and tragedy. (978-1-60282-235-1)

In Plain View, edited by Shane Allison. Best-selling gay erotica authors create the stories of sex and desire modern readers crave. (978-1-60282-236-8)